The Mistletoe Makeover

A SWEET ROMANTIC COMEDY

GRACE WORTHINGTON

Free Novella

SWEET ROMCOM PREQUEL

What happens when you're forced to team up with the MOST infuriating man alive for a research experiment on dating?

You make sure you don't fall for him. Easy, right?
Not when it's the guy known as Dr. Romeo.

The Dating Hypothesis is a free prequel novella when you join Grace Worthington's newsletter at graceworthington.com.

ONE

Mia

"I *hate* mistletoe." I glance over at my roommate, Jaz, from the top of a ladder while wrestling with a tangled fake evergreen garland that's been in storage for a year.

"What did mistletoe ever do to you?" Jaz replies as she digs through a box and plucks a fake mistletoe from the bottom.

"Basically, ruined my childhood." My staunch dislike for mistletoe started early. Every year, my mother forced me to attend our town's annual Maplewood Mistletoe Festival, but after one disastrous Christmas, I vowed I could never look at mistletoe the same again. *And for good reason.*

Jaz twirls the green sprig between her fingers. "If a handsome stranger stops by the house, you'll thank me later." She knows I'd rather get pelted with sharp rocks than forced into kissing a man I've just met. But she also knows how stubborn I am. Too headstrong to fall for a sharp, stubbled jaw and pretty eyes.

If I'm going to fall for someone, it will have to happen naturally and, possibly, against my better judgment.

"You're assuming that I'm desperate," I say, untangling a knot in the stiff garland.

"Holding the title of *never been kissed* until you're forty is not a goal you should strive for." She tosses the mistletoe toward me and I fumble it for a second.

"I have nine years until I'm forty, thank you very much," I add, tossing the mistletoe back at her. I said the same thing about turning thirty, and here I am, still single and never been kissed. I've been so focused on finishing college, getting a job, and supporting my mom that dating in my twenties just wasn't a high priority. But now that I'm settled in Sully's Beach, South Carolina, I probably should at least consider dating again.

"So why all the mistletoe hate?" Jaz asks, setting the mistletoe aside. I have a feeling I'm going to find it later, hanging where I least expect it, and I'll be forced to make a wide circle around it the rest of December.

"For years, my mom has volunteered for the committee that plans the Maplewood Mistletoe Festival in Vermont, which meant our entire fall was consumed by festival planning and stockpiling Christmas decorations. Why do you think I avoid going home for the holidays?" My hometown is overrun with tourists the week before Christmas, and Mom is always in full-on festival mode. "At least I can have a normal holiday here."

"Normal?" Jaz says. "You mean *boring*?"

She doesn't appreciate that my usual holiday plans include binge-watching every holiday movie on Netflix while wearing buffalo-check flannel pajamas.

I climb down from the ladder. "What do you think?" I point to the garland draped over the door.

She presses a finger to her lips. "It needs something."

"You sound like my mother. Her motto concerning Christmas decorations was always *more is more*."

"Then I'd probably love the Maplewood Mistletoe Festival."

"Trust me, you wouldn't," I warn, remembering the obnoxious blinking lights, the fake trees, the garish hand-painted elves next to a hideous plastic Santa Claus I nicknamed *Ugly Santa*. "The festival is dying a slow death. And I'm not sad about it."

For years, the festival covered up the actual issue in our home

—my father's glaring absence. When I was a kid, my dad walked out on us a few days after Christmas, forever tainting what should have been a season of blissful memories.

After that, Mom threw herself into the Mistletoe Festival committee because she thought helping with a massive community celebration was the solution to fixing Christmas. For me, mistletoe became a symbol of forced cheer, of people pretending to be happy, when I knew their circumstances suggested otherwise. Not that I can blame her. I'm just way too realistic to drink the Christmas Kool-Aid.

My phone buzzes in my pocket. "Speaking of Mom." I hold my phone up for Jaz to see.

"It's a sign," she says. "She wants to know if you're coming home for the holidays."

"She knows my answer. I'm staying here with you," I say before accepting the call. "Hey, Mom."

"Are you busy?" she asks. In the background, a blender rumbles to life.

"Yeah, but what's that noise?"

"I'm making a green smoothie. My friend Judy swears by them."

Mom's weakness is falling for every new weight loss item on the market. The ThighMaster. The George Foreman Grill. Every version of Spanx ever invented.

"Excuse me?" I ask. "What green vegetable would you actually eat?" I know my mom's love of vegetables only includes starchy white potatoes. For years, she believed the food pyramid should categorize french fries as a healthy vegetable.

"A pinch of spinach," she admits.

"Mmm. Nothing says Christmas like a green smoothie," I say as Jaz lifts an eyebrow.

"Speaking of Christmas," Mom says. "We're knee-deep in planning mode for the festival."

"Did you already put out the elves? How about Ugly Santa?"

"Believe it or not, we're not using the elves this year."

Judging by the way she says it, this is big news. "I bet that rocked the mistletoe committee."

She sighs. "Well, it's necessary for our survival. If we don't get some new ideas and more money, the festival won't continue after this year."

She waits for a reaction from me, but I can already smell the bait. For years, I've stayed as far away from Maplewood at Christmas as I could. Too many bad memories knotted up like a tangled garland.

"I've told the committee we need to do something drastic," she adds. "We need new decorations, new marketing, and a whole new look. The town is dying, and we need to save it."

I don't have the guts to dash Mom's dreams and tell her they can't pull this off. "It would be difficult to make over the festival without major money and community support."

"Exactly," she says. "We need something *big*. Something that will attract tourists to our little town the week before Christmas."

"Like the world's largest mistletoe?" I joke, remembering the time my mother had the fake mistletoe installed in the town square so that Maplewood would make *Guinness World Records*. The novelty worked until a massive snowstorm hit Vermont and took out the gigantic mistletoe before they received the honor.

Mom pauses. "What do you think about bringing in a big name for a Christmas concert?"

"In Maplewood?" I laugh. Anybody with a name would scoff at performing in such a dinky place, but I don't want to hurt Mom's feelings.

"Obviously, I would have to find the *right* person," she says, noticing my hesitation. "Someone who cares about the town. Ideally, someone who lives here."

I shake my head. "Nobody famous lives in Maplewood."

"Until *now*."

I'm not exactly current on Maplewood news, but I don't remember anyone moving to my hometown.

"Jace Knight," she says proudly.

I frown. "Who?"

She lets out a sigh. "Only the biggest country rock star in America right now. He wanted a log cabin in the Green Mountains and bought a dozen acres of land on the outskirts of town. I hear it's gorgeous."

I'm dumbfounded how my mom knows the latest celebrity gossip before me.

In the background, Mom's spoon clangs against a cup. "I floated the concert idea to the committee as a solution to revitalize the town. Everyone agreed that it's the perfect plan."

"But has he agreed?" I ask. It's not like the town has money to wave in his face.

"Not exactly," she says with some hesitation. "Only because I haven't asked him directly."

"What do you mean . . . *you?*"

"Well," she says, her voice pitching higher. "I was nominated to contact his manager, since I agreed to head up the committee this year."

I nearly drop the Christmas ribbon I'm holding. "Mom, no."

Mom can barely make ends meet working at the local health food shop. If it wasn't for my financial support, she'd have to sell her home. She doesn't have time to be the festival chairwoman.

"Honey, I'm in a different stage of life," Mom adds defensively. "The twins are adults now. And I can still work at the store and act as chairwoman of the committee. But I can't sit here and let the festival die."

"What about Doreen?" She's been the chairwoman ever since I can remember.

"She fell off a ladder and broke her hip."

With Doreen out of commission and the festival in free fall, the town is desperate.

I frown, suddenly feeling this weird tension of having to parent my mother. "You know the twins will not take care of you if *you* fall off a ladder." My younger brothers play hockey and are gone so much, they probably couldn't even keep a goldfish alive.

"Honestly, Mia, I need something to make me excited again."

"Then get a puppy," I suggest, trying to think of anything but letting my mom take on the town festival as chairwoman.

"I don't want a puppy."

"How about pickleball? Isn't that what people do when they get older?"

In the background, I can hear Mom set her glass on the counter. "I'm not bored. I just don't want this tradition to end. If we don't do something, we won't have the funds to continue. And a piece of Maplewood's history will be gone."

"Then let it go," I say, not understanding why this is so important, when all I wanted as a kid was to stop the Christmas festival for good. It always felt like an unwelcome uncle in our house, an exhausting season that kept us from thinking too hard about the past.

"I can't do that. I love this town," Mom says. "And I love Christmas."

While Maplewood celebrates Christmas in a boisterous, over-the-top way, all I've wanted is to stuff it into a bottle, tighten the lid, and toss it into the ocean. Compared to the effort she put into the festival, our own family celebration felt lackluster, like a second thought.

"Half the shops downtown are empty," Mom says. "If you were here, you'd see how it's gone downhill."

I have to clamp my lips to keep from muttering something I'll regret. It's not that I don't want to visit; the real question is *what draw is there to coming home? A mom who's too busy to even spend time with me?*

"How in the world will you convince Jace Knight to do a concert in Maplewood when he could play Yankee Stadium?" As someone who used to plan events for big names, I don't think they have a chance.

"Because Yankee Stadium doesn't want him. Not after what happened with his ex-girlfriend. When they split, the media blamed him for the breakup. Then his new album tanked, and his record label cut short his concert tour. He's returning home soon, and I'm guessing he needs something to bolster his career. Christmas is the *perfect* solution." Without even seeing her, I know Mom's smiling at her clever idea.

I straighten a candle on the fireplace. "I thought you said he's popular."

"*Was* popular. The last six months have been rocky. His manager said he's willing to talk to us. Although he hasn't actually asked Jace yet."

It doesn't sound hopeful. Definitely not something to stake the future of Maplewood on. "It's not like Maplewood is a prime location. It's a small town in the middle of Vermont."

"We have something better than location. We have . . ." She pauses for effect. "*Christmas spirit.*"

I cringe. "That won't convince him." Jace Knight is even less likely to fall for it with this kind of pitch.

"Then what will? Bringing joy to the town? Christmas generosity?"

"Definitely not. Musicians are in it for the same reasons as everyone else. To make money. I don't care if Christmas is involved."

Unlike my mother, I stopped believing Christmas was a magical holiday that solved everyone's problems. Instead, I realized I'd somehow been duped by every Hallmark holiday movie ever made.

Christmas wishes don't come true. People don't fall instantly in love. They don't magically find happiness or angels or talking snowmen.

Maybe Jimmy Stewart did. But not my family.

"Mom, you actually need a marketing plan and some money, as well as someone who's business-savvy enough to draw up a contract."

Knowing the committee members, they'll probably offer him a homemade pie.

She pauses. "Yes, that one missing piece is a problem."

Never mind that I listed three. I thumb through the mail and toss two holiday catalogues in the recycle bin.

"I know the perfect person for this," she says, her voice brightening.

"Who?" I ask, grabbing a banana and peeling it.

"I need an event planner," Mom says, then pauses.

I cough, nearly choking on my banana. "No, Mom. Absolutely not." I shake my head, even though Mom can't see it. No way am I coming home for *that.*

"At least consider it. The town is willing to pay you well."

"I don't understand. The festival is in dire shape, but you can hire an event planner?" This makes no practical sense.

"A wealthy man from Maplewood died and left money in his will to the festival. The committee agreed that hiring a legit event planner to save the festival would be worth it. As long as we make money this year, we can roll the money over to fund next year's festival."

"Mom, I can't."

After years of planning events—from beach festivals to huge concerts to the state fair—I burned out in the end. The events were both massively successful and incredibly stressful. It was hard to find reliable contractors to pull off everything, leaving me working crazy hours at the last minute. It's why I stepped away from event planning last year to recover. In the meantime, I'm temporarily working as a barista at the local coffee shop. After a year of trying to figure out what to do next, my bank account is nearly drained. I can barely pay my bills, much less Mom's. Renting a room in Jaz's home has been a lifesaver.

"I can't, Mom. I promised myself no more big events. And it's so late in the season."

"The committee will assist you . . ."

"My answer stands," I say firmly. "I doubt Jace will even consider it this late."

"His manager said we could talk about it. So what does the committee have to pay you to get you to say yes?"

"Why don't they hire you?" I say, not understanding why they'd overlook Mom's experience.

She doesn't even hesitate. "I can't leave my job at the store. And you've run events all over the South. You've pulled in big acts and negotiated with teams and know how to manage all the details I can't even anticipate. I can hang lights and mistletoe. I just don't know how to take it to the next level."

I sigh and rub my forehead. It would be nice to get an influx of money before Christmas, especially since my bank account looks abysmal.

"Mia, they're willing to give you what you ask," Mom says. "All you're doing is the planning and getting Jace on board. The committee will pull in volunteers to do the rest for you."

It sounds like a dream. Even so, I've opposed the festival for so long, I can't believe I'm even considering it.

Given that I can barely keep up with my bills, and I have zero money saved for Mom's next mortgage payment, this is tempting. If I say yes, I could secretly use the funds to help Mom out. It's either this job or working absurdly long hours at the coffee shop, which will leave me just as drained. I might not love the Mistletoe Festival, but do plumbers love unclogging toilets? Probably not.

Mom goes on, "I have money budgeted for new decorations, and I'll only need you there for a little over a month."

In the scheme of things, it's a good deal. *But can I pull it off?* Doubt spirals inside me like bathwater down the drain.

"Please, Mia, at least consider it," Mom says. "We'd make a good team."

Despite us being vastly different in our feelings about the festival, the last thing I want is for my mom to lose her house. What's one small-town Christmas festival?

I kick a fallen sprig of evergreen out of the way. Maybe if I agree, this will change things for our family. I'm not expecting a miracle, but it would help to finally put the past behind us.

"If you agree to my price, I'll do it on *one* condition: that I can make over the festival. No more Ugly Santa or obnoxious decorations. We turn it into a quaint Christmas town, or else I'm not doing it."

Mom clears her throat. She knows the committee will go down to their graves hanging on to their traditions with white knuckles.

"And you'll get Jace to agree?"

I hesitate. No one can promise that. "I'll try. But that's why I need to change things, to show him what this festival could be."

I'm not even sure I can pull it off, but I can't let on that I'm shaking in my boots.

"Then it's a deal," she says with hope in her voice.

"But I haven't even sent you my price," I say.

"I don't care. You're what Maplewood needs."

My stomach churns. I wonder if I've just made the worst mistake of my life.

"This is going to be the biggest thing our town has ever seen." I hear her relief—and feel the pressure—in that one sentence.

I bite my lip. "I can't do miracles." Even though that's what it's going to take.

"We don't expect miracles, honey. But can you get here by Tuesday?"

"Why Tuesday?" I ask, feeling a slow spike of adrenaline.

Mom pauses, then finally drops the bomb. "Because that's when I told Jace Knight you'd meet with him."

Mia

This is not happening. I stare at the flight attendant with what I hope looks like desperation.

She gazes at me without feeling. "The flight is overbooked. There's nothing we can do," she says with zero pity.

"But I have a meeting to make. It's *today.*" Even in the middle of the Charlotte airport, I'm not too proud to get down on my knees and beg.

The flight attendant shrugs. "All we can offer is a flight tomorrow. Sorry."

"Seriously, that's it?" I mutter under my breath, even though I know others in line are in the same situation—waiting in the purgatory of endless airport delays.

A man behind me, wearing a backwards ball cap and dark sunglasses, pushes up to the counter before I've even moved aside my carry-on. His sharp cheekbones and tousled hair curling out from his hat tip me off that he's stunning under his glasses, while the tight line of his lips gives the impression he's either smoldering or a total grump. And that's the problem with men like him—you can't tell the difference between smolder or grump.

"Oh, hello, sir," the flight attendant says in a cheerful voice.

"Can I help you?" For obvious reasons, she's suddenly way more friendly with him.

He glances over at a middle-aged man next to him with thinning hair and a navy suit. "I know the flight is overbooked. But my traveling companion can forfeit his flight, if needed." He turns to the man. "You wouldn't mind, would you?"

"Mind what?" the other man says, suddenly aware that he wasn't paying attention.

Mr. Smolder keeps talking to his coworker. "I can handle the meeting. Take tonight off. Enjoy a mini-vacation." He smacks his buddy on the shoulder.

"Wait," I say, stepping next to Mr. Smolder, ready to pounce on the one available seat. "I wasn't trying to eavesdrop, but is there a seat open now?"

I point at the guy in the suit, who still looks confused.

"I haven't forfeited my seat," he argues.

"Yes, you have," Mr. Smolder says. "I'm flying back alone."

The traveling companion frowns. "But what if"—his eyes flick to me for a second—"people bother you."

Wow. Mr. Smolder must be a full-on diva if he's that worried about people bothering him.

"We weren't sitting together, anyway." Mr. Smolder shrugs. "I'll be fine."

Why does he need special treatment? And why does the other guy treat him like royalty? It's getting on my nerves.

"Okay, so I'll cancel one seat," the flight attendant says as she changes the reservation. The man in the suit looks distressed. "Can I have your ID?" she asks both of them.

As they fish through their carry-on bags, I belly up to the counter again, determined to snag that extra seat.

"Sorry to interrupt . . ." I say, even though I'm not sorry at all. I'm not usually this pushy, but the whole town of Maplewood is counting on me arriving today. "I'll take the available seat."

I glance at Mr. Smolder again, feeling a need to explain, even though he will not get any special treatment from me. "I have an important meeting today."

He nods, unimpressed. "Me, too."

"Mine's *really* important," I say, defensively.

From behind his glasses, I swear he rolls his eyes.

"Ma'am, can I have your ticket information, please?" the lady behind the counter says. She's suddenly returned to her robotic voice because apparently I'm not as special as Mr. Smolder.

I hand over my ID and catch Mr. Smolder peeking at my ugly license picture, the one that makes me look like a convicted criminal having a bad hair day. "That's a really terrible picture of me, in case you're wondering."

"I wasn't wondering," he says flatly.

"I mean, they won't even let you smile for your license these days, so we all look like a bunch of murderers." When I'm nervous, I turn into my mother and can't stop talking.

From behind his glasses, the crease deepens between his eyebrows. "That's not really a problem for me."

Which is another way of saying, *I always look like a gorgeous guy who women flirt with.*

He steps away just as the flight attendant hands me my ID. "You're all set. You now have a seat in economy class, thanks to this gentleman." She nods toward Mr. Smolder, who looks a bit smug, like he just tossed a couple pennies into my tip jar.

I glance at his ticket and see that he's in first class. Frankly, it seems a little unfair that he flies in first class while his coworker does not.

He turns to the man in the suit. "I'm going to grab some food from the lounge and take a nap until they call for boarding."

Judging by how he's trying to slink away to his special bougie lounge, I actually feel sorry for his traveling companion. It's not right that they fly in two different classes. I follow Mr. Smolder to the entrance of the lounge, wanting to say something but too afraid to tap on his shoulder.

My strong feelings about justice and fairness bubble up inside me, the result of growing up the daughter of a single parent. My mom had to fight for everything.

He turns at the last second to face me. "Let me guess," he says, exasperated. "You want something else?"

"What else would I want?" I crinkle my nose.

"I don't know. A picture?"

The nerve of this guy to assume I want a picture with him. "All I wanted was to say thanks," I blurt. "Even though I think it's unfair that you made your coworker give up his seat. Shouldn't you guys be equals?"

He stares at me for a second, like he's struggling for an answer. "He bought his own ticket," he says flatly.

"Why did you get the first-class seat, then? Did you guys play rock-paper-scissors or something?"

The crease between his eyebrows deepens. "He paid his way. Said he wanted to save money."

I shake my head, still not understanding. "Then why didn't you sit with him?"

"It's kind of hard to . . .in my position." He lifts a shoulder, like he doesn't have another option.

What is he, some special snowflake?

"You should be equals. No matter what position you hold in the company."

"The company?" he says with a laugh.

"Aren't you in business together?"

"Sort of," he says, then stares at me. "He's worked really hard the past several months. I thought he'd like the break." He saws his teeth over his lip, then scans the surrounding area, like he's worried about something. "Believe me, if I could skip this meeting, I would."

"Oh," I say, suddenly feeling stupid. Maybe he's actually doing something *nice* for his coworker, rather than forcing him into airport purgatory.

"I'm sure my manager would appreciate your concern," he adds, "even if you were a bit pushy."

"He's your manager?" I sputter.

"He works for me," he says without explaining more.

My eyes flit over his outfit. He's obviously not in corporate, wearing a henley shirt, ripped jeans, and a worn cap on backwards.

"What's so important that you had to jump on the ticket like a rabid chihuahua?" he asks.

"Hey," I say with a frown, straightening my spine. After stepping out of my career for a year, I feel like a rusty, bent nail that needs to be driven into new wood. "An open seat on an overbooked flight requires doggedness. And if you must know . . .I'm meeting with Jace Knight."

He looks at me for a second without responding. Then he laughs.

"You know who Jace Knight is, right?" I assume he's laughing because he doesn't believe me. "The country rock singer?"

"I know who he is," he says quickly, his sunglasses leveled on me, his mouth twisting slightly, like he's annoyed and amused at the same time. "Do you?"

I shift from one foot to the other. Before I left, I only had time to look up a few pictures of Jace online at a music awards show where he was dressed in a tux. Not exactly thorough research, but I was too busy sending the Mistletoe Festival committee a list of tasks I need done before I arrived, as well as organizing a project management program for everything that needs to happen.

"Of course," I say with feigned confidence. "He has lots of hits."

The corners of his lips curl, and a small dimple deepens in one cheek. For some reason, that dimple looks vaguely familiar, but I can't place where. "Thirteen top-ten hits," he finally says, his dimple still plainly evident.

I bet women love that dimple. Because guys like him? They're always aware of their assets.

I lift an eyebrow. "Well, someone's a Jace Knight fan."

"And you're not?"

I play with the handle of my carry-on, suddenly feeling so called out I can hardly look at him. Why should this guy care, anyway? "Didn't he win some music award last year?"

He grunts. "A few."

For whatever reason, this guy is making me feel woefully ignorant. Shame zips down my spine.

I had planned on doing more research once I arrived in Maplewood and had a few hours before the meeting. Now I'll be lucky to even make it on time. "I hope he doesn't have the inflated ego to go with it," I say, trying to make a joke.

He doesn't laugh, just stares at me, his lips quirking. Even under those glasses, I can tell he's got amazing eyes.

"I'm only doing this as a favor for my mom," I ramble nervously, suddenly feeling the weight of his stare. "And because the money's good."

One eyebrow lifts above his glasses. "So it's about the money?"

"There's more to it," I hint, not wanting to get into my complicated family history. Even now, I can feel the familiar ache at the reminder that I'm going home to face something I've been putting off.

"But the money doesn't hurt, either," he says bluntly.

I shift uncomfortably. "Well, it's been nice meeting you. Thanks again for the seat." Then I offer a weak smile, glad to escape this conversation.

I know my reasons, and I don't have to justify them to him.

I doubt we'll run into each other again since I'll be crammed into economy while he's luxuriously stretched out in first class with all that enviable legroom.

For some reason, his smug look got under my skin, like an itch I couldn't satisfy. Thanks to Mr. Smolder, I'll make my flight home.

I can only hope that when I meet Jace Knight, his first impression of me is favorable. Because if we get off on the wrong foot, it could ruin everything, including Christmas.

THREE

Jace

The log cabin is a welcome relief after spending months touring. As soon as I drop my suitcase to punch in my code for the door, the cats are already curling around my ankles, purring in approval.

"You guys miss me? Did the housekeeper take good care of you?" I scratch their heads, noticing that both cats look a little fatter since I left. Someone must be overfeeding them, although I don't mind. As much as I hate cats, these strays have grown on me since I bought the place.

My phone buzzes in my pocket as the lock clicks open. Allan is already filling my screen with frantic messages.

Allan: Jace, I already told them you'd consider the concert. This won't look good if you back out now before reviewing their offer.

He's concerned about the vague message I left earlier, saying I want to cancel the meeting with the Mistletoe Festival committee. I shouldn't have texted him my decision yet. Ever since my sales have tanked, Allan's blood pressure has sky-rocketed. I had to force him to take a night off so he won't have a heart attack.

The stress feels like it's killing me, too.

All these people rely on me to feed their families, which is why I don't want to bother with the meeting. I can't get their hopes up when I already know I need a month off to recover from a terrible year.

As I drop my backpack on the floor, the sudden ring from my cell phone makes my shoulders tense. I don't want to talk to Allan, who's going to try and convince me to do this. All I want is to sink into my leather sofa for a nap.

I let out a restrained moan, then answer the call. "Listen, Allan, I haven't signed any papers. If I back out now, they can find someone else." I'm not in the mood to discuss my flailing career.

"But I told them you'd consider it," Allan says. "This is only going to tarnish your reputation more if they leak it to the press that you bowed out."

"What reputation?" I say, laughing dryly. "I thought I lost that a long time ago."

I kick off my shoes and sink into the buttery soft sofa that faces a wall of picture windows and a view of the mountains.

After everything that's happened in the last six months, I don't have much of a reputation left. I'm definitely not working with that girl who's supposed to be in charge. Besides her obvious ignorance, she admitted her motivations clearly: She's only doing it for the money.

That's exactly what I don't need. *Someone who's going to use me for what I can do for them.*

"This concert could help your image," Allan explains. "No one can see you as a villain when you're singing Christmas songs."

A grunt escapes my lips. "I'm the villain now? Nice."

"You lost your heartthrob status when you broke up with Ava. The press hasn't been kind to you."

That's putting it mildly. My stomach squeezes. More like a dumpster fire.

"A Christmas concert is always a slam dunk for resurrecting someone's career," he concludes.

"But I don't feel like celebrating. It would be fake," I tell him. Right now, my Christmas spirit is like a truck with an empty gas tank abandoned on the side of the road. I've nothing left to give. "What I need is to write songs again." But only if I can overcome my writer's block. I haven't written even one line for months.

"Then take January off," he urges. "Now's not the time to run away from your career. Christmas could be a profitable month. Use this concert to prop up your sales."

"So you're saying do it for the money? You know I'm not that type." Even if that woman running this event is.

Even now, I'm regretting that Allan knows about my abysmal sales. My album sales have been plummeting, and the ugly rumors in the media about my breakup have only added fuel to the fire. My career is nosediving faster than a stalled airplane.

"I know you care more about the music than the money, Jace. But this is different. It's an easy win for you. At least consider it," he begs.

"I already have," I say firmly, propping my feet up on the coffee table and taking in the stunning view of the valley outside. "My answer stands."

Allan sighs. "One more thing. If you get musically inspired while you're home, write a great song to get your career back on track. If it takes off, that will keep your sales steady in January when you're off."

If only it were that easy.

"Right now, I'd be thankful for any musical inspiration," I say, before hanging up. Ever since I broke up with Ava, I haven't been able to write anything.

Music has always been where I've found my peace. And making other people feel that way—giving them something to hang on to—is why I've continued making music.

For a few minutes, I push off Allan's words: *consider it.*

"Please, Jace."

I sigh. "I'll go . . . so I can turn them down the right way."

I check my watch, wondering if I can still make the meeting.

As much as I don't want to attend, there's one small part of me that needs satisfying.

I want to see *her* face when she realizes who I am.

———

As I head into Maplewood, a light dusting of snow powders the ground around the winding road. My cabin is tucked away on the outskirts of town in the Green Mountains, heavy with the scent of pine and brilliant views of the heavily wooded valley below. In the fall, the view is exceptional, trees lit with blood-red, orange, and goldenrod hues. But now that the leaves have fallen, only barren trees remain. Kind of like my career.

As I take the final curve into Maplewood, a whiff of fresh bread from the bakery hits me. Except for the new sign on the front of the bakery, not much else has changed since I left on tour. The empty stores on Main Street look like hollowed-out shells, their run-down facades a stark reminder that this town needs new life. No amount of lights or decorations can hide how this town is falling apart. It's definitely not the image I want for my struggling career.

When I step outside, the sharp wind makes my breath rise like vapor clouds. Wanda's Diner is next to the bank building where we are meeting, and I have just enough time to grab a coffee beforehand.

The diner smells like a mix of bacon grease and fresh coffee, a welcoming scent after a long day.

"Look who's back," Wanda says with a wink. "You want the usual?"

She knows my regular order of bacon and eggs, over easy, with a side of homemade strawberry jelly on wheat toast, to go.

"Just coffee," I tell her. "Headed to a meeting next door."

Wanda's the type of woman who never asks me personal questions. She's grown old right along with the building. She slides the plain white paper cup across the counter. "Anything else?"

I shake my head and hand her a five even though the coffee is only half that. "Keep the change."

Wanda always treats me like everyone else she serves, even from the first day I walked in.

"You have a good day, Mr. Knight," she says with a nod.

"Same to you."

I wrap my hands around the cup as I brave the short trek to the conference room next door, hoping I don't get stopped. To my relief, no one pays any attention to me. It's the best part of living in Maplewood. No star treatment here. It's like they understand my need for privacy and offer it, no questions asked.

Which is why it's going to be hard to turn down their request today. The people here deserve a concert, even if I want to hide from the spotlight.

A woman with a warm smile and teal glasses greets me at the door. "Mr. Knight! How lovely to meet you. My name is Cora." My manager explained that the pushy young woman I met at the airport is Cora's daughter. I glance around and don't see her yet. Despite getting off on the wrong foot, it's too bad Mia MacPherson came all this way for nothing.

Behind Cora, eight unfamiliar faces nudge each other and smile. They all wear name tags and matching T-shirts, all emblazoned with my picture. It's supposed to be a fun surprise, but it's disturbing to see my huge face plastered across their chests.

"We had these made for you," Cora says, pointing at the shirts.

"Wow," I stammer, because it's all I can say.

Then she hands me a shirt. "A gift for you."

I can't bear to tell her that I'd never wear this T-shirt. I give her a smile and mumble, "I've never seen anything like it."

"I take it your trip home was non-eventful?" she asks.

"Almost didn't make my layover in Charlotte," I say. "But since I'm here, we can begin."

If there's one thing I hate, it's starting late. Punctuality matters in the music business. Proving that I'm a hard worker and not just in it for the money—I pride myself on these qualities.

Cora's eyes skirt somewhere over my shoulder as her brow creases. "My daughter, Mia, should be here any minute," she says, a slight tone of worry in her voice.

Yes, we've met, I want to say, but I'm afraid it will come out as a sneer. *And I'm saving the surprise.*

"Is Mr. French coming?" she asks, wringing her hands as she motions for me to sit at the head of the table. Everyone follows my lead as I take a seat.

"He's stuck in Charlotte," I explain. "But after you hear what I have to say, it's probably unnecessary for him to attend."

"What do you mean?" Cora says, folding her hands in that way women do to prepare themselves for unpleasant news.

"I don't want to waste your time, but I've decided . . ."

The door flies open. "Sorry I'm late!" Mia rushes into the room, hurrying past me.

She's now wearing a fitted, black dress and boots, her strawberry-blonde hair neatly curled into long waves. It's classy in an understated way, and so different from the girl at the airport who wore an oversized sweatshirt and faded jeans.

She doesn't even notice me as she strides in. She drops her laptop bag on the table with a thud. "Sorry to keep you all waiting. My plane was late, and I barely had enough time to change. Has he arrived yet?"

Cora's face freezes into a strained smile as she nods toward me.

"What?" Mia asks, cluelessly glancing around.

"The plane wasn't a problem for me," I say, leaning back in my chair, putting my hands behind my head.

Mia spins around, a look of disbelief, then horror flashing across her face.

"You're . . ." Her voice drops, and her face drains at the realization of our previous meeting finally sinking in. "Mr. Smolder," she whispers.

"Jace Knight," I say with a smug grin.

I was right. *Her expression is priceless.*

FOUR

Jace

Cora places her hand on her daughter's back. "Mia, I'd like you to meet our local celebrity."

Mia blinks, trying to process this news as her cheeks flame. "Jace Knight," she repeats in a strained voice.

I feel sorry for her. *Almost.*

"It's good to *officially* meet you." I hold out my hand, not saying a word about our previous introduction.

She limply shakes it, staring as her brow creases.

"Did you have a pleasant flight?" I ask.

"I did," she says weakly. Judging by how long she's been holding that frown, she's still trying to figure out if I'm going to say anything about our previous interaction. I'm not the type to plot revenge, even if it was thoroughly satisfying to see her face when she realized who I was.

She swallows hard, then says, "Did you?"

"A few pushy passengers," I add, pinning my gaze on her. "But when I stretched out in first class for a nap, I forgot all about them."

She clamps her lips together and looks down at the floor, and I notice red splotches creeping up her neck.

Cora claps her hands. "Let's begin, shall we?" She shuffles

some papers as Mia sits next to her. "Mr. Knight, we're here to talk about a possible concert on the last night of the Mistletoe Festival."

I clear my throat. "That's why I came." My eyes slide over to Mia, who glances down at the table, clearly still avoiding me. There's no point in delaying this any longer. "I appreciate how welcoming the town has been."

The lone man on the committee interrupts. "We were just talking about how your move to Maplewood is the best thing that's ever happened to our town." Then he points to his name tag. "My name is Bob, by the way."

"Well, thanks, Bob," I say slowly, suddenly feeling bad that I'm going to dash Bob's hopes. "I haven't really done anything for Maplewood."

Another woman named Judy raises her hand. "Excuse me, Mr. Knight, but you have done so much. You've given us hope again. We're nearly giddy with excitement about how this concert is going to change our town."

Everyone is nodding and smiling, like I'm some sort of town savior sent to rescue Maplewood. I shift in my seat uncomfortably. It's too much to expect, especially when I can't deliver on this promise. These people are doing this for genuine reasons— because they believe in this town. It's not a matter of money; it's saving a part of their history.

I hold my hands up to stop the committee. "I think that's a little much to expect from one person, which is why I'm not . . ."

"We don't expect anything, Mr. Knight," Bob says. "We already think you're great!"

"But I'm not a miracle worker."

"You're being modest," Cora purrs with an adoring smile. "You're one of the most popular country rock stars ever. We're so honored to have you in Maplewood. We'll do everything we can to make this your best concert ever." Then she leans toward me and pats my hand. "We know this year hasn't been easy."

I frown. *That's one way of putting it.*

Mia covers her eyes, embarrassed by her mom's concern.

"That's kind of you, to want to help," I begin, trying to steer this ship back to why I'm here. "And there's nothing you or I can do to fix this year." Especially when my career is in the tank. "Unfortunately, I need some time to recover from things."

Cora's mouth sags. "Do you mean you can't do the concert?"

I bristle under her devastated look. "I'm afraid you'll have to find someone else."

"But there *is* no one else," Cora insists, then glances at her daughter for help.

Until now, Mia has been staring at the table in humiliation. Her mother's gaze seems to shake her from her silence.

"Can't?" Mia asks. "Or won't?"

"Both," I say.

She hesitates, then taps a finger on the edge of the table. "How much time do you need? Could you take a few days and then decide?"

"That won't help," I reply, even though I know I'm in no place to decide right now. I'm exhausted, and this meeting clearly came at a bad time.

"We'll do everything for you," she says. "Marketing, tickets, promotion. And it's a Christmas concert. Different from your others."

"My team is tired. I don't even have a personal assistant right now. She quit on me last week."

Cora's face brightens. "I know someone who'd make a wonderful assistant for you." She turns toward her daughter. "Mia has loads of experience assisting famous people."

"Mom," she says, through clenched teeth. "I already have a job, remember?"

"But you're incredible at managing events *and* people. Remember when you were the manager for that indie rock band?"

"What band was that?" I ask, curious.

"An all-female metal rock band called The Terminators," Mia says.

Cora leans toward me. "Not really my style. I'd much rather hear you sing any day of the week."

"They're no longer together," Mia adds. "And why don't we get back to the topic at hand, which is whether Mr. Knight can do this concert?" She straightens her spine, like she's shifting into a new role: businesswoman.

"I can't," I say firmly.

The committee looks around.

"What kind of offer do you need?" Mia asks. "We're willing to negotiate."

"I don't want an offer," I reply.

Allan's voice echoes in the back of my head, but I don't want to listen.

Mia glances around at the committee. "Look around this room, Mr. Knight. These people put their hope in you to save the festival. Your concert could work wonders for our community. But that's not why I'm asking you to do it. It's because we're losing a piece of our history. Maplewood needs you."

Her charm almost works on me. But I've been in the music industry long enough to know when someone is trying to use me for their gain.

"You should be a lawyer," I say, not hiding my sarcasm.

Then I glance around. The whole committee is focused on her rousing speech. Bob nods dramatically. Patty blinks back tears. Donna clutches her heart.

Maybe Mia wasn't making up a speech to manipulate me.

"Okay, Boss Lady, what are you offering?"

Her face flinches before she folds her hands. "My name is Mia."

"Okay, Mia. Let's talk through what Maplewood has to offer."

She swallows and glances at Cora. "Mom, could I have a moment alone with Mr. Knight?"

Cora shrugs. "We'll step into the hall for a break." She motions for the rest of the committee to follow as Mia closes the door behind them.

She remains standing, crossing her arms, leaning against the conference room door, eyeing me. "I don't know what you're up to since you weren't exactly forthright at the airport, but I want to know what your game is."

A humorless laugh escapes my lips. "There's no game. I'm just not that interested. Maplewood isn't exactly a stage singers would die to play on."

"I know that. But the people of Maplewood believe in you. They're willing to do whatever it takes to make this a success."

"Including you?" I ask, tilting my head.

She drops her arms to her sides. "Why wouldn't I be?"

"You admitted why you were doing it."

She hesitates before sitting to face me. "Is that why you're so opposed to this? Because of my stupidity at the airport? It wasn't exactly fair of you to not tell me who you were."

"I wasn't the one who didn't do my research ahead of time."

"So I googled a few pictures of you at a music awards show. You weren't wearing glasses or a hat, and definitely not dressed like that." She waves toward my ripped jeans. "I'm sorry if I offended you. But don't hold it against the people of Maplewood. Give me one last shot for the community." She stops and waits for an answer.

"Tell me what you're thinking."

Her mouth curls before she flips open her laptop and brings up a page that looks like a complicated spreadsheet along with a detailed list and timeline.

"Well, this entire town needs a makeover for Christmas. New decorations. New events. The whole Christmas enchilada. If we can get some local media coverage of the Mistletoe Festival, it will build up to the pinnacle event—your concert. What if we stream your concert live on YouTube? Then we could get even more publicity."

"I don't stream my events," I insist. "That's like giving away your good stuff for free."

She narrows her gaze. "I think that depends on your goals. The old downtown theater can only hold so many people. The YouTube event could make you money and give people the chance to see you differently."

"I don't want to become a YouTuber," I argue.

"That's not what I'm suggesting," she says. "It's all about perception."

"Ah, yes." I nod. "Now you sound like my manager. He thinks I need to work on repairing my reputation and believes Christmas is the perfect time to do that."

"He's not wrong," she says. "A Christmas concert is an easy solution for you. How can anyone imagine you're a Scrooge if you're crooning about snuggling by the fire?"

I let out an unexpected guffaw. "I don't sing about snuggling. I sing about partying. Have you listened to my music?"

She shifts uncomfortably. "I listened to one or two songs."

"One? In that case, you probably don't know that I'm not that type. I prefer breakup ballads."

"Well, breakup ballads don't really work after the year you've had," she says. "Your fans want to hear about falling in love at Christmas."

"Have you been talking to my manager?" I ask, annoyed. "I don't write sappy songs."

"Then what do you listen to at Christmas?" She tilts her head.

I shrug. "I don't really listen to the fluff they play on the radio. I'm more likely to choose Christmas carols with soaring violins and piano."

She studies me, like I'm a puzzle she can't figure out. "But you're a country rock singer."

"It's not what I perform. But there's a familiarity with those old songs. Every time I hear them, it's like stepping into my grandparents' church."

She points at me. "That's your concert. You do the familiar

songs, but you do them your way. And then sprinkle in a few new ones."

I shake my head. "Nobody is going to go for a country rock singer doing Christmas carols."

"I disagree," she says. "People want what's traditional at Christmas. And by doing a mix of carols and your own songs, you'll win them over. Easy, right?"

"Hardly." I run my hand across the back of my neck. "But I'm still not sure my team can pull it off."

"What do you need help with?"

"Everything." I feel like I'm being swept away by a current I can't control. *Man, she's persuasive.* And for some reason, I don't hate it. "I need someone to pull together the logistics. My manager will help remotely. And I'll make sure the band is ready."

She nods and thinks for a second. "What about your assistant? Is this something I could help with for this concert?"

I lean forward, resting my elbows on my knees. "I thought you were already the event planner for the festival?"

"I am." She leans back in her chair as she looks at her spread-sheet. "If I can bring in a few friends to help me, then I can do both. And I'll have insider info on the festival, so it will be easy to coordinate."

"And more money, right?" I give her a pointed look.

"I didn't ask you to pay me," she shoots back.

"But money doesn't hurt."

"Look, I quit my event planning business a year ago, and I'm trying to figure out what to do next. So yeah, I'm kind of desperate for work." She looks at the door, making sure the committee isn't listening. "If you must know, I help my mom with her bills. But I know I'm good at what I do. Even though we got off on the wrong foot, I hope you won't hold it against me. I'm here for work, but also because I want to help my mom preserve this town's history . . . for the future of Maplewood."

"So you love the Mistletoe Festival?"

"Not at all," she says, then notices my surprise. "Christmas

has never been the most wonderful time of year for me, honestly."
Then she glances away like she's uncomfortable.

"That's something we have in common," I say, leaning back in
my chair. Christmas is not a happy holiday for me either. Ava and
I broke up around the holidays, and the association was
automatic.

"Then maybe we both need this Christmas to be different," I
say. "Even if that means we have to put up with each other."

Her eyes flick toward me, and I can feel the doubt rolling
off her.

It's going to be hard to change Mia's mind about me after the
airport incident. But doing something for the town of Maplewood is the first thing that's felt right. Because it's no longer
about me.

Even if this doesn't fix my career, it gives me something to
focus on. An event that's more than fame or money. And if it
helps Maplewood, this could be the legacy I leave. No matter how
much Mia dislikes me, I can't let her interfere with the concert.

"If I agree to this concert—will you play by my rules?"

Her lips quirk, like she's trying to hold something back. "Yes."

I tap my knuckles on the table. "Then I'll do it."

FIVE

Mia

"I think I just made a deal with the devil," I tell Jaz over the phone. I tap my bright blue fingernails on Mom's dining room table, which is also my current office. It's a little less than ideal to live in my family's tiny home along with my twin brothers, but given that I'm low on cash until I get paid, it's my only choice.

My brother Vale pounds on the drum set in our basement like he's in a heavy metal band. I rub my forehead as cymbals crash repeatedly, like someone's driving nails into my head.

"Who is making that awful noise?" Jaz asks.

"My brother's new hobby," I moan. "How am I going to survive until Christmas?" Both my brothers are massive creatures, mostly from lifting weights and playing hockey. But they're also loud and always in my space, and this house is way too small for all of us.

"Maybe the committee could pay you early so you can rent an apartment?" she suggests hopefully.

Even if they pay me early, I'm too broke to spend money on something I don't need.

"The town doesn't pay me until the festival is complete. And

Jace . . ." I pause, unsure how to explain that I've already botched our relationship. "He detests me."

"There's no way. He hardly knows you," she assures me.

"The way he looked at me at the airport when I confronted him . . . it was like I was the most disgusting creature alive." I shake my head. "How was I supposed to know who he was when he was wearing a disguise?" Not that a hat and sunglasses are a foolproof disguise, but they clearly threw me off.

"I'm sure you're not the first."

"I'm probably the first to say something stupid."

It's only been two days since I talked to Jace, but I'm wondering if I'm in over my head. None of the volunteers know how to plan a big event, much less a concert. "I'm freaking out here, Jaz. What if I can't deliver on what I've promised? What if the festival is a total flop?"

"You couldn't be a flop if you tried, Mia. You research everything. Your spreadsheets are so mind-boggling, they make my eyeballs roll back into my head."

"I'm not sure that's a good thing."

"It is for certain situations. I'm missing your organizational skills at home. And I could use your expertise with planning my new fashion website."

"But I don't know anything about fashion."

"That doesn't matter. I need someone to organize all the ideas in my head."

In our friend group, I'm the person who finds problems and fixes them. Jaz is the fun one—the life of the party who's always dressed to kill. But my research skills don't apply to my dilemma. "I told Jace I could plan the festival *and* be his assistant. I can't be everywhere at once. This is Jace Knight we're talking about—he's at a massively different level than The Terminators."

"And far better looking," she adds. "In case you haven't noticed."

I have noticed, but I won't admit it. Jace Knight can't even stand me right now.

"It's why women fling their clothing at him during his concerts," I say.

Jaz snort-laughs. "I bet he has quite a collection of ladies' underwear."

I grimace. "I don't want to know. The only collection he should have is something boring. Like paperclips."

"He can't help that he's gorgeous in that rugged country-boy way. I bet he'd look great shirtless on the back of a horse."

"Will you stop? I want to poke my eyes out now." I rub my forehead, trying to wipe that image from my mind. "The town has so much potential. I just need to find someone who's got the style to turn this town into a Hallmark Christmas movie."

"What about someone from the committee?"

"No," I say. "They don't have the design skills, like you and Ella."

There's a pause on the other end. "Is this your desperate plea to get me to work for you?"

Ever since Ella opened up her interior design business in Sully's Beach, Jaz has been helping her while trying to get her fashion design business off the ground. My offer might not be the same as designing a Christmas festival, but it's close enough.

"I could pay you," I add. "And Ella too. The committee has a budget that I'm allowed to use at my discretion. Plus, I need you as my emotional support." Between my meddling family and Jace's big ego, I need someone who will keep me sane.

Jaz lets out a sigh of defeat. "When do you need me?"

I jump up from my seat so fast I knock my papers off the table. They float to the floor as I pump my fist in the air.

"You won't regret this. The people here are lovely. And Maplewood will put you in the Christmas spirit."

"You had me at the mention of Hallmark Christmas movies," she says. "I'll get to work on a design for Main Street right away."

"Let's chat about the details after I meet with Jace."

I slide back into my chair and a message pops up on my computer screen.

Jace: Can we move our meeting up an hour?

I lean on the table, suddenly aware that Jace is no longer a famous star on the other side of a screen, but a real person who invites me over. My stomach flutters. I'm not someone who rubs shoulders with celebrities. I'm just an unemployed thirty-one-year-old temporarily living with my mother.

"Listen, Jace just moved our meeting up, so I gotta run."

"You're meeting with Jace Knight right now?" The wonder in her voice makes me even more nervous.

"Yeah, why?"

Jaz squeals on the other end. "I got shivers just thinking about seeing his place."

I roll my eyes. "I'm his employee, not a guest."

"I know," she says. "But he's inviting you over. Do you know what a privilege that is? He doesn't even let the press into his home."

"We've got a concert to plan in a very short time." I don't say it, but it's in the back of my mind: *And a reputation to fix.*

"Maybe this will be the best thing that's ever happened to you." I can hear the smile in her voice.

Or the worst. I just don't know which way it'll go yet.

———

I arrive at Jace's cabin on the outskirts of town with five minutes to spare. Since a security gate blocks his sprawling property, I check in with my own passcode and then travel the winding drive through the middle of a dense forest. If Jace wanted privacy, this is definitely the equivalent of getting off the grid.

About the time that I'm sure this drive will never end, his log cabin comes into full view. The modern luxury cabin looks newly built and has massive windows and a large porch. A Jaguar sits in the drive outside.

I step outside my car and shiver as the wind tosses my hair in my face. It's not that I'm nervous about today, it's that every time I'm near him, I get this strange jumpy feeling in my chest, like my heart is about to leap outside my bones.

Maybe it's because he's Mr. Smolder himself, dubbed the *Dark Knight* because he's the poster child for *tall, dark, and handsome* with that mysterious dimpled smirk.

No matter how I try to paint our newfound working relationship, I distinctly get the feeling he doesn't like me. After lecturing him at the airport and then arriving late to my last meeting, I need us to hit it off today. And if I do my job well, an endorsement from Jace would be huge for any future career prospects.

As I walk to his front door, something brushes my leg, and I nearly stumble over it, catching myself at the last second before I fall on my face.

"What was that?" I mutter, trying to find whatever nearly tripped me.

"Stray cat," a husky voice says. Jace leans against the doorframe with an amused glint in his eye. A ginger cat skitters by, hiding behind a bush.

I straighten, trying to pick up whatever's left of my pride. "Were you standing there the whole time?" That wasn't how I wanted to make a first impression.

"Long enough to see you almost face-plant." The orange cat leaps out from the bush as Jace moves to block the door so the kitty won't sneak inside. "If you want to come in before Tabby bolts in here, I'd appreciate it."

"Tabby? You name your strays?" I glance at the ginger feline who caused my humiliation.

"I found them in the woods as kittens and they followed me home. The other cat is Blackie."

"Let me guess . . . she's black?" I lift an eyebrow.

Jace shrugs. "I'm not very creative with names," he admits, reaching down to scratch Tabby behind her ears. "Even though I have a small heated shed for them, they act like they want to be indoor cats."

"Maybe you should let them," I suggest. "Cats know where they belong."

"I tried, and all they wanted was to bolt outside. I think they want whatever they can't have. And since they can't make up their minds, I keep them outside."

Even though Jace seemed standoffish and smug the first time I met him, this makes me think there's more to him than meets the eye. A guy who takes in strays can't be that bad, right?

As Jace waves me inside, Tabby attempts to follow my lead, and Jace makes a swift movement to stop her and bumps into me instead. As my hip brushes him, his bicep presses against my arm to steady me, and I immediately notice that he's solidly built—a fact that makes me jump away from him in embarrassment.

"Sorry," he mumbles as Tabby slinks away. "Do you want to have a seat?"

When I turn, my breath catches. This place is just as gorgeous as I imagined. A grand entry opens up to a spacious living room with reclaimed wood floors, an enormous stone fireplace, and leather furniture that looks so buttery soft, I could melt into it. A modern chef's kitchen is off the living area while an open stairway leads to a loft where I assume the bedrooms are. My favorite part is the wall of picture windows in the living room, boasting a stunning view of the sloping mountainside, overlooking the valley below. No wonder Jace wanted this property. The cathedral ceilings and breathtaking views are priceless.

"This view," I whisper, taking in the snow-dusted fir trees dotting the mountain. "It makes me feel like I'm outside with the cats."

"It's the reason I bought this property," he says, his eyes roaming across the valley. "I wanted a place in the mountains where the surroundings inspired me. After traveling by tour bus and plane for weeks on end, this place is my shalom."

"Your what?"

"It means peace in Hebrew."

I can see why. A grand piano sits in the opposite corner,

begging to be played. According to the brief bio I read, he plays guitar, so I'm not sure why he has a piano unless it's to impress people. The whole feel of the place makes me want to curl up on a leather sofa with a cat tucked on my lap.

Jace sinks into an armchair and motions for me to do the same. He props his elbows on his knees, suddenly turning into Mr. Smolder, ready to do business.

I erase all thoughts of lounging around in this mountain retreat and open my laptop. "I have some ideas I want to run by you. And then you can tell me what you need me to do."

"I won't need your ideas," he states. "And I'll send you a list of things I need done by email." His words pinch, throwing off my newfound confidence. He's totally dismissing me.

"Uh, I thought we were discussing concert preparations and how we can tie it into the festival."

He grabs his phone off the coffee table and swipes the screen, ignoring me. What happened to the Jace who wanted to help the community?

"Jace?"

He puts a finger up to let me know he's busy. "I'm responding to a message from my manager."

He might be a big star, but my time is worth something too. I rest my chin on my hand and stare at him while he types a text.

"Uh, sorry." He sets down his phone. "I gave it some thought, and I want a small concert. My manager is picking some pop songs that are Christmas-themed."

I frown. "What about our original idea? The carols you like along with a few new songs?"

"I'm not sure now. And I don't want to include any new songs." His eyes flit out the window. "There's not time. And no offense, but it's just Maplewood."

My shoulders sink. What happened to the Jace who wanted to help Maplewood and restore his career? He's totally giving up on this before we've even started.

I glance down at my list of carols, which Jace refuses to look at. I wish I'd printed them off. At least then I could wad up the paper and throw it at him in frustration. It's not like I can tell Jace Knight what to do, but he seemed genuinely interested in performing something totally different. And it made me feel like he valued my opinion.

"I'm keeping the concert easy," he says. "That's my style."

"I thought your style was party songs with a side of breakup ballads?"

Jace gives me a little smirk. "Normally, yes. But not this time. I mean, really, I don't care as long as it makes money." He gives me a look that's not so much the *Dark Knight* as it is *Ebenezer Scrooge*.

He might be one of the most famous music stars in America, but I will not let him ruin this concert because he's too tired to care.

I shut my laptop and pause. I'm not going into this conversation with fists swinging, but I need to know why he's already given up before we've started. "This doesn't sound like you at all."

"Because you know so much about me?"

I glance away for a second, feeling embarrassment creep up my spine. "I made a mistake of not doing my research before we met. To be honest, I'm not really into celebrities. But I was hoping to get an impression of you. An *unbiased* one."

He stares at me like he's trying to figure out whether he should believe me. "So you didn't look up all the dirt on me?"

I shake my head. "My mom mentioned you've had a difficult year, but I don't keep up on celebrity gossip. Honestly, I didn't want to know about your personal life. Because it's none of my business." Even though I heard about his breakup, I didn't want to taint my view of him.

"Well, that would be a first." He stares at me long enough to make me uncomfortable.

"Listen, I know Maplewood might be peanuts to you, but this concert is a big deal. We're going to turn it into the cutest little Christmas town ever."

"What does that have to do with me?"

"It has everything to do with you." I set my computer down on the expensive-looking coffee table made from reclaimed wood and metal. "If we create this idyllic small town where people want to bring their families and make Christmas memories, then all those good feelings transfer to you. It's a win-win for both of us." Even as I say it, I hope we can pull it off. I'm making big promises that I'm not even sure I can deliver.

Jace shakes his head. "Do you really think Maplewood can live up to that image? Especially with the way it looks now?"

"I hope so." But I'm not sure I believe myself. Nothing in our town looks promising, not even the theater where he'll be performing. No wonder he doesn't want to put much effort into this.

"Have you ever been to Evergreen, New York, at Christmas?" I ask.

He shakes his head. "Never heard of it."

"It's this little German village decorated for Christmas. But five years ago, it looked like a deserted town," I say. "They've transformed the place. Quaint shops. Street performers. Gourmet food. There are people dressed in lederhosen, singing 'O Tannenbaum'"

His eyes widen. "Are you expecting me to wear lederhosen? Because that's a definite no."

"Of course not," I say, stifling a smile as I imagine Jace dressed as one of the Von Trapp Family singers. "What if we went on a field trip to Evergreen next week so you can see what I mean? I'm not too proud to bribe you with a homemade cinnamon roll."

I'm hoping the idea of warm bread drenched in butter and brown sugar softens his stone-cold heart. Because I don't know what happened since our last meeting, but something has shifted.

"We're already running late on planning," he says with a concerned look.

"It's just one day. Come on, Jace, don't be a humbug. It'll be fun!" As I say it, I can feel my growing desperation. Even though

Jace agreed to the concert, he's not putting any effort into it, and I don't understand why.

"So you're forcing me to go?"

"I have a feeling that nobody can *force* anything on Jace Knight."

"If I do this road trip, you'll stop nagging me about the concert?"

I hold up a hand. "Scout's honor," I assure him, even though I don't have a plan if this doesn't work.

Embarking on a quick trip with Jace means we will be alone together for a whole day. And I don't know how I'll bite my tongue when we can barely get along for an hour.

But I'm willing to do whatever it takes if it means getting him to buy in to my big Christmas ideas.

SIX

Jace

The snow falls lightly, spiraling from the sky like dandelion seeds as I load my backpack in the trunk for our excursion to Evergreen. My phone buzzes in my coat pocket, and I take a deep breath to release the stress ballooning inside me. If I pretend I'm alright, maybe Allan will buy it.

"Hey, Allan," I say. "I'm on my way to Evergreen today."

"What's in Evergreen?"

"Oh, men in lederhosen and a German village."

"Huh," Allan says, trying to hide his worry over my nonexistent new songs I'm supposed to be writing. "How's the songwriting coming?"

"Same," I answer, which is short for *nothing yet*. My songwriting dried up when everything tanked in my life. Every time I sit down to write, my mind goes blank.

"Your record label is begging for something," Allan says. "The concert would be the perfect time to try out a new song."

"Yeah, but that means I need to write a new song first." Based on the last few months, it's not just a dry spell. It's more like I'm lost in the Sahara with no GPS. I've never had a case of writer's block this bad. But I've also never had this much pressure to deal with either.

"I know, but I can't debut a song I don't have." I pull on my beanie to cover my ears. "It's not that I'm not trying. There's just nothing to inspire me."

"I'll tell the record company you're working on a surprise," Allan says. "But I don't know how long I can keep them from demanding a song."

"I'll come up with something," I reassure Allan, even though it makes me feel even more pressure. "I've got ideas rolling around in my head. This month at home is just what I need to recover from the year."

"Well, don't take too long," Allan reminds me.

It's already been too long. I've been home for over a week, and I still can't find inspiration.

A trip to Evergreen won't solve it either.

When Mia arrives, she climbs out of her car, holding two cups. I glance down at her dress boots, which seem like an odd choice for a winter day.

"Are you sure about those boots?" I ask, lifting an eyebrow.

"What's wrong with them?" she asks.

"Impractical, for one. And two, they won't keep your feet warm."

She waves my concerns away. "I've worn these all day and my toes are toasty."

"Outside?"

"Does it matter?" She takes one look at my face and holds out a white cup. "You look like you need this."

"Uh, thanks," I say, wondering what's under the lid.

"Don't worry," she says. "Wanda told me you like your coffee black."

"You got this from the diner?"

"I saw you had coffee at our meeting. I did my homework." She smiles, clearly trying to make up for the first time she didn't do her homework.

"My last assistant just asked me what I wanted."

Something's different with her, and I can't put my finger on what. She's being *too* nice. Like she's trying to win me over.

I hold up the cup before taking a sip. "Did you poison this or something?"

She frowns. "No! I was trying to surprise you. It's called a *nice gesture*." She digs one hand into her winter coat as snowflakes coat her hair. "That's what a competent assistant does. Makes your life easier so you can be the creative genius."

I let out a humorless laugh. "I'm not a genius at anything these days."

"I think you're wrong."

"You think that a lot."

"No, I don't!"

"I made my point."

She frowns again.

"Lately, my creative muse is missing," I say.

She grabs a large bag from the passenger seat. "That's why you need to go to Evergreen."

"Right," I mutter, unconvinced that Evergreen will solve my problems. "The only thing that sounds good is a vacation on a remote island."

"Pretend you're having fun," she says. "Although that will require you to act like you enjoy being with me."

Does she think I can't stand her? Because that's not what I was trying to say.

Mia looks around, like she's missing something.

"Were you expecting someone else?" I reach to open her car door, but she jumps in front of me and pulls it open herself. She must be one of those women who won't let a man help her.

"I thought you'd have someone with you," she says. "Like a bodyguard or a driver."

"I enjoy driving. Clears my mind. And I already have someone with me." I climb into my vehicle, pulling on sunglasses and starting the engine. "You."

She glances at me. "But what about crazy fans? I don't even have a weapon."

I laugh and nod toward the large leather carry-on she brought. "You could do a lot of damage with that."

She clutches her bag to her chest. "I'm not wasting my designer bag on you."

I give her a side eye. "For your information, I walk around Maplewood and no one bothers me. Not in my usual disguise." I point to my hat and sunglasses.

"But this isn't Maplewood. It's more crowded. And it's a well-known venue for celebrity sightings."

I shrug. "My disguise kept you from recognizing me at the airport."

"But I didn't even know who you were, so that's not a good comparison. I thought you don't want to be bothered." She knots her fingers and looks out the window as the snow falls harder, coating the windows.

"You heard about the fan who jumped on me?" I ask, keeping my eyes on the road.

She glances over for a second, measuring my reaction. "No."

"It was at an awards show." I didn't worry about fans before, but after this year, I've had to guard myself.

"So what do you want to do in Evergreen?" she asks with a cheery smile, trying to change the subject to something lighter. "Snow carving contest? Ice-skating? Or we could watch the guy who makes reindeer balloon animals."

I give a vague grunt as I turn onto a back road.

"What's that supposed to mean?" she asks.

I lift an eyebrow. "Reindeer balloon animals?"

"Okay, so what do you find fun, Mr. Humbug?"

"Nothing commercial. No Santa Claus or Mrs. Claus," I say. "Or anything involving balloon animals."

She chugs down the last of her coffee like it's taking some restraint not to react. "If you don't like Christmas, then tell me what you do like."

"I never said I disliked Christmas."

"You implied it," she says.

"So did you." I glance at her.

"Maybe it's not my favorite," she begins, "but I still enjoy things *about* Christmas. Like cheesy Christmas movies, the smell of gingerbread cookies, walking through the snow." She pauses, looking out the window.

"For me, it's driving." The snow is falling harder, covering the road like a clean white sheet. At least it's a pretty day for a drive, even if the roads aren't great. "When I'm on tour, I don't drive much, so this is fun."

"Is that why you're taking the long way to Evergreen?" she says, glancing at the map on my phone.

"You ever heard of the road less traveled? Some people find that fun."

"Yeah, but Robert Frost wasn't saying to try it during a snowstorm. Evergreen received six inches last night. And that doesn't count what's coming today."

I shrug, unimpressed. "The news always makes it sound worse than it actually is. Trust me on this, okay?"

She gives me a doubtful look before pulling out her phone and scrolling as the silence grows between us. If we're going to Evergreen, I might as well attempt to find some common ground with her; otherwise, this day is going to feel like forever.

"What other Christmas plans do you have?" I ask.

She looks up at me, eyes wide. "Other than pulling off the two biggest events for this season? Absolutely nothing."

"You should really get a hobby."

"You are my hobby," she says. "Which means I'm your *ride or die.*"

I laugh. "I wouldn't say we're *that* close."

She smiles. "By the end of this year, you're going to wonder how you survived without me."

When she grins like that, her whole face lights up.

"I meant, what are your plans after the concert?" I ask.

"My mom always hosts dinner at her house on Christmas Eve, but most years, I stay in Sully's Beach, South Carolina, and celebrate with friends. It's easier than being home, honestly." She pauses, then glances out the window. "Do you see family for Christmas? I bet it's hard for you to get time off."

"My parents decided to book a Mediterranean cruise this year, which means I'll be alone, watching football."

She stares at me for a long second. "That doesn't seem right."

"Not getting together with my parents is actually preferable than dealing with them." I grip the steering wheel, feeling the roads grow more slippery as the snow intensifies. "My family isn't close. My parents only want to talk about money. It's not really relaxing."

"I'm sorry," she says.

"Don't be. I prefer to be home alone for Christmas."

"Even though I'm just your assistant—a term I'm not fond of, by the way—being alone for Christmas seems kind of sad. You should plan something fun."

"Thanks for your honest opinion of my nonexistent social life," I say dryly. "But lying on the couch and watching football *is* fun. And since you hate the term assistant, what would you prefer to be called?"

"How about your minion of happiness?"

I burst out laughing. "My minion?"

"Of happiness," she repeats. "I don't take care of cats or do dishes."

"Tabby and Blackie will be very disappointed to hear that."

"I know, but I more than make up for it with my special talent for putting together amazing playlists."

"You mean a mix tape?"

She nods. "Only better. Just give me a few songs, and I'll put together an entire soundtrack for our drive."

I suggest an eclectic mix of country, jazz, and classic Christmas numbers, and she quickly swipes through the options, calling the playlist, *Your Christmas Mix Tape.*

Pretty soon, we're careening through the snowy hills while listening to Elvis's "Blue Christmas," a country version of "Jingle Bell Rock," and a slow jazz version of "I'll Be Home for Christmas." Before I realize it, I'm humming along to them and in a much better mood than when we left. I'd hate to give her the satisfaction of actually being right, but this list is amazing.

It's so good that I hardly notice how much the road conditions have deteriorated in the last hour. I can barely see the road ahead of me.

When I slow down for a curve, my tires hit an icy patch, and the Jaguar breaks loose, sliding sideways. I turn the wheel in the other direction to correct my slide, but my maneuvers are no match for the ice, and the curve is too sharp. It's like I'm careening across a hockey rink.

"Hold on," I say, trying to avoid the steep ditch on my right.

Mia instinctively braces as we hit a bump before the vehicle pitches forward into a shallow ditch, whipping us both forward.

When we finally stop, I immediately glance over at Mia. "You okay?"

She's breathing hard, staring at the enormous tree we missed by a few feet. "Just saw my life flash before my eyes, but other than that, I'm fine."

"That curve was all ice. Let me try to back us out."

I put the car in reverse, but the tires spin uselessly in the snow.

"Stay here for a second." I climb out to survey the situation. The vehicle looks fine, but there's no way I'm getting this out of the ditch without a tow truck. I bang on the window and call through the glass, "We need to call a tow truck."

She looks over at me. "In this weather?"

"You have a better suggestion?"

She shakes her head.

For the next thirty minutes, I google tow trucks while Mia and I tag-team, calling every number with no luck.

One tow truck driver laughs when I tell him I need pulled out as soon as possible.

"So do hundreds of other people."

"But we need to get to Evergreen today," I plead.

The man roars with laughter. "Every road to Evergreen is closed because of the weather. The region has declared a travel emergency. You're not going anywhere."

"Then how much do I have to pay you?" I beg, willing to fork out whatever it takes.

"I don't take bribes."

"It's not a bribe," I explain. "I'm Jace Knight."

"Yeah, right," he says, before hanging up on me.

I stare at my phone in shock. "Can you believe that guy?"

Mia bites down on her smile.

I frown, not seeing the humor. "Why are you happy about this?"

"Because that guy didn't believe you were Jace Knight. Guess the joke's on him."

"Except we're still stuck. And we can't wait here all day." The temperatures have already dropped ten degrees since we left Maplewood, and the snow is only getting worse.

I knew this was a bad idea. I should've listened to my gut and stayed home.

She opens her maps app. "There's a motel only a half mile from here. If we walk there, we can wait in the lobby until a tow truck arrives."

I don't like that option, but it's the only choice we have right now. The motel will have heat, and I can buy something from the vending machine before my stomach consumes itself.

Mia props open her door and swings her legs out.

I nod toward her useless dress boots. "Are you sure you can walk that far in those?"

"Of course I can," she says, jutting out her chin. She climbs out and takes two steps before slipping in the snow and falling to her knees.

"I'm okay!" she squeaks, popping back up and wiping herself off.

"Those boots won't keep your feet warm for ten minutes."

She puts a hand on her hip. "It's not like I expected to get stranded today."

I hold out my hand, offering help. She stares at it like I'm holding fire.

"Why are you not accepting my help?" I know she doesn't like me, but I didn't think she'd be so obstinate.

"Because I don't need it." She attempts to take another step and slips again. This is not going well for her.

I cross my arms, stifling a laugh.

She frowns. "Stop laughing. It's *not* funny."

"You know what's funny? Refusing to accept my help because you want to prove you can walk in those ridiculous boots. But if that's what you want, be my guest."

She glances at her boots and takes another step.

I walk away, just as she slips and falls again.

She punches the snow. "Okay, fine," she growls.

I turn back with an amused grin.

"Are you going to rub it in or help me?" she says, annoyed.

"I'm waiting for you to say please."

She rolls her eyes. "Please."

I step forward and put my hand out.

As she hangs on to me, her feet slip in the snow, forcing me to wrap my hand around her waist to keep her upright. The warmth of her body and the soft curve of her waist are distracting.

"Thanks," she murmurs as soon as she reaches the road. "I think I can stay upright now."

"So, where is this motel?" I ask. "From here, it looks like we're in the middle of the forest."

She nods at the snow-covered road ahead. "If we follow this farther, we'll run into it."

The road is thick with snow, and our short walk takes much longer than it should, especially since Mia's being careful not to slip again.

But walking this slowly gives me a chance to see the forest

blanketed in snow, and a movement in the treetops catches my eye. I tip my chin, watching two eagles slowly circle overhead.

"Look at that." I point at the birds.

Mia glances up. "Um, what am I supposed to be looking at?"

"Eagles."

She squints, and then looks back at me, unimpressed. "They're just birds."

"Not just any bird. They're an eagle pair."

"Are you sure? They could be two random birds who hunt the same area."

"Not likely. They're probably a pair. Eagles mate for life. And this is most likely their winter home."

"Forever?"

"Pretty much. But since a lot of birds migrate, you don't see many birds that actually stick together through the winter."

"Maybe they could give us directions before my toes fall off."

Mia grimaces in pain but continues to hobble along, trying to keep up with me. I slow down so she doesn't have to push too hard, but I'm also concerned about her getting frostbite. The sooner we can reach the motel, the better.

After what seems like forever, we finally see a shoddy half-lit motel sign up ahead. The rusted metal sign from the seventies is so faded I can barely make out the words *Pine Paradise Motel*.

I stop. "This looks like a place where people come to be murdered," I mutter, noting the faded chipped paint and a neon sign that blinks *open* in the lobby. I wonder if there is anywhere else we can wait. Even a gas station would be preferable.

She turns to me. "Do you have a better suggestion?"

"Well, it doesn't look like much of a paradise."

"We're not staying here overnight," she says, limping toward the lobby. "It's temporary until we can get a tow truck." She looks around at the cramped parking lot. "Can it be that bad if all these people are here?"

"Maybe they're desperate like us."

The tiny lobby is vacant and boasts a lone metal chair and a broken bell on the counter.

After a long wait, an older lady with teased silver curls makes her way to the desk, wearing a crooked name tag that reads "Edith."

"Can I help you?" she says in a croaky voice that sounds like she's a chain smoker.

"Do you mind if we wait here? My vehicle's in the ditch." I step forward, waiting for Edith's eyes to widen when she recognizes me.

"Suit yourself." Edith nods blandly toward the metal chair.

It shouldn't surprise me that she doesn't know who I am. From my guess, she doesn't look like she's listened to music in this century.

Even though I'm dying to sit, I offer Mia the chair since her feet are killing her. She plops down onto the metal surface like it's an overstuffed La-Z-Boy and kicks off her boots.

"I heard there won't be tow trucks out tonight," Edith says. "The emergency travel warning is forcing them off the road."

Mia strips her socks off and rubs her toes. "But we can't get home without a tow truck."

Edith shrugs blandly. This isn't her first snowstorm. "Maybe tomorrow."

I glance at Mia's bright red toes. There's no way we can walk anymore today. "Maybe we should get two rooms, just in case."

"At this place?" Mia whispers, trying not to hurt Edith's feelings.

"If a tow truck somehow miraculously shows up, we give the rooms to some other stranded travelers."

Mia bites her lip, like she's afraid to tell me something. "Um, could I borrow the money for the room and pay you back later? I'm running a little short this month."

I knew Mia's financial situation was bad, but I didn't know it was this terrible.

I shake my head. "Don't worry about it. I'll take care of it since you're working for me."

She gives me a relieved nod, then lifts a hand to get Edith's attention. "We'd like to make a reservation for two rooms."

"Got one," Edith says without looking up from her paper.

"She said two rooms," I add, certain she misheard us.

Edith flattens her newspaper and glares at me, while plucking a cigarette from the pocket of her shirt. "There's only *one.*"

The lighter flicks, then a bright flame appears before a puff of smoke crowns her head like a halo. I'm pretty sure it's illegal to smoke in a hotel lobby, but I'm not about to ask. She's probably been smoking longer than the laws for smoking have been around.

"Take it or leave it," she says as the cigarette dangles from the corner of her mouth like a loose crumb. "All the other rooms are occupied."

Mia stares at the lady, her mouth agape, like she can hardly believe our luck. Maybe my bad year is rubbing off on her too.

"Do you want it or not?" Edith asks, the cigarette barely hanging on to the wrinkled corner of her lips. "Because if you don't, I bet this guy will." She nods toward a man beelining toward us in the snow.

"Let me discuss it with my friend," I say to Edith, before turning toward Mia.

"Discuss what? There is nothing to discuss," Mia says in a determined voice. "We can't stay in the same room."

"We'll freeze in the car. Or you'll lose your toes. Either way, a terrible idea."

"There is no way I'm staying here with you," she mutters under her breath.

"That's funny," I say. "Because there are loads of women who'd pay money to be in your shoes."

She folds her arms. "Well, I am not one of them."

Whatever progress we made earlier has been obliterated by the tension between us now.

I frantically glance outside as the snow whips furiously in the wind. "You were the one who planned this stupid Christmas trip."

Her mouth falls open. "It's *not* stupid. And it's not my fault you took the scenic route. We'd probably be there by now if you'd taken the highway like a normal person."

"Clearly, we're both abnormal. Why else would you wear dress boots in a snowstorm?"

I glance up in time to see the man from the parking lot outside the lobby door. I've got to do something before this stranger takes the last room.

The man opens the door as the wind rushes in like an answer to prayer.

I wheel around to Edith, who's blowing white halos of smoke as she watches snowflakes somersault from the sky.

I leap toward the counter, cutting the man off. "We'll take the last room."

SEVEN

Mia

Based on the state of this decrepit motel, my life has become a Stephen King novel. I don't even have a clean pair of underwear with me.

"Humph," I mutter as we trudge through the snow to our motel room. I can't feel my toes, and Jace won't have any sympathy for me anyway, so I bite my cheek and pretend my feet are not painful blocks of ice.

"Here we are," he says, swinging the door open to a dark, musty-smelling room. "Welcome to paradise."

I step inside and take in the room.

Paradise is a stretch. The sagging bed is topped with a faded blue bedspread that looks like it's thirty years old. The wallpaper is peeling at the corners, and the carpet is so worn, it's duct-taped to the floor like a patchwork quilt. The lone table is leaning precariously to the left, and the single wooden chair looks like they rescued it from a trash pile.

"Wow. Nice," I say in a monotone voice. *This is where I'm going to take my last breath.*

"Doesn't sound like you approve," Jace remarks dryly.

"I'm pretty certain this room was a crime scene once. Maybe

we should check some true crime podcasts and see if *Pine Paradise* comes up?"

"Don't you think the motel would've changed their name?"

"I'm pretty sure Edith wouldn't care a hill of beans about whether we froze in the storm or died in our sleep. Why would she bother telling us we're sleeping in a room where a murder happened?"

Jace laughs, and the sound of it rings through my body. *I made Jace Knight laugh.* That knowledge is unexpectedly sublime, even though our circumstances are not.

Ever since we first met, getting him to smile has been nearly impossible. No wonder people call him the *Dark Knight*. This isn't an act; he's serious in real life too, although I'm one of the few with an inside glimpse. Because of that, his laugh is like a rare coin I'm tucking away for keeps.

I sink onto the bed and strip off my boots again. We still haven't figured out how we're going to survive tonight, but right now, I just want to feel my toes again.

"Do you want me to call more tow trucks?" I offer, hoping someone can rescue us before we have to decide who gets the bed.

"I doubt we're going anywhere tonight." Jace flops down in a tired-looking chair, looking just as exhausted as this room. He pulls a snack from his pocket—a bright yellow bag of dried onion rings. "I grabbed the last package from the vending machine. You want some?"

I wrinkle my nose. "I detest onions. But I have two granola bars."

"Keep them," he says. "I'm scared to see what Edith might offer us for breakfast."

"Probably small children that she's fattened up on bread crumbs like the witch in *Hansel and Gretel*."

Jace's mouth quirks at my dark humor. "Um, okay. Not the direction I was going." He tosses a dried onion ring in his mouth.

"How are they?"

"Underwhelming. But right now, my stomach doesn't care." He dumps a handful on the table and keeps eating.

"At least we have coffee." I motion toward the cheap-looking coffee maker sitting next to the TV.

"You're going to need a strong stomach to drink Edith's coffee. No fancy drinks here."

"How did you know I was a coffee snob?"

"The overpowering scent of hazelnut wafting from your travel cup."

I shrug, trying to prove I can handle this rotten situation. "This motel won't break me. But what I wouldn't give for a Reese's Cup right now."

"I don't have chocolate, but you can take the bed tonight," he says, propping his feet on the bedspread and leaning back in his chair.

That's when it hits me: *I'm sharing this room with Jace Knight.* I can't take the bed. I forced him into this trip. The least I can do is let him have the only comfortable place to sleep.

"I'll be fine on the floor." I rub my feet as my toes throb painfully.

"That's the same thing you said about those boots." He gazes at me with an amused look.

"Okay, wise guy. I'll admit, I shouldn't have worn the boots. And if I'd listened to you, we'd be home, instead of stuck in a creepy motel where stranded travelers get murdered."

"We are not getting murdered," he says. "You're lucky Edith only had one room. If we're together, I can protect you."

"If we don't kill each other first." Like he would protect me. If an axe murderer barges in, he'll probably push me toward him.

"We can survive one night," Jace says. "I'm even willing to stop complaining about going to Evergreen."

I frown at him, trying to figure out what's the catch. "Did Edith put a spell on you?"

"Nope," he says. "I figure if we're stuck here, might as well make the most of it. You want to head outside so you can pelt me with snowballs?"

I look over at him like he's crazy. "Tempting, but no."

"Why? You scared?" His eyes flicker in mischief. I don't know what happened to grumpy Jace, but suddenly, it seems like he's trying to make the best out of an unpleasant situation.

"Jace, this is a snowstorm," I remind him. "And I just started to feel my toes again."

"I'm only going to the parking lot. It's two steps from the door. This is your last chance to take out your frustration. Unless you're chicken . . ." He pauses, giving me a smile that's infuriating, then heads outside, leaving the door hanging open.

"Jace," I call after him. "The door!"

When he doesn't return, I walk over to shut the door and that's when it happens. A cold, wet snowball smacks me in the shoulder and disintegrates on my sweater.

If there wasn't smoke curling from my nostrils before, there is now.

"Hey!" I yell. "I said I'm not playing."

From ten feet away, Jace is smiling at me in triumph, while forming another snowball. "Just in case you're wondering, it feels fantastic to hit you."

I lift an eyebrow, daring him to do it again. "Oh, really? You wanna play dirty? I'll show you." I slide on my boots, not caring if my feet are still hurting. All I want is sweet revenge. Music star or not, nailing him in the head will be *so satisfying*.

As I step outside, I spot Jace across the parking lot.

"What are the rules for playing dirty?" Jace asks, mischief playing across his lips.

"First rule: you can't hit someone when they're inside." I bend over to gather some snow in my hands. A snowball smacks me dangerously close to my butt.

I growl, "And you can't hit me when I'm bending over."

"Too late," he says and then laughs.

I toss a snowball at him that barely grazes his shoulder.

"Missed me, missed me," he mocks without finishing, *now you've gotta kiss me.*

Jace is definitely not kissing anything but my snowball.

"I don't want to play with a cheater," I taunt.

"Then why'd you come out here?" I look around. Everyone is holed up in their rooms because of the storm. The parking lot is ours for a showdown.

"Because you left the door open."

"Excuses," he says, throwing another snowball my way.

This time, I jump before it hits me. The wind whips my hair around my face, and my sweater is clinging where it's wet from snow. That's when I realize I forgot my coat inside. Probably because I was so mad at Jace for hitting me first.

"I don't want to get wet," I complain. I scoop up another handful of snow, packing it into a ball.

"Then go back inside," he says. "Nobody's forcing you to be out here."

As if I can. Jace is challenging me to a snowball fight. And it's too tempting to put him in his place.

"But what if I stay?"

He opens his arms wide, like he's offering to be my target practice. "Hit me with your best shot," he invites. "Except you probably throw like a girl."

It's the last straw before my restraint crumbles like a house of cards.

I throw the snowball as hard as I can, and it sails through the air, pelting Jace in his stomach. For a fleeting moment, victory swells in my chest . . . until Jace looks up at me with a wicked grin.

"You're going to pay for that," he says.

This time, he isn't kidding.

"Oh, shoot," I mutter and do the only thing I can think of. *I run.*

Jace immediately launches a round of snowballs that pelt me across my back, shoulders, and legs. While I scramble to collect more snow, Jace throws another, and I'm forced to sidestep awkwardly in my stupid boots, tripping and falling into a pile of snow.

So this is how it ends.

I cover my head with my hands, waiting for Jace to use my fall to his advantage.

I'm expecting Jace to throw a half dozen painful snowballs at me. Instead, nothing happens.

I crack open one eye.

Jace kneels next to me, gently pulling my arms away from my face, cradling my head. "You okay?" he says, breathing hard, a crease lining his forehead.

Is Jace concerned about me? Or is this just a prank?

I blink once, expecting him to pull out a hidden snowball and drop it down the back of my sweater. Instead, his eyes skate over my face in concern. That shakes me more than the fall did.

"Um, yeah." There's no way he's concerned about my well-being. "Just wet and cold."

His eyes fall to my sweater, which is covered in melting snow.

"For what it's worth, you're not bad at snowball fights," he says, his dimple deepening, making my heart trip.

His eyes catch mine, and our gazes hold a few seconds too long, my heart skittering across my chest like a car sliding on ice. I sit up, uncomfortable with the weird way my heart is erratically bucking against my ribs.

"You forgot I have two brothers who play hockey. When I play with them, there is no mercy."

He holds out a hand to help me stand, and this time, I don't hesitate to take it, even though it's like touching a fallen wire. *Is he trying to act like a gentleman and mess with my emotions?* Because this isn't the old Jace who would make a snarky joke about me falling in my boots. Mr. Smolder is making everything inside me go up in flames.

I look at my sweater so he doesn't see my face flush. "I probably should go inside and change," I say, before realizing I don't have any clothes to change into. I was stupid enough to wear these dress boots, and now I'm kicking myself for running outside without a coat.

It's not until we return to our room that I notice his cheeks are tinged pink from the cold. He rubs his hands together, blowing on them to warm them up.

"I could use a hot shower," he says, shutting the door behind us.

The finality of that door slam is jarring. *I'm alone with Jace.* Not only do I have to stay in the same room, but I have to do everything else with him nearby too. Except for my friends, my world is pretty small. I don't even like using public restrooms.

"Do you want to go first?" he asks casually. This setup doesn't seem to bother him at all, while I'm a nervous wreck.

"I guess," I say. "But I don't have dry clothes."

"Is there a blow-dryer?"

I hurry to the bathroom and find an ancient one under the counter. "This might work."

"While you're in the shower, leave the door unlocked, and I'll get the sweater and start blow-drying it."

I glance at him like he's crazy. "Um, no. I've watched *Psycho* too many times."

While some women might not have second thoughts about leaving the door open for Jace Knight while they shower, that will not work for me.

"I was trying to help you, not murder you," he says with a puzzled smile.

His dimple flashes, and I wish I'd stop noticing, because every time I do, it's like my insides turn to jelly.

"Why don't you throw the sweater out the door, and I'll see if Edith has a clothes dryer," Jace offers.

It's a less-than-ideal plan, but it's the fastest option at this point.

As I crank the water to extra-hot, it turns gloriously steamy, fogging the bathroom mirror. Hiding behind the door, I chuck my clothes into the room, and then step into the shower, hot enough to scald my skin and erase every thought about my precarious situation.

When I finally dry off, I peek out the door, checking for Jace.

The bedroom is empty, which I hope is a good sign that he found a dryer. A neatly folded henley shirt waits on the bed with a message scribbled on the motel's notepad.

Feel free to take my shirt until your sweater is dry.

Since Jace wore a henley under his flannel shirt, he technically has two.

I grab Jace's shirt and slide it on. Almost instantly, his smell washes over me. Pine and musk, an intoxicating mix that smells better than a Cinnabon. Which is saying a lot, since a fresh-from-the-oven Cinnabon is the best smell in the world.

I wipe the mirror so I can see how ridiculous it looks on me.

It's oversized, the sleeves nearly covering my hands, while the hem of the shirt hits just above my knees. Every time I move, the soft cotton brushes delicately against my skin. It isn't terrible. In fact, some people might even like it. My stomach flip-flops, and I quickly erase that thought.

Not Jace. He's used to dating celebrities and movie stars.

Maybe if I hike up the sleeves and tuck the shirt into my jeans, it will look decent. But when I check the bathroom, I can't find my jeans either. I'm searching the room when Jace returns, and I freeze, because I don't know what else to do. Even though his shirt is as long as a dress, my stomach drops when his eyes graze over it. He probably thinks I look stupid.

"Um, thanks for the shirt." My voice cracks.

He quickly looks away, realizing I caught him staring, but I can't read his expression. He's probably biting back a comment about how I look like an elf wearing a giant's shroud. An awkward pause hangs between us before he drops his eyes to the garments in his hands.

"I'm glad you found it," he says.

"I'm surprised you aren't making fun of me," I blurt, unable to hold it in any longer. If he's going to make a joke about my appearance, he might as well start now.

He frowns. "Make fun of what?"

"Oh, just . . . how I look ridiculous in your shirt," I say, pulling at the hem, trying to shield myself from his little jabs.

He stops, his eyes locked on mine, and then mutters, "I would *never* make fun of how you look."

My breath hitches for a second, like someone's squeezed the air out of me. I glance away, sure I misinterpreted his meaning. "Okay, well, it wouldn't be the first time."

"When have I made fun of how you look?" he asks in a voice that sounds almost offended.

I give a weak shrug, sorting through our endless petty arguments in the short time we've known each other. "Well, you made fun of my boots."

"That wasn't because . . ." He runs a hand over his stubbled jaw. "I mean, they're impractical. Not because of how they look on you."

I frown, finally seeing the truth in his eyes. He didn't hate me in my boots.

"You liked my boots?"

"They look great. You *always* do." His voice drops off, and my brain stops on the words that shake me. *You always do.*

He drags his hand through his hair. "I just wish you wouldn't always think the worst of me, Mia."

My eyes drop to the ground. "I don't think the worst . . ."

"Except when you do," Jace adds, dropping my clothes on the bed.

He knows that from the first day we met, I've always second-guessed him. And it's not his fault, either. It's a hard lesson I've been fighting ever since my father left.

"You're right," I mumble, feeling so called out, my cheeks burn. "From now on, I won't jump to conclusions."

He nods once, before brushing past me, keeping his eyes just over my shoulder, like he's avoiding looking at me in this shirt.

"You didn't find a dryer?" I ask.

"No dryer," he says, holding up my wet sweater and jeans. "And no Edith. I think she was taking a smoking break."

"Or burying dead bodies," I add.

His lips quirk, the tension between us broken by our mutual hatred for the Pine Paradise.

"If you don't mind, I'm going to shower next and then head to bed." His eyes graze over the single bed between us. "And I'll sleep on the floor. You take the bed tonight."

"Are you sure you're okay on the floor?" I ask, sweeping a toe over the duct tape that's holding it together.

"What other choice do we have?" he says, slamming the door to the bathroom.

My heart hammers in my chest. *I can think of one.*

After all, we're not a couple, and there's no chance that anything could happen between us.

Because after we leave, we'll forget all about tonight. This shirt. His smell.

You always do.

EIGHT

Mia

I close my eyes and force myself to sleep, but right now, adrenaline is coursing through my veins. A famous music star is showering six feet from my bed. *And humming Christmas songs.*

I'm dying to tell someone. I roll over and fish my phone from my bag and text Jaz as I snuggle under the covers. *I'm stuck in a snowstorm with Jace Knight.*

It takes less than a second for her to respond.

Jaz: WHAT?! Where are you?
Mia: An awful motel. I'm talking horror-movie bad.
Jaz: Jace is IN your room?
Mia: There was only one room. He gave me the bed. This is so awkward.
Jaz: Do you know how many women would DIE to be in your place?

Right then, Jace comes out of the bathroom and I hide my phone under the covers so he doesn't see that I'm texting.

"Are you ready for lights out?" he asks, dressed in the same jeans and shirt he wore earlier since he has no other clothes. I'm letting my outfit air dry overnight, which is convenient since that means I get to wear Jace's shirt longer. The cotton is so luxuriously soft, it's like I'm swaddled with a herd of alpacas. I can only imagine the exorbitant cost and how many women would sacrifice their firstborn children to be in my place.

"Ready when you are!" I say as he settles on the carpet.

I peer over the edge of the mattress. "I wouldn't sleep on . . . that." I point at the duct tape and the mysterious brown stain nearby.

"Uh, maybe I'll sleep in the chair."

"You mean the chair that's about to fall apart next to the frosty window? I can't let you do that." I peel off a thin, white blanket from the bed. It's not much, but it's better than nothing.

"Don't you need it?" he asks, taking it.

"I still have this." I point to a dubious-looking comforter.

Jace shakes his head. "You keep the blanket. I'll use my jacket. Does it seem cold in here?"

"Yes," I say, relieved. "I didn't mention it because I thought you liked to sleep in an igloo."

Jace pushes a few buttons on the heating unit and nothing happens. Then he bangs his fist against the side. Still nothing.

"No wonder it's cold. The heater is broken."

"I'll call Edith." I pick up the ancient-looking landline. There's no tone, so I punch a few buttons to see if I can magically revive it. "It's dead. This really *is* like a horror film," I groan, slamming the receiver down. "Haven't you noticed that in every horror movie, the phones never work? And with no way to contact the police, we're dead."

Jace's eyes fall to my cell phone. "Except we have modern technology, as well as one other key difference."

"What's that?"

"We aren't stupid. Haven't you noticed how movie characters always do the exact *opposite* of what they should? Like, *Let's go into this creepy old shed where all these saws and sharp tools are . . .* and bam! They get axed. Stupid people do stupid things. But we are not that stupid."

"So maybe Edith is trying a different approach and freezing us to death?"

"This isn't exactly the Ritz." Jace glances out the window. "Looks like the front desk is closed. The chance of someone repairing this tonight in a snowstorm is probably zero. Maybe it will come back on during the night."

"And if it doesn't?" I ask, wondering how cold this room will get and whether this is the last time I'll feel my toes before they're amputated from frostbite.

Jace shrugs. "We hunker down until morning."

This has gone from bad to worse. Not only am I stranded at a creepy motel, I'm now going to freeze. "This reminds me of the time I camped out with my brothers in the backyard and the temperature dipped below freezing. We were determined to stay outside. So we climbed into one sleeping bag."

Jace frowns. "How did you do that?"

"My brothers were six and I was eight, so we all fit inside like a burrito grande. And boys are like little ovens, so we survived."

"We're not going to die tonight, either. Promise."

"Well, you're a lot bigger than me," I say. "I'll be an icicle by morning."

Jace pauses, then looks through his bag, pulling out two rectangular packages. "Try this." He tosses them on the bed.

"What are these?"

"Heat warmer packs. I bought them when I had an outdoor concert this fall so I could warm my fingers before playing guitar. But I forgot to use them."

I shake my head. "I can't take both. You don't have any covers."

He pulls the thin blanket up to his shoulders, but it's too short to cover his feet at the same time. "I'm bigger than you. Like a little oven."

"Or not so little," I say, unwrapping one of the heat packs. I nod toward his exposed socks. "Your toes are going to freeze."

"Maybe we could share," he says, trying to readjust the small blanket so it covers his feet.

"Share what?"

"Forget it," he says. "Dumb idea."

"There are no dumb ideas. Not when our feet are about to turn into ice blocks."

He readjusts the blanket, but it's not going to fit him no matter how hard he tries. "It won't work anyway."

"Just tell me, Jace."

He pauses, his eyes sweeping over the bed. "Well, two people make more heat than one. Just like you and your brothers."

It takes a moment for the idea to sink in. "Are you suggesting we share the bed?" I say slowly.

"I told you it was a dumb idea."

"No, it's not dumb at all. I mean, this is an emergency. It's not like . . ." I stop myself, realizing where I'm about to go with this conversation. It's not like *there's something between us*. We're trying to survive. People have done far worse to survive.

"We don't have to do it," he says, dismissing the idea.

"No, I'm okay with it. As long as we both stay on our side of the bed. We'll put our heat warmers under the covers, draw an imaginary line, and stay on our designated side." I mime drawing a line down the center of the bed. It's no different than two people sleeping on an airplane next to one another.

"Are you sure about this?" Jace asks, a bit worried.

Not at all. Because right now, I'm freaking out.

"It's fine," I say breezily, even though the blood is pounding in my ears.

How am I going to sleep with Jace Knight next to me? I don't have a clue. I leave one warmer pack on his side of the bed, then place the other near my feet.

Then I fall back onto my pillow and pull the covers up to my chin.

Jace makes his way to the bed, slowly slides in, and stays by the edge of the mattress like he's afraid of getting even remotely near me.

I'm sure I look odd with my covers up to my earlobes, staring at the ceiling, like this isn't awkward.

"Good night," he murmurs, then reaches over and turns off the bedside lamp as the room plunges into darkness.

"One more thing," I say. "Do you snore?"

"I don't think so. Why . . . do you snore?"

"Of course not! I just wondered whether you did."

He pauses, then says, "Well, if you do, I'll tell you in the morning."

I slap his arm in the dark.

"Ouch. What was that for?"

"Like this isn't already weird enough."

Even without looking, I know Jace is smiling in the dark.

"I was joking!" he says. "But I'll still tell you if you snore."

———

I don't remember falling asleep, but at some point, I drifted off. Between the hand warmers and our combined body heat, I'm snug and toasty, cocooned under these covers. That's when the fragments of last night's dream take shape: An arm slung around my waist. Someone's breath warming the curve of my neck. My body tucked against the wall of someone's chest. I'm trying to remember the rest of the dream—who the mystery person is and why we're tangled together—when I feel something move. Something that's touching me.

My eyes fly open. Is that a cockroach? Rats? At the Pine Paradise, anything is possible.

Without moving my body, I squint in the hazy grey light and see something move under the covers. I slowly lift my head to figure out what is happening.

Is that Jace's arm . . . *on me?*

Don't freak out, I tell myself, even though I'm most definitely freaking out.

During the night, I must have rolled near his chest—probably for warmth—although I don't remember moving.

And now, his arm is slung over my waist so naturally, it's like it's made to be there.

I stare at the wall, trying to figure out how to get out of this situation before Jace wakes.

And if he does wake, what do I say then? This is worse than the time I ripped the crotch of my pants in the third grade. Or when I realized I was in the men's room at a travel stop . . . while I was on the toilet.

My heart races frantically, and I want to shake myself, but that would require moving . . . which I can't do without bumping Jace.

I attempt to slip out from under his arm, but as soon as I move, Jace stirs.

I hold my breath. Either I roll over in one swift move and pretend that we accidentally bumped each other, or I confess to our accidental cuddling, which might look like I'm subconsciously attracted to him.

There's really only one option—sneak out of his embrace as quickly as possible and hope he doesn't wake.

Three, two, one . . .

With a quick motion, I roll to my right and fall onto the floor as Jace's arm flops onto the bed.

The thud my body makes as I hit the floor sounds like I dropped a bowling ball, and I bite my lip to keep from screaming in pain.

Jace stirs. "Is it morning?" He lifts his head over the side of the bed and frowns at me. "Why are you on the floor?"

I stand and glance around like I have no idea. "I fell . . . getting my glasses," I say, reaching over to snatch them off the nightstand.

Jace must believe my excuse, because he doesn't ask any more questions about why I'm on the carpet. He digs one palm into his sleepy eyes, looking adorable with his tousled curls. It's not even fair how good this man looks with bedhead. I'm tempted to roll right back toward him.

I run my hand through my hair and feel strands sticking up on the top, like some freakish Halloween wig. I do a quick double take in the mirror and see lines imprinted on my cheek from sleeping on my side. And is that *drool*?

"Is it still snowing?" I ask, hoping he'll check the window and ignore me for a few seconds.

He reaches toward the blind and peeks through as I furiously rub my cheek, trying to erase the pillow lines and dried drool.

"It stopped, but it's a winter wonderland out there," he says.

When he turns back, I pretend to fiddle with the coffee maker, pouring the mysterious packet of no-name coffee and filling the water tank. As soon as I push start, a burning stench fills the air.

"What's that smell?" I crinkle my nose.

Jace sniffs. "Smells like you're about to burn down the motel . . . which might be the best thing to ever happen to this place."

Above the coffee maker a puff of smoke rises like an ominous cloud. "Um, Houston, we have a problem." Even though burning down the motel sounds good, I don't want to be stuck in the snow either. I unplug the machine. "Despite its name, this place is *not* paradise."

Jace's mouth curls slightly. "It probably wasn't good coffee, anyway."

"Maybe today's the day I give up my caffeine addiction."

"Do you have another option?"

"Not really, but I'm trying to see the silver lining in all this."

"You think there's a silver lining in getting stuck at the Pine Paradise Motel?"

I suddenly realize how terrible this experience has been for him. He's used to luxury hotels and being waited on. The poor guy had to eat generic Funyuns for dinner last night.

There's no silver lining except getting as far away from this situation as possible. Because I'm certainly not the type of girl he'd choose to get stuck with.

His eyes drift over his shirt, which I'm still wearing, and I cross my arms, suddenly self-conscious.

"You probably want your shirt back." I turn toward the bathroom door, grabbing my clothes and shutting myself inside.

As I change into my sweater, I slide my hand over the curve of my waist and think of his arm slung over me.

I won't bring it up, I tell myself, folding his shirt into a neat square. *Pretend it never happened.* Even now, it's hard to ignore the fact that the shirt smells like him, which means I'm wearing his scent. Pine and musk. His arm wrapped around me. *That dimple.*

How am I even going to survive today?

When I step out of the bathroom, the room is silent.

I glance outside and track Jace's footsteps in the snow, headed toward the road, but he's nowhere in sight.

Jace is gone.

NINE

Jace

Everything shimmers in the soft morning light, making me hope today is going to turn out better than yesterday. Even the Pine Paradise looks improved with a fresh coat of snow covering its faded exterior.

But it doesn't help me feel better. Because I still don't know how to make sense of what happened last night.

When I woke this morning, my arm was wrapped around her waist, and she was cocooned against my chest. Both of us were clearly violating the imaginary line, making it unclear who was responsible.

Given our history, I don't want to bring it up and make things worse. It's already bad enough that I can't stop thinking about it.

When I enter our room, Mia's sitting on the bed, dressed again in her sweater and jeans. She stands, a puzzled expression on her face. "You're back."

"Of course I'm back. Where'd you think I'd go after a snowstorm?"

She lifts a shoulder. "I thought you left for good."

"I tracked down our old friend Edith. I hoped she might have coffee."

She tilts her head. "Let me guess . . . she didn't."

"Welcome to Pine Paradise. A true budget motel." Then I hold up two drinks. "But she told me about a gas station not too far away."

I hand her a Styrofoam cup that's still warm, and her face brightens like I just gave her a winning lottery ticket.

"Is this . . ." She sniffs at the plastic lid. "Heaven?"

"As close as you're going to get." I take a sip from my cup. "It tastes like coffee-flavored dirt, but at least it's hot. Yours is a gas station version of a mocha."

"Otherwise known as chocolate-flavored dirt," she says and grins.

"Look what else I found." I pull out several packages from my pockets: two yogurt cups, three cereal bars, and a Reese's Peanut Butter Cup. "I thought this might make your day better."

"You remembered?" she gasps, before tearing open the package and dunking the peanut butter cup into her coffee.

I laugh. "You must be hungry. Because this is the worst meal I've ever bought for someone."

She sits at the lopsided table while I divide the food. Right now, whatever awkwardness was between us has quickly been extinguished by our hunger pains. It's amazing how people can set aside their differences when they're forced to survive.

As I inhale the cereal bar, my phone buzzes. "Looks like we're getting out of here," I tell her, turning my phone so she can see the text from a tow truck driver I called yesterday. "There's a truck available to pull us out."

"Oh . . ." she says. "That's great." Judging by her tone, she doesn't sound as thrilled as I expected.

"I thought you'd be jumping up and down about not having to stay another minute here."

"I am!" she says, but something sounds off. "I'm sure you want to get home."

"I'm not planning on going home." She looks up, puzzled, as I lean back on my elbows. "We're going to Evergreen."

She shakes her head. "You don't have to, after what happened yesterday."

I sit up. "I didn't come all this way to stay at the Pine Paradise."

Her eyes flick to the bed, like she's remembering last night. "It was a terrible idea, anyway." She scoops a bite from her yogurt cup.

Is she talking about what happened last night? Either way, I'm not about to get this far without going to Evergreen now. I need something to inspire me to write music again.

"Well, I'm not a quitter," I tell her. "And you said I'm your ride or die. That means we're headed to Evergreen." I crumple my wrapper and shoot it toward the trash can, hoping I don't regret this decision. The wrapper circles the rim and falls in.

When I glance over, there's a spark in her eyes, like she's questioning whether this is a good idea.

I have to believe it is.

———

Despite the snowstorm only a day before, the roads are passable, thanks to the plows having resumed early this morning.

But that's not the reason my stomach is knotted up. Something else is bothering me, because it feels like I'm about to step off a cliff and plummet toward a cluster of sharp rocks.

Just around a curve, a sign for Evergreen appears, painted in red and green. "Is this it?" I ask, glancing at a few run-down houses, a gas station, and a dollar store. "Not very impressive. How long ago were you here?"

She hesitates. "Maybe fifteen years?"

"That long? Are you sure this place is as magical as you remember?"

"No, but things can only get better after yesterday, right?"

"That's a very dangerous thing to say."

As I follow the signs that point downtown, I finally turn onto

Main Street and feel like I entered a portal to Bavaria. The entire street looks like an old-fashioned European town, decorated with candles, garland, and bright red ribbons. A giant Christmas tree that rivals the one in Rockefeller Center stands in the middle of town, shimmering with gold and silver bulbs.

I had pretty low expectations for this trip, but already this is looking more promising than the Pine Paradise Motel.

Since the snowstorm shut down the town, few visitors braved the roads today, which is a good sign. If I'm lucky, I can slip through town unnoticed.

"What do you think?" Mia asks, clapping her hands together. "I knew it was going to be wonderful."

I glance at her. "I think you're going to freeze."

She self-consciously runs a hand through her hair. "I'll be fine. I meant the town. Isn't it amazing?" She looks like a kid visiting Cinderella's castle.

I shrug, not wanting to show too much excitement. "It looks decent."

"*Just* decent?" she repeats. "Don't you feel as if you've been transported to a small German village a hundred years ago?"

"A hundred years ago, they would have had real candles," I say, pointing to the battery-powered ones in the windows. "I work in show business. Everything is big and bright and mostly fake. I'll make a judgment after I taste the food. Do you know any good breakfast places?"

She smiles. "Just the place." She hops out her door and nearly trips over a snowdrift. She shoots me a look that warns, *Don't you dare say a word about my boots.*

As we step inside the bakery, I'm immediately hit with the scent of warm cinnamon. In a display case, warm apple streusels, decadent caramel rolls, and cranberry orange muffins dripping with glaze tempt me.

Despite wanting one of each, we both order cinnamon rolls and settle at a café table in the corner.

Mia sinks her fork into the roll as she pulls up a document on her phone. "I revised our agenda for today."

"I thought we agreed on no balloon animals?"

"This list doesn't include balloon animals. I think you'll approve." She shows me a schedule on her phone. "We'll start with strolling Main Street, then stop to listen to the carolers, and head over to see a demonstration from a woodworker who makes homemade Christmas ornaments. After that, we'll grab lunch, go on a sleigh ride, and end our day with dinner. How does that sound?"

"Exhausting." I stare at her for a second. "I bet you'd make an exemplary tour guide. You're just the right blend of bossy and sweet."

She frowns. "Isn't this what you're used to? Having a timed schedule and a handler who takes you from point A to point B?"

"Yes, and that's exactly what I *don't* want today. My whole life is running from one meeting to the next." I take another bite of the sweet roll and close my eyes. I haven't had a roll this delicious since my grandmother made them. "When I have a day off, I prefer a more leisurely schedule."

She glances from her tidy schedule to me. "Okay, Mr. Spontaneity, let's leisure it up today."

I grin. "I'm not sure that's the way you're supposed to use that word."

"I'm being leisurely about my use of the word *leisure*," she says, her lips curling in amusement. "Whatever makes you happy."

I point my fork at the roll. "This makes me happy. If the rest of the town can measure up to this . . ." I lean forward. "I just might have fun today."

When we finish the cinnamon rolls, we stroll down Main Street and head inside the Christmas market. The sun is finally out, making the snow shimmer, and they've plowed the walks, so Mia doesn't have any problems with her boots. The Christmas market is filled with hand-carved ornaments, fluffy knitted woolens, and homemade fudge that we sample every chance we get. Mia stops at a booth with handmade stocking caps made from soft alpaca wool.

The woman selling them gives Mia a friendly smile. "You're welcome to try one on."

"Oh, I couldn't," she replies.

"Why not?" I ask. "Because right now, you look cold."

Her cheeks are bright pink, and she's clutching her coffee, trying to warm her hands.

"I'm not that cold," she argues.

I hand her a hat. "Try it."

She glances at me with a sigh before sliding it on.

It fits her perfectly, and the teal yarn brings out her eyes. "That looks fabulous on you," I say. "You should get it."

She quickly tugs it off. "Thanks, but I can't." She places the hat back on the table.

As she walks to the next vendor, I fall in step with her. "Didn't you like the hat?"

"Yes," she replies, not meeting my eyes.

"Then I don't understand. You're shivering and need a hat. Or do you prefer being miserable instead?"

"No," she says, pausing. "It's just . . ." She looks around, hesitating. "That hat was way more than I could afford. I know it's handmade, and that lady probably spent hours knitting it. I don't want to offend her."

I remember our conversation about not having enough for a hotel room, and I mentally kick myself for making her feel ashamed.

I glance around. "I need to look for a bathroom. You go on without me."

I head toward the bathrooms, then spin around and sneak back to the hat lady.

I quickly scan the table for the hat Mia tried on.

"Where is that hat?" I ask. "The one we were trying on."

"I'm sorry, but that lady over there just bought it." She points at a woman who is walking away with Mia's hat.

"Do you have another in the same color?"

She shakes her head. "I'm afraid not."

I look over the rest of the hats, but none of them are the same, so I take off after the lady who bought Mia's hat.

"Excuse me," I say, waving her down. "Sorry to bother you. But how much do you want for that hat?"

She looks at me like I'm crazy. "I just bought it as a gift for a friend."

This is a going to be harder than I thought. I fumble for my pocket. "Would you take a hundred dollars for it?"

She shakes her head. "I'm sorry, but it's not for sale."

"Then two hundred dollars," I say, more urgently, pulling out the money.

"For a hat?" the woman asks, her eyes widening. She pauses, then shakes her head. "I'm sorry, but I really like this one."

She turns to leave, and I realize I need to do something drastic. I tap her on the shoulder one more time. When she turns around, her brow creases in frustration.

"It's me again," I say with a smile.

"I know," she barks, obviously annoyed. "I thought I told you no already."

"It's just . . . I really like that hat." I slide off my sunglasses and wait to see if she recognizes me. It's not like everyone knows who I am, but I'm gambling on the fact that this lady might.

Her mouth slowly falls open. "Wait, I know you. Are you that singer?" She stops and tries to recall who I am. "What's his name?"

"Jace Knight?" I prompt, hoping this works.

She snaps her fingers. "Yes, that's it!"

"I am." I nod toward the hat. "I was hoping to get that hat as a gift for my assistant. And I'm still willing to pay whatever you want for it."

She pauses, then smiles. "Would you take a picture with me?"

I grin. "You bet."

She hands over the hat without hesitation.

As I hand her the money and pose for a picture, a few people look up and start snapping pictures. If I don't hurry, I'm going to get mobbed by the small crowd that's gathered around us.

When I glance around for Mia, she's standing at the candle booth, and our eyes finally meet across the room.

She frowns, like she's trying to figure out why I'm surrounded by people taking my picture. She's never seen me with my fans before, and something passes across her face.

When I finally finish, I hurry across the market to catch her, hiding the gift behind my back.

I tap her shoulder. "Miss me?"

"You were gone like five minutes," she says with a laugh. "What was going on over there?"

"I had to take some pictures with fans." I pause, then pull out the hat. "I couldn't leave without buying this."

She stares at it for a moment, shocked. "You bought it . . . for *me*?"

"Yeah, some lady purchased it first, so I had to get it from her."

"Wait. You took a hat from someone?"

"I didn't take it—I offered her a price she couldn't turn down." I won't tell her I paid four times the price for it.

Her brow creases, like she's trying to make sense of this. "You didn't have to do that."

"Yes, I did. You're cold. Don't you know how much body heat you lose from your head?" I slide the hat over her strawberry-blonde hair to prove my point.

"But you just blew your cover," she says, still frowning. "What if you get followed today? Or someone hassles you?"

"I know what you're thinking," I say. "And it won't happen here. Evergreen is like Maplewood. And I wanted to surprise you. Despite being a Scrooge, I don't like to see people suffer in the cold."

She touches the hat, like she's amazed I went to all this trouble for it. "Thanks," she says softly. "I'm not taking it off for the rest of today."

A slow grin curls the edges of her lips, and my heart does this weird squeeze, like there's something wrong with it. The problem is, I know what's wrong . . . and I need to forget it. Because I already promised myself I'm not dating anyone. Not after what happened with Ava.

"Where to now?" she asks, looking at the schedule on her phone.

"I'm kind of hungry for lunch."

Her mouth twists into a disbelieving grin. "Lunch? We just ate breakfast."

"Well, I'm still hungry."

She shrugs, like she's officially given up on her schedule. "Then let's eat our way through Evergreen."

For the next few hours, we eat and shop, munching on fresh gingerbread cookies, chocolate-covered nuts, a white chocolate trifle, and circling back to the bakery when they pull out fresh apple strudel from the oven.

When the carolers stop on the street corner, we join in singing carols until Mia checks her watch. "Oh no, we're late for the next sleigh ride."

"What sleigh ride?" I ask, taking the last bite of a buttery sugar cookie that melts in my mouth. "And do I have to go? Sounds kind of cheesy."

"You need the full Christmas experience, Jace. Our day wouldn't be complete without it."

She grabs my arm and tugs me toward a shortcut to the barn. We hurry down an alleyway and then turn off on a side street before we arrive at a barn on the edge of town.

For someone in dress boots, she sure can run when she needs to.

"You didn't tell me it was a race," I say, panting hard from our mad dash across town. I lean against the fence for a break.

"You're not tired, are you?" she says with a grin. She barely looks like she's broken a sweat.

"No," I say, even though I'm sweating under my coat. "But I'm still not crazy about this idea. I'm not a big horse fan."

She stares at me, then bursts out laughing. "Aren't you a country singer?"

I frown. "What does that have to do with anything?"

"Because people expect you to like big trucks and farm animals."

"I do," I say, shifting uneasily. "Just not horses. I fell off one as a kid."

"Let me guess . . . now you're traumatized." She doesn't buy my fear of horses.

"I could've been trampled," I insist.

A man bundled in a heavy coat approaches us. "You here for a sleigh ride?"

"No," I say.

Mia gives me a look. "Yes."

"We'll be leaving soon. Climb on in." He nods toward a sleigh. It's tiny—only enough room for one driver and two passengers—and I'm sure it could easily flip over on a slippery curve.

"See? It's not so bad," she says under her breath. "You're not even close to the horse."

"It's like a death trap on blades," I mutter.

When I don't move, Mia grabs my arm and tugs me toward it.

I pull my arm away. "I'm perfectly happy in my horse-free life."

"But you never know when you might need to pose for a picture, riding a horse, bareback on the beach." She bites down on a laugh.

"I'm not Fabio. I wouldn't be caught dead doing that."

"This isn't just about horses," she says. "I want you to face your fears."

Ah, there it is. She's running my life again. "I didn't hire you to be my therapist."

She rolls her eyes. "Fine." She climbs into the sleigh. "But you're missing out."

"On what?" I say, trying to hide my FOMO.

"Oh, I don't know . . . *fun?*"

"I like to play it safe."

"Whatever." She turns away, scrolling through her messages. I can tell she's annoyed with me, but there are some things I'm weird about, including horses.

"You ready?" the driver announces.

After what happened last night, she probably already thinks I'm an egotistical jerk. This is my chance to make up for yesterday's debacle.

At the last second, I haul myself into the sleigh. Mia turns to look at me, but doesn't say a word as the horse takes off.

I clench my fists, aware of every bump under the sleigh.

"Just relax," Mia whispers.

"I can't," I say through gritted teeth. Not only am I afraid the driver is going to lose control, I'm also jammed in this small seat next to Mia. With every bump and turn, our legs crash together, like we can't avoid touching each other.

"Would it help if you focused on something other than the horse?" she asks, grabbing my arm. Her touch sends electricity through me, and my body stiffens in response.

I don't look at her. "What do you mean?"

"You've been staring at the horse the entire time."

That's because I'm trying not to focus on you. "What am I supposed to look at?" I huff, trying to avoid her eyes, which are just as distracting.

"How about the beautiful landscape? It's gorgeous out here. And you need to loosen up." She tries to shake my arm loose, but it makes my shoulder tighten even more.

"I'm too worried about how I'll escape if this horse runs wild."

She tilts her head. "I didn't know you were such a control freak."

"I'm not," I grumble.

She raises her eyebrows.

"Okay, I am."

"What if you pretend you're enjoying this?" she suggests. "Not that you'll take my advice, but it might be a start. Just trust me."

I let out an unconvincing grunt. I wonder if she realizes that's the same thing I told her before we slid off the road.

She looks out at a snowy field. "What if you forget about the danger and imagine it all works out?"

If this year has taught me anything, it's that you can't wish your way out of things.

"Is that even possible?" she asks, waiting for me to answer. Until now, I would've said no without hesitation. But I'm rolling this idea around in my mind.

"Maybe."

I can't fix what's wrong with myself, but I can pretend that things are different. That I'm just a normal guy, out with a beautiful girl.

Who even gets to do that? Me, that's who. I'm the luckiest guy in Evergreen.

I take a deep breath, my shoulders loosening. As I lean back, I feel like, for once, my luck is shifting.

And that's when I see *her.*

My body freezes and my fingers tingle as I stare hard at the blonde woman in a nearby parking lot.

"There's no way . . ." I squint my eyes, sure that it's a mistake.

Not a mistake. Ava's standing next to a massive black SUV. A man approaches, and she latches on to his arm and throws her head back in laughter.

"It can't be," I mutter, trying to figure out why she's in Evergreen.

"Who?" Mia asks, frowning.

She follows my gaze to the parking lot.

"Are you talking about that woman over there? How do you know her?"

"She's my ex," I say, trying to hide my disgust.

"Do you know that man she's with?"

"Oh, I know him," I grumble. "But there's no way I want to run into them today."

TEN

Mia

Jace sits stiffly next to me, taking another glance at his ex. It's obvious his thoughts are a million miles away. He probably wishes he was too.

"What do you think of Evergreen so far?" I ask, trying to get his mind off of Ava.

"Now that my ex is here?" he sputters.

"It's my attempt to distract you." I blame myself for how badly everything has gone. How was I supposed to know his ex would show up and ruin everything?

"Well, it's not working," he says.

"Listen, just because your ex is here doesn't mean we'll run into her. This is a popular place."

"You don't know how unlucky I am."

"It's not about luck," I reassure him.

He grunts, but doesn't comment.

As the driver pulls next to the barn, Jace is the first to hop out of the sleigh. The relief on his face is obvious.

"Never again," he mutters. His eyes skirt the perimeter, like he's checking for her. "Are you ready to head back?"

"Jace, stop worrying. We shouldn't leave early because of one person. We'll probably walk around the rest of the day without seeing her."

A blonde woman rounds the corner of the barn and halts when she sees him. "Jace?"

I'd recognize Jace's ex anywhere. Besides being a superstar country singer, she's also gorgeous.

I glance from her to Jace and watch the color drain from his face. His body immediately stiffens, like he doesn't know what to do with his arms.

Ava brushes a wisp of bleach-blonde hair behind her ear and gives a shy smile, highlighting her perfect cheekbones, bright blue eyes, and button nose. It's no wonder Jace fell for this woman. She's like a living, breathing Barbie. When she and Jace were a couple, they were hailed as a powerhouse duo, two superstars who only bolstered each other's country star fandom. Like *JLo and Ben. Harry and Meghan. Beyonce and Jay-Z.*

From what Mom told me, Ava started dating someone soon after their breakup and reported to the press that "she'd never been so happy."

"I told you I was unlucky," he mutters under his breath before looking at his ex with a guarded expression. "What are you doing here?"

She turns to the guy next to her, an equally stunning man dressed in mirrored aviator sunglasses and a silver ski coat that's so reflective I can almost see my face in it.

"I've never visited this town before," Ava says. "Benedict wanted to show it to me."

Benedict? What kind of name is that? I nearly choke with laughter but pass it off as a cough. Jace elbows me in the ribs and shoots me a look. Benedict is strangely silent. There's an obvious showdown going on between him and Jace.

"Well, enjoy your visit," Jace says in a wooden voice, indicating he's done with this conversation.

Ava's eyes fall on me. "Who's your friend?"

I glance at Jace, unsure how to answer. Should I admit I work for him? Or does that make him seem more pathetic because he doesn't have a date?

"This is Mia," Jace answers, then fiddles with his gloves, like he's unsure what else to say. Judging by his silence, he wants to leave as quickly as possible.

"Oh," Ava says, waiting for more. She's trying to figure out what our relationship is. But Jace's obvious silence is making this encounter even more awkward.

I panic, unable to stand this any longer. If Jace won't do something about her, then I will. Because he deserves so much better than her judgement.

I jut my chin out. "I'm Jace's girlfriend."

Ava's smile drops, before her eyes flick to Jace's. "Really?"

"Yes, really." I grab his arm and pull myself into him like I'm totally comfortable with no personal space between us. Every muscle in Jace's body stiffens as he turns his head to me in shock. I refuse to meet his eyes, afraid of what I'll see there.

"We just started dating," I say, then drop my voice. "No one knows. It's a big secret."

"Until now," she says.

"I guess the secret's out!" I let out a bubbly laugh that sounds nothing like me. I just hope Ava buys it.

I wrap my arms around Jace's middle and force myself under his arm. I'd never noticed before, but Jace's abs are like rocks, and it's startling.

"Are you here for the day?" she asks.

"Yeah," I say, my anxiety skyrocketing, making it so that I can't stop talking. "I made him come to Evergreen to have our Christmas *dream* date." I give her a big smile and squeeze Jace so hard, he coughs.

He's going to be furious about this.

"Good thing you missed the snowstorm yesterday. I hear it was a doozy," she says.

Jace slowly wraps one arm around my shoulder. Maybe my

plan is working and Jace wants to pretend he's not lonely and single, trying to recover from his worst year ever.

"Oh, we didn't miss it," I blather. "We got stuck in the snow and had to get a room at a motel. It was quite a memorable night," I conclude, before realizing what I've mistakenly suggested.

Ava's face drops as Jace coughs harder, like he's choking on something.

I smack Jace's chest, helping him catch his breath again. "Are you okay, sweetie?"

"No, I'm not," he sputters, giving me a mortified look. *I am so dead.*

Ava's eyes skirt over me, like she's made up her mind about me. "We should probably go," she says, grabbing Benedict's hand. "We're here to catch the next sleigh ride."

"Perhaps we'll see you later and we could do dinner or something?" As the words fly out of my mouth, my stomach drops. Jace looks at me in panic.

I don't even know why I offered it, other than when I get nervous, I say really dumb stuff.

"We already have reservations. For two *only,*" Jace growls, eyeing me.

"We do?" I ask Jace before realizing he's making this up to give us an out. "Oh, right! We do!"

"Where?" she asks. "We're looking for a nice restaurant after our ride."

Jace stares at me in panic again. He doesn't know what restaurants are here because he preferred no agenda. For once, my planning has paid off.

"The Belle Mansion," I say automatically, choosing the most expensive restaurant in town, and then realizing the last thing Jace needs is to run into Ava there. "But it's very exclusive," I backpedal. "I bet they're full tonight. Actually, we'd better get going before we miss our reservation."

I link my hand with Jace's, twining my fingers through his,

like we can't get enough of each other. "Right, honey?" I've never called anyone honey in my life and it sounds ridiculous.

Jace frowns slightly, like he's going to strangle me with his bare hands. "Right, *sweetheart*," he mutters.

Then he yanks me away before striding in front of me in dead silence until we're out of earshot.

"Um, Jace?"

He doesn't stop, just keeps one step ahead of me, his jaw set.

"Are you mad at me?"

He stops and wheels around. "What in the world, Mia?"

"I was trying to help you."

"By telling her we're dating and suggesting we *slept* together?" he nearly shout-whispers at me.

"Well, technically, we did."

"Not *technically*. We slept *beside* each other. There's a difference," he says, then drags his hand through his hair. "Why couldn't you just stop talking?" He grunts, then storms off.

I blink as he leaves, realizing I've ruined everything. Not only this day, but this whole trip. I'm the worst assistant ever.

"I'm sorry, Jace," I say, trying to catch up. "I thought you might appreciate having a pretend girlfriend to make your ex jealous. I was doing this for you."

"For me?" He wheels around. "Do you know what you've done?"

For once, I have nothing to say.

When I don't answer, he continues, "Now we need to pretend that we're dating."

My thoughtless decision means we have to keep up the charade, at least for today.

"No one else knows," I say. "Once we leave Evergreen, it'll be a funny story between us. Just like the Pine Paradise Motel."

Jace stares at me for a long second. "That wasn't funny, either."

Is he referring to our accidental cuddle session? If it's that bad of a memory for him, then he must find me totally repulsive.

"Then let's just go home. I didn't know I was that much of an embarrassment to you."

I brush past him, shame burning inside my chest. He grabs my arm, not letting me go. "Mia, I didn't mean that. You're not an embarrassment to me. I would never feel that way."

Even though I'm hurt, my heart feels like it's galloping across my chest, like the beat of a hundred horses.

He shakes his head, then rubs the back of his neck. "We should at least get dinner before heading home."

"Even if Ava shows up?"

"If she does, we'll deal with it." He looks over my shoulder, where Ava is heading off on her sleigh ride, then back at me, his lips curling. "When you told her we were dating, her face was priceless."

"She seemed so smug about Benedict. Even his name sounds like a snooty Englishman."

Jace bursts out laughing.

At least now we're not feuding. We're on the same team.

"We don't have to go to the Belle Mansion," I say. "I was totally making that up."

"If she shows up and doesn't see us there, she'll know you weren't telling the truth." His eyes catch mine. "What if I take you on a date to the Belle Mansion . . . my treat?"

The way he's looking at me, his lips in a lopsided smile, his dimple showing, there's no way I can say no.

ELEVEN

Mia

The Belle Mansion is located on a hill outside of town, a towering stone Romanesque mansion I could never afford in my wildest dreams. As soon as we step inside, we're transported into another time. A sweeping curved staircase, like something out of a fairy-tale castle, fills the lobby, while gleaming mahogany woodwork and golden sconces line the walls.

The hostess takes us into the ballroom, where golden candles flicker on tables and an impressive chandelier twinkles above, creating a magical circle of light.

She seats us at a cozy table close to the massive fireplace, where we can hear a violinist playing a soft tune. If I wasn't determined to keep this dinner strictly professional, this would feel like a lavish date. Not only is the Belle Mansion the kind of place where you take someone to spoil them, the prices inside the menu are jaw-dropping.

When our server comes to take our drink order, Jace orders a hot tea while I ask for water.

I frown. "I didn't know Nashville boys drank English Breakfast tea."

"My grandmother's fault." He rubs his hands together like

he's still trying to warm up after our walk. "She was a proper Brit."

"She was? But weren't you born in the South?"

"Born and raised. But my English grandmother always tried to make sure I had some British influences. She's the reason I started my musical training. She paid for my piano lessons."

"You play piano?" I think back to the grand piano in his living room, the one I thought was just for show.

"I don't tell many people. I learned classical piano first, and guitar came second. Sometimes I still play a few classical pieces."

I shake my head. Jace Knight, with his tousled hair and ripped jeans, has another side. What else don't I know about him?

"Do you ever play piano at your concerts?" I ask, intrigued.

He shakes his head. "My public image is forever tied to a guitar, so I've never tried to alter that. It's kind of a country music staple."

"Maybe you should."

"It'll probably just bring out the haters on social media. I seem to be good at that."

I lean back in my chair, the warmth of the fire relaxing me. "You're good at more than that."

"Name one thing," he says.

"Arguing with me."

Jace laughs. "I'm not sure that's a positive thing."

"Depends on how you look at it. I enjoy the mental sparring."

He hesitates for a beat. "Me too."

Our eyes catch, and his gaze shakes me a little. We're starting to feel like friends on this trip, but will it be the same when we return? Truthfully, I'm afraid that if Jace sees the real me, he might not like it. Maybe that's why it's easier to hide behind petty arguments and quick comebacks than show people who I really am.

Just then, the server arrives with our drinks and fresh bread from the oven, and I'm grateful for her timing. When I get nervous, I talk too much, and that means I'm more likely to say something stupid.

"Do you mind if I ask you a question?" Jace looks at me with a curious expression.

"Be my guest," I say, taking a sip of water. "I'm an open book."

"Are you dating anyone?"

I immediately choke on my water, and it almost comes out of my nose. I cough, and Jace looks at me in concern.

"Are you okay?"

I nod, catching my breath. "I didn't know we were getting personal so quickly."

"I didn't think it was that personal. I need to know if your boyfriend is going to be mad at me."

"For what?" I look at him like he's insane.

"If you were my girlfriend, I wouldn't be happy about you staying overnight with another guy."

"If I *had* a boyfriend—which I do not—I would tell him it was that or freeze to death. A matter of survival." Even if I can't get it out of my head now.

"So those friends you mentioned in Sully's Beach," he says. "You aren't dating any of them?"

"The only guy who's still single is Brendan. And no, we don't see each other like that."

His eyes drop to his tea as the steam curls into long ribbons. "What I'm trying to say is that I don't need more bad press . . ." He hesitates, then glances at me. "I hope you won't say anything about what happened at the Pine Paradise."

"Why would I say something?" I assure Jace. "I want this concert to be as much of a success as you do. And I didn't mean to tell Ava. It was a stupid mistake."

His shoulders relax, and I realize he's been worried about me telling everyone that I shared a hotel room with him. To be under public scrutiny is terrible, but even more so when someone betrays you. Maybe the fact that he trusts me a little means we're making progress.

The waitress comes over and takes our order. I choose a salmon dish I can't pronounce, while Jace picks filet mignon.

"Can I ask you a question now?" I unfold the cloth around the warm bread and offer him a slice.

He plucks it from the basket. "It's only fair."

"What's your family like?" I ask. "I know you said you're not close."

"They were helicopter parents before there was such a thing. My parents pushed me into show business when I was a kid, always signing me up for auditions. I'm grateful to be where I am, but they always made me feel like I wasn't their son. Like they were fulfilling their own dreams through me. And that it was all about money." He eats his bread and doesn't say anything else, and I get the feeling he doesn't want to talk about it.

"The invitation to spend Christmas with my family is always open," I offer. "They're slightly dysfunctional, but they make up for it by being highly entertaining. And I balance out the crazy."

Jace laughs. "Do you think your mom and brothers would care?"

"Care? They'd be thrilled. They've already roped me into cooking."

"You're staying for the holidays? I thought you hated Christmas?"

"I have a love-hate relationship with the holidays," I say with a shrug, wondering if he'll let it go. "Sometimes my mom and I don't get along."

"Hate is a strong word." His eyes stay on me. "Why do you dislike it?"

I set my bread down and wipe off my hands. "My dad left a few days after Christmas when I was a kid. Even though it was a long time ago, I hate that I still connect the holidays with that one event."

I let the news fall between us into the stony silence.

"I'm sorry about that," he murmurs, his eyes softening. "No one should leave on Christmas. Or anytime, really. Do you have contact?"

"After he left, we didn't hear from him for a long time. I always thought that someday, we'd reconnect and I'd finally find out why he left—and we'd make up for lost time. But he never came back. Then last year, Mom got word that he died unexpectedly in a car accident, and I knew I'd never get the answers I needed." I swirl my straw around, avoiding Jace's eyes. "Sorry to be such a downer. I didn't want to mention it."

"I'm glad you did. Now I finally understand why this Christmas festival means so much to you."

I lean forward so no one else hears. "You want to hear a secret? I kind of *hate* the Mistletoe Festival."

"Then why'd you agree to plan it?"

"I thought I could make this year different for some kid who's had an awful Christmas. And that maybe it would help my family. Isn't that stupid?"

He leans on the table, his eyes studying me. "It's not stupid at all."

"It feels like an impossible wish. Kind of like those people who only date at Christmas because they feel lonely and think a Christmas romance will fix it."

Jace smirks. "You know, a couple of the guys in my band are single. I could set you up."

"Um, no." I shake my head. "I don't date when I'm planning a big event. There's no time. And new relationships are time-sucks."

"That's a bad excuse," he teases. "You're supposed to *want* to spend time with people you like."

I try to avoid the peacock blue of his eyes, but I can't. When Jace looks at me like this, it makes something inside me come loose. "I'm a terrible girlfriend. Especially when I'm focused on something else. And in case you haven't noticed, I'm kind of bossy."

Jace laughs again, making everything spark in my chest.

"That should be your goal," he says. "Go out more. Get a date for Christmas."

I don't know what to say to this. *Fat chance? I'd sooner win the lottery?*

I break off an enormous piece of bread and slather butter on it. "I'm perfectly happy watching Hallmark movies and living vicariously through them. Plus, I don't have time for fun or dating."

"Now who's the Scrooge?" he says, his lips quirking.

"In case you've forgotten, I have a job to do for a big music star. And I want to do it right."

"You are doing it right," he says with a grin. "But your Christmas needs more fun." He smiles, like he knows the effect his dimple has on me.

Is he flirting with me? I feel like he's flirting.

Or maybe I'm just delirious.

"What if we both have more fun at Christmas . . ." he suggests. "We've both had a bad year, so why not try to change that?"

I frown, not understanding. "It doesn't work that way. It's not a contract you make with yourself. Sometimes, life just sucks and there's nothing fun about it."

"That's one way of looking at it. All I'm encouraging you to do is chase the fun. It doesn't have to be dating."

I laugh and shake my head. "I'm pretty lame if I need you to help me with that."

"Well, if you're lame, then I am too."

"I doubt that." I break off another piece of bread. "I don't see the point when I'm already so busy."

He studies me for a second. "What are you scared of?"

"What? I'm not scared. Why would I be afraid? That's ridiculous."

Jace shrugs. "Because if you try to search for happiness and you don't find it, you're afraid of what that might mean."

I crinkle my nose. "I'm not afraid to be happy."

He levels his gaze at me. "Then I dare you to try."

The way he's looking at me with those ocean-blue eyes makes me almost feel like I could. But how can I believe things will be different this holiday? Everyone is counting on me. Mom. The Mistletoe Festival committee. Jace. The entire town of Maplewood. I can't let them down. There's no time to consider my happiness when I have everything else to take care of.

"Happiness is a luxury for people whose lives are going right."

"No." Jace shakes his head, his jaw set. "You deserve it."

The way he pins me down with a look makes me want to agree to anything. I'm willing to take this happiness dare and fall headlong into it. I've let the weight of my past become a slow drag on my life for far too long.

I play with my straw, making endless circles in my water. "I'll try," I finally say. *What do I have to lose?* "At least until the holidays are over."

He gives me another lopsided smile. Then he holds up his glass, offering a toast. We clink cups to our new agreement, finally unified on one thing. "Here's to our happiness."

"And chasing the fun," I add. "No matter how impossible it is."

As soon as I say those words, I feel like I've erased my chances. You can't find happiness just by making a deal with someone.

And now I'm waiting for the other shoe to drop.

Jace's eyes flick over my shoulder, his dimple disappears, and a deep crease forms between his brows.

"What's wrong?" I ask.

I wheel around in my chair, and my breath catches when I realize what he's staring at.

Ava and Benedict have just walked into the restaurant.

TWELVE

Jace

"Don't panic," Mia says, even though she's clearly panicking. "What'll we do?" She swivels around to me, her face pleading for an answer.

"Why are you looking at me? How should I know?"

"I don't know," she says, glancing around the room like she's looking for an escape route. "You have better instincts than me. I talk too much when I'm nervous."

"She still thinks we're dating." I glance back at Ava and Benedict who are now making their way across the room.

"What's wrong?" Mia asks, turning toward Ava.

"Don't look, but they're coming this way," I mutter under my breath.

Mia grabs my hand from under the table and pulls it up so that it's clearly visible. Our linked hands are blatantly on display for the entire room to see.

"What are you doing?" I whisper under clenched teeth.

"We're going with my plan. Pretend to be crazy about me."

Then she turns and waves to Ava and Benedict, like they're good friends.

Ava's eyes skirt over our hands before she pastes on a fake smile. "I hope you don't mind, but we took your advice. And wow, this place is gorgeous!" Her gaze drifts over the ornate wood-work and the grandiose chandelier.

"Jace would only choose the best for me," Mia coos, squeezing my hand and giving me a wink. "He's always spoiling me with dates and gifts." She rubs her thumb over my hand. Even though I know it's an act, my body tenses.

Ava's mouth tightens for a second before she glances at Benedict, who hasn't bothered to acknowledge us.

Our waitress returns with our food, giving us an immediate out.

"We should probably go, but enjoy your meal!" Ava smiles again and grabs Benedict's arm.

Relief floods through me as they return to their table.

I pull my hand away from Mia's. "You could've warned me first," I whisper. "I jumped when you grabbed my hand." I take my knife and slice a piece of filet.

Mia stares at me. "I had exactly two seconds to figure out what to do. I almost hopped onto your lap, but I thought that might be too extreme."

"Thank you."

She glances to where Ava is sitting. "What now?"

"It's not like we need to touch all the time. But we should keep up the charade."

"How do we do that?" Mia asks with a puzzled look. "I haven't exactly dated a lot."

"But you've been in relationships, right?"

She pauses. "None of them have lasted long. A few days."

I stop eating and stare at her. "You haven't been in a relation-ship for more than a few days?"

"I'm *very* picky," she says. "Plus, it's not cool when you're smarter than your date, and they break up with you because of it."

I frown. "Why would they do that?"

"It makes them feel dumb." She takes a bite of her salmon. "No guy wants to feel like that."

I shake my head. "Finding a smart woman is like gold. It doesn't take away from a guy's worth. It makes him even better."

"Tell that to all the bums I've dated. Not that there have been many."

"But you've held a guy's hand before, right?"

She frowns like she's trying to remember. "It was a long time ago."

"So was kissing a long time ago, too?"

Her eyes drop to her fork as she picks at her salmon. "I've never been kissed."

I drop my fork on my plate, and the clanging echoes across the room. "Never?"

Mia freezes, then glances around. "Could you keep it down? People are staring."

"I'm sorry. I was just surprised," I whisper. "I've never met a girl who hasn't been kissed."

She tilts her head. "You're making me feel like a freak."

"You gotta admit, it is unusual."

She shakes her head. "That is not helping."

"So, this whole pretend dating scenario right now is a real stretch, huh? Because you don't throw yourself at anyone."

"Only you, apparently. And I'm the worst actress."

I stop eating and stare at Mia. "You weren't terrible. Ava totally bought it." And I did too.

"We need to figure out how to keep up the act when we leave," she says.

"Let me take care of it," I insist. I hadn't realized how much of a sacrifice this has been for her. She wasn't trying to make me feel awkward. She was saving me from the humiliation of facing my ex.

She frowns. "Does that mean we're going to run out of here as fast as possible?"

I shake my head. "Not if I can help it. Just follow my lead."

An expression passes over her face that I can't read. I'm not sure if she's terrified of what I'm suggesting or revolted by it, but she's willing to go along with the plan.

After finishing our meal and paying our bill, I glance over at Ava who's shoving a shrimp appetizer in Benedict's mouth. Their flirting makes my stomach turn. "Are you ready to go?"

Mia nods. Maybe it's my nerves, but knowing how Mia's touch caused my body to react last time makes me wonder if I'm going to internally combust on my way out the door.

And the worst part is that I have to pretend I'm not reacting, which is so exhausting.

I hold out my hand. She glances at it, like she's considering whether this is a good idea.

"It's okay, Mia. I promise I don't bite."

When she takes my hand, it's so warm and soft and distracting, I forget my nerves. All I can think about are the fireworks going off in my body.

From the corner of my eye, Ava's gaze is on us the entire way out.

"Is it working?" Mia whispers as we head into the foyer.

I don't even bother looking back to see if Ava is watching.

"Just in case, we should keep this up until we leave Evergreen."

———

When we finally reach my car and escape to the privacy of the back roads, Mia finally pulls her hand from mine. For the first time since we saw Ava, we can relax because there's no chance we'll run into them anymore.

"What did you think of Evergreen?" Mia asks. "I want the truth. And pretend you didn't see your ex there."

"That definitely colors things. But it wasn't as cheesy as I thought," I add, not wanting to admit how much I liked it. "The food was amazing. It makes me wonder if Maplewood can pull off something similar."

"In its heyday, Maplewood had the best festival around. They were known for their mistletoe contest."

I narrow my eyes. "You're kidding, right?"

"Back in the day, it was the contest all the newlywed and engaged couples talked about. They gave you a time limit to show off your best kiss, then the judges scored you and announced the winner at the end."

I let out a laugh of disbelief. "What did they rate it on? Most creative? Longest and most passionate?"

"I'm sorry, but we are a PG-rated festival," she says, lifting a brow. "It wasn't just about technique. Every couple had to talk about how they fell in love."

"Like watching *The Bachelor* before reality TV?"

"Yes, but they wanted couples who were mad about each other. Most of the older folks in town love reminiscing about the mistletoe contest."

"Then why not bring it back?"

"Seriously?" she asks. "The committee would love it. But I wish there was a way for it to generate income. The festival desperately needs funds if we want to continue the event after this year. They received a big donation recently, but next year, we'll be stuck without money."

I think for a minute. "Why not do a fundraiser? Like a charity auction for something people would pay big bucks for."

She frowns. "Like what?"

"A date to a high-end restaurant or a popular event."

"There aren't any fancy restaurants in Maplewood, and the only big event is yours."

"No promises, but I'll see what I can do," I say. "It would be even more fun if there were volunteers involved."

"What do you mean?"

"Like dinner with the mayor," I suggest. "Or a date with you."

She looks at me in horror. "I'd rather die."

"When was the last time you dated?"

She looks out the window. "A few months ago, Jaz set me up on a date that was a total flop. I think it was because I told him my hobby was collecting houseplants." Then she glances at me. "Do you get why I scare men off? I'm a barrel of laughs."

"Houseplants are riveting," I say, stifling a smile. "Who doesn't love a woman obsessed with them?"

"Not just any houseplants . . . succulents. When I mentioned them, his eyes glazed over."

"For what it's worth, I don't find you boring at all," I admit. "And I'm fascinated with birds. Ava always found that weird, but I like people who have interests that are more than money or success."

"Thanks for making me less of a weirdo," she says.

We talk about eagles and succulents and the stray cats who followed me home. Before I realize it, we turn into my drive, and I'm disappointed the trip is over.

I put the car in park as Blackie and Tabby run across the drive to greet us. "Do you want to come inside for a few minutes?"

She glances at me uneasily. "Thanks, but I should probably head home and get a good night's rest." She grabs her bag from the back seat. "I've got work early tomorrow."

As much as I want her to stay, both of us need time to clear our heads and get Evergreen out of our system.

But that's the problem. *I don't want to get her out of my system.*

Ever since she mentioned that she's never been kissed, I can't stop thinking about what it would be like to give her the first one.

"Wait, Mia." I circle the car, stopping in front of her, my heart beating wildly. "I feel like I should at least say goodbye."

For a split second, she looks confused. "Yeah?" Everything about her body language is closed off, guarded.

"I enjoyed our trip to Evergreen."

She crinkles her nose. "You did?"

"Nobody is more surprised than me. And I wondered if . . ."

The pause hangs between us as something ripples behind the deep green pools of her eyes.

"Wondered what?" She swallows hard, and my gaze drops to her lips.

Then I realize my mistake. It's one thing to pretend we're dating. But she hasn't given me any hint that she wants something more.

"If I could give you a hug?" I blurt instead. "As a way of saying thanks for making me go on this trip."

"Oh, of course," she says.

I step forward and slide my hands around her back as she leans her body into mine. It feels as wonderful as this morning when I woke up with her in my arms. My cheek brushes her hair, and I get the heady scent of warm vanilla, the same intoxicating fragrance I breathed in sleeping next to her.

She gives a small laugh as she pulls away. "For a minute, I thought you were . . ." She pauses and shakes her head.

"Thought what?" I frown.

"Never mind." She waves her hand in the air, dismissing the idea.

I shove my hands in my pockets, suddenly aware of the heat flaming in my chest, the memory of her skin against mine, the first kiss that almost happened.

THIRTEEN

Mia

When I meet Jaz at the airport, she's dressed to kill. Apparently, when I explained it was winter in Vermont, she thought that gave her an excuse to buy a pink faux-fur coat that's ideal for an Instagram shoot, not for an *actual* winter. Contrasted against her light brown skin, the color looks perfect.

"Jaz!" I wave, then run over to her. Hugging her in this coat is like hugging a bear, but I don't care.

"I've missed you!" she squeals, her arms squeezing the breath from my lungs. "I brought you a surprise!"

"What's going on?" I frown, pulling back. "What surprise?"

"I decided not to tell you before I arrived. Because I knew you'd say no."

"Not tell me what?" I ask, suddenly concerned.

From around the corner, Ella jumps out.

"Surprise!" She runs toward me and falls into my arms. Her brown hair is pulled into a ponytail, and she's dressed in a ski jacket.

"What are you doing here?" I ask, feeling like a sandwich between my two best friends.

"You asked me to help design the festival and I talked Ella into coming. Isn't that wonderful?" Jaz pulls away so I can catch my breath before her fake fur suffocates me.

"But I can't pay you both," I say, looking between them. "I don't have the budget for it. The committee only gave me permission for one person."

Ella waves a hand in the air. "Don't worry about paying me. I'm just here for a quick girls' trip. Once we work out the design concept for the Mistletoe Festival, we can do fun stuff, like a spa day, before I head back to Grant. My husband won't want me gone for long."

Jaz and Ella look ecstatic, like they're expecting me to drop everything and get a facial right now.

"But I have so much to do for the festival and the concert," I moan. "I can't possibly take time off for a spa day."

"That's why we're *here*," Jaz says. "To make things easier on you so you don't work yourself to death."

"That's so sweet of you, but . . . I can't." I shake my head, torn about having my friends here when I'm swamped.

Ella's face drops. "Can't?"

"The festival is starting in a few weeks. And we're already so far behind. I'll be lucky just to get everything done in time."

"Honey," Jaz says, linking arms with me as we head to the parking lot. "I could tell you were worried over the phone. Between working for Jace and managing the festival committee, you're totally stressed out. We're here to make things happen."

"Who knows?" Ella grabs my other arm. "Maybe this gig will lead to a permanent contract working for Jace?"

"I don't think so," I say. My friends want the best for me, but I need to make it clear: working for Jace isn't a good fit. The best thing I can do is ignore my feelings for him and pretend they don't exist until this is over.

"Jace would be crazy not to hire you after this concert," Ella says. "We all know how insanely talented you are."

"I wouldn't even consider it," I insist.

Jaz shoots Ella a worried look. "Wouldn't consider it because you have a better option? Working as a barista is not a long-term solution for your money problems."

"I don't think working for Jace is either," I say, avoiding their eye contact.

Jaz stops in the middle of the parking lot and grabs my arm so that I'm forced to stop. "That's not the reason. I can see it in your face." She points at me, her smile spreading slowly. "You like him."

My mouth drops open. "I do *not.*"

"You do." Then Jaz turns me toward Ella. "Look at her face."

Ella studies me, then crosses her arms. "You're right."

I shake my head, even though my cheeks are heating like an oven. "No, I don't like him. Not like that."

Jaz rolls her eyes. "You haven't noticed he's a gorgeous human being?"

"He's . . . not horrible looking," I stammer.

"I knew it!" Jaz says, smiling. "You have the worst poker face."

"That doesn't mean I like him," I argue.

Both of them erupt into laughter.

"I'm serious," I say.

"What about sharing a motel room?" Ella says.

I turn to Jaz. "You *told* her?"

Jaz lifts a hand. "You know I'm terrible at keeping secrets."

I'm never going to live this down. "It wasn't my fault," I insist. "The snowstorm hit, and we were stuck in this awful motel with one bed."

Jaz raises an eyebrow. "How convenient."

I ramble on. "The heat didn't work in our room, and Jace was going to sleep on the disgusting motel carpet."

"So you sacrificed half the bed?" Ella shakes her head. "Sleeping beside Jace Knight was probably so hard for you."

Jaz snorts with laughter.

I storm toward my mom's car and climb into the driver's seat. "You won't tease me about what happened with Jace."

Jaz slides into the passenger seat while Ella climbs in the back.

"I'm curious." Jaz glances at me. "Does Jace snore?"

"No, he doesn't."

"Does he look cute when he sleeps?" Ella asks.

"I'm not answering that." I turn toward the highway, glancing at Ella in the rearview mirror. "And I wasn't staring at him like a stalker. I couldn't even see him."

"What do you mean you couldn't see him?" Ella asks.

"He had his arm on me," I blurt before realizing my mistake.

"Wait." Jaz frowns. "Why was his arm on you? Unless he was . . ." Her mouth falls open, and her eyes widen.

I shouldn't have let that slip.

When I don't answer, Ella leans forward. "Why didn't you tell us?"

"It wasn't like that!" I throw my hands in the air, exasperated. "Nothing happened between us. His face was next to my shoulder, his arm across my waist, and I froze. I mean. What would you have done?"

Jaz smiles. "I'd have taken a selfie. Because no one is going to believe this."

"I don't want proof," I insist. "I want to forget it happened."

"Did it come up afterward?" Ella asks.

"Every time I wanted to, I was too embarrassed to bring it up."

Jaz shakes her head. "You should've taken that selfie."

"So he could fire me?" I say. "He's still nursing a broken heart from that very public breakup with Ava. And I don't want to ruin things before his concert. In person, he actually seems . . . *nice*."

"Nice?" Jaz turns to Ella and they exchange a knowing look.

"What?" I ask.

"You never say that about any guy," Jaz warns.

"I can't have feelings for Jace. Why would a music star fall for me?" I take a quick glance at Jaz, who still looks doubtful. "You don't believe me?"

She sighs. "I've been your friend long enough to know how you are."

"I don't like him that way." Even as I say it, my stomach squeezes. I'm getting too caught up in defending Jace because something has definitely changed between us. Jace is charming, but I won't fall so easily. "Why do you think I haven't kissed anyone yet? I'm not exactly throwing myself at the first available man. I don't have time for a relationship, even if he did like me." Which he doesn't. We're too different.

Ella stares out the window as we enter Maplewood's downtown.

"Welcome to Maplewood!" I say, glancing over my shoulder. Both of the girls look concerned.

"Wait, is this it?" Ella asks.

"I know it doesn't look great, but think of what it was in its heyday. There's so much potential!"

Neither of the girls says anything as we pass the empty storefronts and drab downtown. As the silence lengthens, I suddenly realize just how much work this town needs. It doesn't look like a Christmas town. It looks like a set for a post-apocalyptic movie.

"I thought you said this place was cute?" Jaz asks. "Where are the coffee shops? The boutiques? The bakeries with mouthwatering desserts on display?"

"We have a diner," I say, pointing to Wanda's restaurant. "But we've lost a lot of businesses."

"This is going to be . . . interesting." Jaz bites her cheek. "How much money do we have to work with?"

"I have a spreadsheet with the budget numbers," I say. "And we have tons of decorations stored in one of the empty storefronts."

"Are the decorations in good shape?" Ella asks.

"Some. You'll also have a few thousand to spend."

"A few thousand *dollars?*" Jaz asks.

"Yeah," I say, realizing that's far too little. The big donation is mainly covering my salary and Jace's concert.

I pull into a parking spot and fish the budget records from my bag. Ella and Jaz look over the numbers.

"That's impossible," Jaz says as she looks over the sheet.

I turn to them. "Listen, I know it's a challenge. Especially given our limited resources. But try to keep an open mind. The committee will volunteer all their free time to bring this festival back to life. It's that . . . or the town dies."

Jaz stares at me. "So you want us to work a miracle? Is that what you're saying?"

"If there's anyone who can do it, it's you. And I'm working on a fundraiser that will help us make more."

I take them to the abandoned storefront where we keep the Christmas decorations from past years. Most of them look like they're from fifty years ago, but the committee can't part with them. When we step inside, a man with wrinkly skin steps around a large aluminum Christmas tree.

"Nolan, I didn't know you'd be here," I say, then turn to Ella and Jaz. "This is Nolan Whitmore, our resident handyman. He can fix anything."

They both shake Nolan's hand as he gives them a nod. Nolan remembers the good old days of the Maplewood Mistletoe Festival. He's probably the only one, other than my mother, who believes I can restore it to its glory days.

"Nolan, we're going to have a look around and see what's salvageable."

Now that Jaz and Ella are here, I'm wondering what I've gotten myself into. Everything looks like trash. Ella and Jaz spread out, combing through boxes. Then Jaz moves to the back storage room and discovers something covered with a tarp.

"An old tree from a shop window," Nolan says. "No one has used it in years."

Ella looks it over. "It's in decent condition. The only problem is that it's a monstrosity to put together. But if we didn't have to buy everything, that would save us money."

Knowing that we have little to work with, it's a start. "Let's put it on our list as a potential decoration."

Ella stops in front of a vintage light-up Santa. It's enormous and would probably cover the entire side of a building.

"I have an idea," Ella says, her eyes skirting over the room. She tilts her head in that signature way when her design wheels are spinning. "I can't believe how much vintage stuff is tucked back here. Some of it is junk. But others are classic. What if we clean up the good stuff and make the downtown look vintage-inspired?"

"I think the idea of bringing back old Maplewood is fabulous," Jaz says, clapping her hands together. "What do you think?"

"I love it," I say, throwing up my hands and giving the girls high fives. If anyone can make this town come back to life, it's Jaz and Ella. "If you decide what's salvageable and put together a sketch of the Main Street design, I can assemble a crew of people to set up the decorations."

My phone rings and Jace's name pops up on my screen.

"I need to take this," I say, wondering when I'll stop getting tiny zaps of energy when he calls. Apparently, my body didn't get the memo about ignoring my feelings.

"Hey, what's up?" I say casually, making sure I don't sound too excited.

"Where are you? I just passed your car parked on Main Street."

"In the old mercantile building sorting through Christmas decorations."

"Are you free?"

Excitement zips down my spine. Of course I'm free. Especially when Jace calls.

"Sure. When will you be here?"

"How about now?"

I spin around. Jace is standing in the door, wearing a henley shirt with an open flannel shirt, looking as dreamy as always. "Hey, Mia," he says with an easy smile.

My heart leaps as I try to tamp down my excitement. "Oh, hey," I mumble.

"You roped Nolan into helping?" Jace waves at the older man across the room.

"He's volunteered for years. You know him?" I assumed Jace didn't know many people in Maplewood.

"Nolan is the guy I call when things break at home," he says. "Since I know nothing about fixing things."

Jaz and Ella shoot me a look, begging to be introduced.

"These are my friends Ella and Jaz. They're helping with the festival design."

"Nice to meet you," Jace says, shaking their hands and showing off his dimple.

For once, they're both speechless. I've never seen Jace have this effect on people.

"Could you help Mia have some fun so she doesn't work too much?" he asks with a grin.

"I am having fun," I insist.

"We'll force her to take some time off at the spa," Jaz volunteers.

"Do you mind if I steal her from you?" Jace asks.

"Go right ahead," Jaz says, giving me a look.

"Are you sure?" I ask them. "You don't know where anything is."

"Nolan will help us find things," Ella insists, nudging me toward Jace. "You two have fun!"

They both wave as we walk outside.

"Where are we going?" I ask.

"It's a surprise."

I stop on the sidewalk. "I thought after the Pine Paradise Motel, we don't do surprises."

He grins. "I promise, this is better."

Jace starts up his car and heads out of town, speeding across country roads surrounded by pine trees.

"Do I get any clues about our destination?"

"Ever since we went to Evergreen, I can't get that violin tune out of my head. When I got home that night, I wrote a new song based on a few chords and sent a rough version to my band. They loved it and said we should release the single as quickly as possible." He looks over at me. "And I wanted to play it for you . . . as a test."

I shake my head, unsure why he invited me. "Why me?"

"I need your honest opinion."

"But this isn't the way to your house."

"That's the surprise." His eyes light up, like he's excited about something. "I'm taking you to a barn."

"A barn? But why?"

"You'll see. Since you forced me to go to Evergreen . . . I figured I'd return the favor."

I hold up my finger to stop him. "I didn't force," I interrupt. "Maybe pleaded and begged."

"If Evergreen inspires me to write one song . . . then the Pine Paradise was not a waste."

"I'm not really a farm girl," I admit.

"It's not that kind of barn," he clarifies. "It's a renovated round barn that someone turned into an event center. And it's located right outside Maplewood."

As he turns onto a long lane, I suddenly remember where we are. "I know this place. It used to be a farm years ago."

"The owners sold it two years ago, and they built a stage and seating but kept the gorgeous vintage structure."

He pulls into a clearing, where the round barn sits on the top of an immaculate hillside. The renovated circular building is striking against the snowy backdrop, like it should be on a postcard.

"But why are you playing the song here?"

He parks the car and looks at me. "This is where I want to have my concert."

"What?" I say. "But we already reserved the old theater downtown. I know it's not in great shape, but it's better than a barn."

He shakes his head. "Wait until you see this place."

When we step inside, my mouth drops. The circular ceiling

stretches high above us like a cathedral. Rough-hewn beams and an old wood floor give the place character.

"What do you think?" Jace says.

"It's gorgeous," I murmur, awestruck with this hidden gem. "It would make a stunning backdrop for the concert. There's only one problem."

"What's that?"

"The size," I say. "We need a bigger venue."

"The downtown theater isn't much bigger, and it's not as unique as this place. I like the idea of playing a small venue." He hops onto the stage and spins around. "This feels intimate. Like the gigs I used to play when nobody knew my name."

He sits at the piano and plays a few chords, and it's so obvious that music is his first love. On stage, Jace looks like he belongs here. This venue fits his music, even if it means we'll have to limit tickets.

He stops, suddenly aware that I'm staring at him. "Come on up." He pats the space next to him on the piano bench.

I shake my head. "Behind the piano is a really great look for you."

"You need to see the view from here. And you make me nervous when you're watching from the audience."

"Me?" I say, surprised. "But you've performed in front of thousands of people."

"I still get nervous. It's easier if you're beside me. It feels less like a performance that way."

As I sit next to him, I avoid looking directly at Jace since we're almost touching. Ever since the Pine Paradise, it's like my body is constantly aware of where his body is, like one magnet pulled toward the other.

His eyes flick toward mine, and I can see the curl of his lashes. "Since you're officially head of the festival, can I move the concert here?" If he wasn't already convincing enough, he flashes an adorable smile that makes his dimple show, and my body instantly melts. *How am I going to say no to that?*

"We'll have to change all the promotional material. But I can do it, as long as you make it up to me." I give him a teasing smile.

Jace laughs. "How about I'll make you dinner some night?"

"You cook?" I don't know why I imagine that Jace Knight eats out every night. Maybe because he can.

"It's not *exactly* cooking," he explains. "I have a chef who stops by a few times a week and preps meals for me. I know it's cheating, but it's better than eating chips every night."

He has a chef, in addition to a housekeeper? *What does this guy not have?*

"That's not cheating. It's *amazing*." I don't want to admit that I've eaten chips more nights than I can count.

"It's not like I've always been able to afford a chef. When I was on my own for the first time, I worked at a warehouse during the day and gigged at dive bars in the evening. Most nights, the people were so drunk they talked over my songs and booed me."

"It's hard to imagine anyone doing that to you."

"Well, it's not all awards and high-profile parties. Sometimes I actually miss those days of being unknown."

"Why?"

He stops playing and looks over at me. "Fame is like being in a fishbowl. Everyone is watching you, but it's a lonely place. People take normal life for granted. And anyone I date has to accept that my life is anything but normal."

I want to ask him what he means, but the barn door squeaks open and a young woman with bright pink hair steps in. "Hey, Jace, sorry I'm late." She looks around. "This place has some great vibes. Perfect for TikTok."

Jace leans over to me and whispers, "This is my social media manager, Cammy."

Cammy sets up her lights and microphone while Jace practices his new song. When he's not looking, I soak him up—the music, his dimple, his scent. He's so insanely talented, and I'm more than happy to be the girl he practices his songs for.

Cammy climbs up the steps to the stage. "Are you Jace's new hire? I've heard a lot about you."

"I am," I reply, suddenly curious about what Jace said about me.

"How do you feel about being on camera?" she asks.

"What?" I reply, shocked. "You don't want me. I'm really terrible on video."

"Don't worry. I'll focus the camera on Jace the whole time. His last video got a million shares."

"A million?" I pause, my mind reeling.

"Free promotion for the festival," she hints.

With our limited budget, I'd be a fool to pass up this opportunity. "Okay, I guess."

"It's easy," she promises. "And Jace will be the star. Just let him do his thing."

Before I can ask her what she means by "do his thing," she turns to Jace. "Let's run the song again with background tracks so you don't have to play the whole thing. And could you interact with Mia? Pull out your signature move, like you throw into every concert."

She gives me a quick wink, like I should know what she's talking about.

As my heart bounces against my chest, I whisper to Jace, "What does she mean?"

There's a wicked gleam in his eyes. "You don't know my signature move, do you?"

"I don't. And no sarcastic remarks about how I should've done my homework. I've been busy."

"The fact I'm going to surprise you is even better," he says with a low chuckle.

"Jace," I growl under my breath. "This is not funny."

Cammy holds her hand up from behind a camera. "Okay, Jace. We're ready to roll. You can start singing to her."

"To me?" Sweat suddenly breaks out on the back of my neck, and I wonder if I look as scared as I feel.

"There's no one else here to sing to," Jace replies, like this is the easiest thing in the world for him.

But it's not for me. I'm not used to the limelight or being on camera for millions of fans. I've never wanted fame, and I'm perfectly happy being unknown.

He starts the song and concentrating on the keys, which gives me a few seconds to pull my thoughts together.

Then he sings,

I built my walls so high, swore love couldn't find me,
Locked my heart away, believed I was finally free.
But then you walked in, stormed into the night,
Tore down my defenses, couldn't put up a fight.

As soon as our eyes meet, my stomach starts doing cartwheels. I know Jace isn't singing this to me, but my body doesn't know that. Before now, I could always count on stuffing my emotions into a locked container inside my chest. But now it feels like those emotions are spilling out, like a shaken bottle.

Jace stops playing, letting the background music take over. He moves off of the piano bench and takes my hand. I'm confused about what's happening, but Cammy told me to follow Jace's lead. And right now, I'd let Jace take me anywhere.

He gathers me in his arms, pulls my body next to his, and starts to dance with me in the middle of the stage. As we find a slow rhythm together, his body brushes mine, and for a second, I forget that I'm on camera because my heart is beating wildly inside my chest.

Jace's hand sweeps across my lower back, shooting sparks where his fingertips move. For a moment, it almost feels like we're alone until Cammy yells, "Keep dancing. This will make great B-roll!"

Jace shifts his hands tightly around me and pulls me even closer so that I can hardly breathe. With my body next to his, I'm overwhelmed by his scent.

Why did I have to fall for someone so perfect? So unattainable? There's no question. I'm out of my league.

"Are you having fun?" he whispers in my ear. "Because if I remember right, we made an agreement to have more fun."

"If you call making a fool of yourself on camera fun, then no, I'm not having fun."

He chuckles. "Then forget the camera. Pretend this is spontaneous," he whispers, sending shivers down my arm.

If only I could forget that I'm slow dancing with Jace.

"And what part, exactly, is your signature move?"

"It's a thing I do at my concerts with a woman from the audience."

"You slow dance with a stranger?" I repeat, finally understanding why he pulled me into his embrace. It's not me he wants to dance with. It's his publicity stunt.

"You're not a stranger," he whispers. "That's why this is more fun."

Jace is having fun with me? I know it's only for the camera, but he's outstanding at playing this role. With his lips close to my ear, my brain turns into a thick soup, making it hard for me to think straight.

The problem isn't the dancing. Every place he touches me is melting with heat.

"Maybe I need more practice," I say. "Before it becomes fun."

Jace pulls back so he can look at me. "If you need someone to practice with, I'm available."

"Okay," I say, my heart twirling in my chest. Did I just agree to dance with Jace again? *Who have I even become?*

His gaze holds mine for a moment, and I swallow, suddenly wishing we weren't just pretending.

"And cut!" Cammy yells as she shuts off the camera.

Jace's eyes flick away, and he drops his arms, the moment evaporating between us like a magic spell.

"Was that enough B-roll?" he asks Cammy, stepping away from me.

She gives Jace a thumbs up.

The warm pressure where his fingers splayed across my back is still pulsing.

Jace takes off his baseball cap and drags his hands through his hair.

"Was that okay?" I ask, suddenly wondering if I'm the only one who felt something between us.

He holds my gaze for a second. "Perfect."

This was all for the camera, right?

Jace isn't looking for a girlfriend after what happened with Ava.

And I'm not looking for a Christmas fling . . . even if it is with Jace Knight.

FOURTEEN

Jace

For the next few days, I can't forget that dance, even though I've tried.

I should've known not to dance with Mia after how I felt at the motel. But when I wrapped my arms around her, it seemed like the most natural thing in the world.

Which is why I can't stop watching the video. Or replaying it in my mind.

When Cammy brings it up while taking some photos at my house, I immediately tense up. "Did you hear? Your video is going freaking crazy."

"Yeah, I heard." I pluck a few guitar strings, loosening my fingers for my three-hour music practice session later today.

"I think this might be the start of turning things around for you," she says, taking another picture.

"As long as they like the song, I don't care about anything else." That's really the only reason I still use social media. To build buzz and get traction on the charts.

"They like the song." Cammy takes a few shots of me with my guitar. "But they also love her."

I glance up in surprise. "Mia?"

Cammy pauses behind the camera. "She was the perfect choice, Jace. She's not the Hollywood type, like Ava was. Nobody knows her, and that makes her more relatable because she's the girl next door."

"I want to keep it that way," I mutter. *For Mia's sake.* She doesn't need the paparazzi all over her because of this video.

"Good luck with that," Cammy says, chuckling, then glancing over her camera. "Your chemistry on screen was off the charts. I think everyone wants to *be* her."

Even now, I can't forget the feeling of my hands skating across her back, her body pressed close to mine, the warm vanilla scent driving me insane.

I'm obsessed with her scent the way my cats are obsessed with catnip.

"The attraction between you two . . . I almost believed it," she says, watching me closely.

"Maybe I'm getting better at acting," I lie, trying not to react. She's fishing for some hint that there's more going on.

"Or maybe it wasn't acting?" Cammy suggests, lifting an eyebrow.

I shake my head. "I couldn't put her through that. Not after Ava."

"What? Dating you is that bad?" Cammy laughs.

"Dating a celebrity. The whole life of dodging cameras, wearing disguises. Even Ava struggled with it, and she *is* a celebrity. For a small-town girl, it would be overwhelming. She didn't even know who I was when we met."

Because that's what makes her different from every other girl I've dated. She doesn't care about my celebrity status or fame.

"That's why the video worked," Cammy adds. "She wasn't posing for the camera. She was looking at you. It was refreshing to see someone so in the moment. She's endearing, really."

Exactly. It's why Mia has gotten under my skin in the worst way. Every moment with her reminds me how my life could be different if she were in it. No cameras. No fans. Just us, slow dancing in the living room alone, every touch setting off the fireworks inside me.

One night with her at the Pine Paradise made me fall hard. Now, I can't stop dreaming of waking up with her in my arms every day.

Cammy stops shooting long enough that I know what's about to happen. She sits on the coffee table. "Jace, you know I don't give personal advice very often."

"Oh, really? You've been hinting about Mia for the last five minutes."

She shrugs. "I'm a matchmaker because I like to see people happy instead of miserable and depressed."

"I'm not miserable or depressed . . ."

Cammy shakes her head, her pink ponytail swinging across her shoulders. "Ever since you and Ava broke up, you've been in a funk. I know you're trying to push away all your feelings after Ava. But instead of telling yourself why you can't date someone new, try to imagine how you *can*."

"That's the problem. I can't imagine dating someone, especially after what happened. I don't want to drag someone into my very public life and see them get hurt."

"But don't you understand, Jace? It's not your fault things ended up so messy. Ava spread some things about you that weren't even true. It's not fair you were the one the press blamed for the breakup."

I still haven't gone public with the truth—though I have my reasons.

The front door opens, and Mia walks in, holding my dry cleaning. "Oh!" she says, looking between Cammy and me. "I didn't know you were busy."

I'd told Mia that she didn't have to knock when she dropped off my dry cleaning.

"We were just finishing up," I say. "Cammy wanted a quick photo shoot."

Cammy grins as she looks from me to Mia. "Thanks to you, everyone is asking for more of Jace."

Mia frowns. "Me?"

I look at Cammy. "Told you she doesn't know." Then I turn back to Mia. "Our video went viral."

Mia looks at me in amazement. "It did? That's great, right?"

"Yeah, really great," Cammy says. "If it were up to me, I'd have you dance with Jace for *every* video."

Mia shakes her head. "I'm sure you could find lots of girls for that job."

"Nope. The public has spoken, Mia," Cammy says, putting her camera away. "You're the *it girl.*"

She crinkles her nose. "I don't want to be anyone's *it girl.*"

She doesn't want the attention of millions of fans. Maybe Ava loved that part of our lives together, but Mia would hate every second of living in the spotlight.

"You don't have to do any more videos," I insist.

She didn't choose this life; I did. Just because she's filling in as my assistant for one concert doesn't mean she has to experience the dark side of fame.

"Come on, Jace," Cammy urges as she hauls her backpack over her shoulder. "This will help your concert sales. And your image problem."

"I don't care about my image problem," I grumble, tired of Cammy and Allan bringing it up. It's been a topic I've been dodging all year.

"Well, you need to care," Cammy says. "Or else this concert is in trouble."

"That's why I stopped by. I have some news." Mia drapes my dry cleaning across a chair. "Tickets for the concert sold out in less than twenty-four hours."

"They're all gone?"

"Yep, and Mom wants to celebrate. She wondered if you're available for dinner tonight. I may have dropped a hint that you frequently eat alone . . . after our conversation about Christmas.

You can call it your holiday dinner dry run. If my family drives you bonkers on a normal night, then you do not want to visit on Christmas Eve." Mia tilts her head and frowns. "Why are you looking at me like that?"

"Like what?"

"Like you're shocked."

"It's just . . . normal people don't invite me to dinner."

"Um, you are normal," she says.

Cammy steps between us. "Sorry to interrupt, but he'll be there." Cammy shoots me a look that reveals she's not sorry at all. "It's just what he needs. What time do you want him to stop by?"

"You know, I'm sitting right here," I grumble. "I can answer for myself."

"I didn't want you to turn this dinner invitation down." She gives me two thumbs up behind Mia's back on the way out.

She is totally trying to play matchmaker.

"There's no pressure," Mia says. "But dinner is at six."

"I'll be there. Should be fun, right?"

"Interesting? Yes. Fun? As long as you can handle the twins . . ."

I frown. "Why would your brothers be a problem?"

"They can be a bit protective of me and Mom, and they like to take it out through hockey."

"I don't even play hockey," I say with a laugh.

Mia crosses her arms. "That's never stopped my brothers before."

———

When I step onto Mia's front porch a few hours later, the first thing I notice is the acrid smell of burned food.

The door flies open and Mia's eyes widen. "You're not the pizza man." Her mouth twists in distress as she looks over my shoulder.

"That's definitely not the greeting I was expecting."

She frowns before shaking her head. "Sorry . . . welcome to my humble abode." She motions for me to come in. "Okay, it's not my home, exactly. But the humble part? Totally true."

"It's quaint," I say, as I squeeze into the tiny foyer. Everything feels miniature-sized here, like I'm a giant in a doll's house. A faint whiff of smoke permeates the air. "What's that smell?"

"My mom burned the meatloaf for tonight's dinner, which is why we're waiting on carryout. But that's not the worst of it . . ." She rubs her forehead. "When I arrived home, Mom said we had a leak from a broken pipe in the ceiling over my bedroom. The ceiling collapsed, and now everything in my bedroom is wet. As we were cleaning up, Mom forgot about the meatloaf."

The doorbell rings and I open it, since I'm closest to the door. The pizza man hands me the boxes, which I dutifully take.

"Follow me." Mia leads me through the tiny combined living and dining room. She points to the couch. "Now that my bed is wet, that's where I'll sleep tonight."

"That looks as uncomfortable as the chair I tried to sleep in at the Pine Paradise."

In the kitchen, Cora is scraping burned meatloaf from a pan. When she sees me, a smile spreads across her weary face.

"Jace, welcome." She opens her arms and gives me a momma bear hug.

Ever since my grandmother died, I've missed these kinds of hugs. My parents aren't big huggers, and the fact they don't visit much only worsens the problem.

"Make yourself at home," she says. "The twins are outside playing hockey, if you want to join them."

I glance out the window to see two hulking young men racing around a small frozen pond, swinging madly at a tiny puck. I'd be insane to even try.

"You have your own hockey rink?" I ask Mia.

"If you call a makeshift ice patch a hockey rink, then yes," she says. "The twins figured out how to make your own backyard rink when they were ten, which involved some digging and flooding of our yard, much to my mom's dismay."

I glance outside again. The rink isn't fancy, but it's big enough to skate on when they can't make it to the practice rink.

Cora sets her pan aside to dry. "When they were little, I thought hockey would be a good way to get their energy out, if they didn't kill each other first. They played in college and now both play on a minor league team, so I guess it wasn't a far-fetched dream."

The boys scramble into the house, their faces tinged red from the cold and exertion, their hockey gear wet with snow. They pile their skates on the floor and take a sidelong glance at me.

"When's dinner?" one asks.

"I'm starving," the other says.

"Boys, we have company. Say hello first." Cora nods my way, and their eyes skate over to me.

"Jace, these are my brothers, Brax and Vale," Mia says, pointing to each one. The twins look exactly alike—brown hair, piercing eyes, broad shoulders—and except for Vale's longer hair, I could never tell them apart. Brax gives me a quick nod, while Vale looks me over. I can only imagine how much worse this would be if Mia and I were actually dating.

"Let's eat before the pizza gets cold," Cora says, directing us to the table.

Brax and Vale scramble to one side of the table, while Mia and I claim the other, leaving me to endure their steely gazes the entire meal. I feel like I'm under interrogation instead of enjoying a family meal.

"So, you play hockey?" I ask, trying to make conversation as Cora serves pizza.

Brax and Vale look at me for a second without blinking, like the answer is obvious. It's a lame question, and there's no way to backpedal after saying it.

"You play?" Vale asks.

"Oh, no." I chuckle, remembering what Mia warned me about earlier. "Not at all."

"I'm sure we could teach you a few things," Brax says, eagerly.

And eat me for breakfast too. I shake my head. "I don't skate very well."

"We'll take it easy on you," Vale promises, but given his wide shoulders and giant frame, it wouldn't take much to knock me down.

I shoot Mia a panicked look. She responds with a shrug and another bite of pizza.

"He has a concert to prepare for," Cora interrupts, dishing out a slice of deep dish for herself. "He doesn't have time for hockey or injuries. And frankly, neither do you. I need your help with the festival setup."

Both of them groan. Brax and Vale are clearly not as excited about the festival as Cora is.

"Have you shown Jace the schedule yet, Mia?" Cora asks.

"No, I was waiting to see if the committee approves it first."

"Of course they will," she says, reaching over to the counter and handing me a paper.

"Jace doesn't really need to see that," Mia says, looking embarrassed that her mom is fussing over the festival details. She knows I don't really care about the festival, other than my part in it.

"I don't mind." Maybe if I study this, Brax and Vale will forget about hockey.

Cora continues as she cuts her pizza. "The paper lists an hour-by-hour schedule of events for kids and adults, along with local musicians and vendors."

I skim the list, and my eyes stop on one event. "You're reviving the mistletoe contest?"

"With a modern twist," Cora says. "Mia mentioned dropping the contest and creating a mistletoe picture booth. The committee thought it was a fabulous idea. People can take their own selfies under the mistletoe."

"Did she mention her other idea?" I ask. "About the fundraiser auction?"

I glance over at Mia, who's staring at her plate, avoiding my gaze. Ever since it came up, I've been thinking about how perfect it would be for raising money.

Cora tilts her head. "No, she didn't."

"You should hold a fundraiser auction, but with a twist, like a dating auction. Get a few recognizable people from Maplewood and auction off a date with them to the concert."

"Where in the world would we get tickets?" Mia says. "The concert is sold out."

"I could pull a few strings. They always save me a few tickets to give away. And I'd be willing to donate them to this fundraiser."

"I love this idea!" Cora says. "Everyone's trying to find tickets for your concert."

Mia frowns. "No one would willingly volunteer to be auctioned off on a date, even if it was to his concert."

Cora puts down her fork and looks at her daughter. "I know a few people on the committee who would be delighted to, because they couldn't get tickets. And it doesn't have to be a date. Just a fun night out at Jace's concert."

"Exactly," I say, glancing over at Mia. "It's supposed to be fun."

"I think Mia should do it," Brax says.

Mia shoots her brother a dirty look. "Nice try, but no."

I put my fork down. "Right now, you don't have a ticket to my concert."

Mia cuts her pizza with her fork. "Yeah, well, I don't need a ticket, because I'll be backstage helping you."

"You can't see from backstage. And once the concert begins, I won't need your help."

"Why, that's perfect!" Cora says. "Mia could use a date."

"Mom!" Mia exclaims.

Brax and Vale stifle laughs.

Mia frowns, shooting me a look that says *I'm going to kill you later.*

Cora doesn't notice the look exchanged between us. "This would be perfect for raising funds for next year's festival."

Mia shakes her head. "I think we should do something else, like sell caramel apples."

Cora raises her eyebrows. "Do you know how many caramel apples we'd have to sell to make enough money? Thousands. But one Jace Knight ticket will probably raise hundreds of dollars *each.*"

Mia looks from her mom to me. "Seriously?"

"I usually get front-row tickets," I explain. "I don't know how much they'll sell for, but it would definitely raise the money quickly. And it would help you reach your personal goal too."

"What goal is that?" Cora asks.

"To have more fun. Mia works too much, and this would be the perfect reward for a job well done."

My personal motives are pushing a hidden agenda now. I want to see Mia in the front row. Having a familiar face there would calm my nerves when I debut my new song. But there's something else that I can't admit yet—I don't want to dance with anyone else but her.

Mia holds up her hand to clarify. "That's not exactly what we agreed to. You said to *chase the fun.* It's different."

"Wouldn't front-row tickets make you happy?" Brax asks, finally siding with me.

"They would," Mia says. "But I'd like to pick the company."

Vale laughs in disbelief. "Like *you'd* ask someone out."

"I might," she says weakly.

Brax and Vale laugh more loudly this time.

Cora shoots her sons a look. "Jace is donating these tickets to the town as a fundraiser, and we desperately need the money. So unless Mia agrees, I'll ask someone else."

"I volunteer," Brax says, raising his hand.

"Me too," Vale says.

"You both can't volunteer," Mia says, looking between them. "The committee gets first dibs."

I look at Mia. "But if you aren't taking a ticket, why not give your brothers a chance? They want to have fun, even if you don't."

Mia glares at me. She's just competitive enough that she doesn't want her brothers to steal her ticket. But she also hates the idea of participating in a dating auction.

"I'll think about it," she grumbles. "But I'm not making any promises."

———

"You want to join us on the rink?" Brax asks me after dinner. "We'll take it easy on you. Promise."

The twins slide on their jackets as Mia and Cora clean up dinner.

I shove my hands in my pockets. "Sounds fun, but I don't own skates."

Mia stops with a stack of plates in her hands. "Oh, we have skates." Then she opens a closet door and shows me an enormous pile. "What size?"

"Um, ten," I say, praying there are no tens in the pile.

She hands off the plates to Brax and pulls out a pair. "These should work."

"See you out there," Vale says as he heads outside.

"I should help your mom clean up," I say. "Shouldn't I?"

"No. You owe me this."

"Owe you?"

She crosses her arms. "The fundraiser auction."

"I didn't make you agree. I suggested it, and your brothers were more than willing to participate. But I'm so proud of you for saying yes."

"There's still time to back out," she grumbles.

"If you go through with it, I'll make sure the concert is fun," I promise.

"As fun as a root canal?" she says, still looking doubtful. "Or as fun as playing hockey against my brothers?"

I turn to Mia. "Tell me one thing . . . am I going to die?"

"Not die," she says. "But you might not get out of bed tomorrow."

I swallow hard. "Can I sneak away?"

"Oh, no," she says, nearly shoving me out the door.

"Suggesting you participate in a fundraiser is entirely different from me getting destroyed by your brothers."

"Not really. I'd say it's just as painful." She hands me a hockey stick. "I'll watch you play once I finish cleaning up. Good luck!" She gives me a satisfied grin before slamming the door.

I sigh as I wobble across the yard.

It's been at least a decade since I've even stepped on the ice. As soon as I try, I flail like an idiot—arms windmilling, ankles shaking, before I find my balance.

"Try some drills first," Vale says, pushing a puck toward me. I attempt to hit some pucks toward the net and miss every shot by a wide margin.

"Did I mention I'm bad at hockey?" I say.

"We don't have to keep score," Vale says, practicing some fancy footwork as he glides across the ice.

I attempt to follow him, trying to remember how to balance on skates. Just about the time I feel confident, he passes me a puck. I stretch to reach it with my stick, but it throws off my balance so badly, my feet slip from under me and I fall backwards on my butt.

"You okay?" Vale calls across the rink.

"Sure," I say, rubbing my aching hip while I get to my feet. I paste on a tough look even though my backside is screaming in pain. "I'm really terrible on skates. Music is my thing. Not hockey."

"You can't be any worse than our sister," Brax says.

"I heard that," Mia shoots back.

I spin around on the ice and almost fall for a second time.

Mia's sitting on a bench in the yard, looking like she's enjoying every minute of my humiliation. "And I'm not *that* bad."

I can't resist the bait. I raise an eyebrow. "Then prove it."

"I don't want to take you down," she says with a spark in her eyes.

"I think she's scared," Vale taunts.

"I'm not scared of you," she says. Then she grabs some skates that are under the bench and slides them on.

Without hesitation, she glides across the ice like an Olympic skater.

"Oh, shoot," I mutter under my breath. She can take me down.

"What was that?" she asks with a grin, speeding up.

"You didn't tell me you were a good skater," I say.

"You didn't ask," she says, turning around so she's skating backwards, toward me. "I've been skating since I was four. I wanted to become a figure skater until I broke my ankle when I was twelve."

"A career-ending injury?" I ask.

She nods. "I missed tryouts for the biggest ice-skating competition that year. After my ankle injury, it was never strong enough for all the jumps."

"But plenty strong enough for hockey," I note, watching her thread through her brothers as they pass the puck back and forth.

Mia turns as her brother passes the puck to her. With seemingly no effort, she hits the puck toward the net and nails it.

"I thought you didn't play hockey," I say.

"I don't," she says. "Except with my brothers."

"But they're professional players."

One of her brothers hits the puck so hard, she has to accelerate to catch it. "I don't mind a game of friendly competition." She whacks it toward me, and I stop it with my stick.

"Are you challenging me to a game?"

She skates over, making a hard stop in front of me. "In case you didn't notice, I'm chasing the fun. And seeing you get beat makes me *so happy,*" she adds, referring to my little happiness dare.

"I'm glad my humiliation is so entertaining," I tell her with a smirk.

"Then may the best person win," she says, readying her defensive stance.

I don't care that I'm about to get beat by a girl.

She drops a puck between us and hits it toward the goal before I can even react.

"Hey, I wasn't ready," I complain, hurrying after her.

"I can't help it if you're slow," she tosses over her shoulder.

Her challenge pushes me to skate faster, and I catch her just as she swings her stick. I don't block it. Instead, I do the only thing I can think of: I bodycheck her.

As she slams into me, we tumble down together, and I reach out to buffer us against the fall. The cold shock of ice hits my arm, and I cradle her against me so that I take the brunt of the impact.

As I hover over her, her eyes flutter open, and we stare at each other for a second. I'm only inches from her lips and my hand is still wrapped around her waist.

"Good catch," she murmurs. "But that move was *so illegal.*"

"Illegal . . . but necessary," I reply, my body heating from the adrenaline pumping through my veins. "I couldn't let you win. In this sport, everything's legal." *Except the way I'm feeling about her now.*

I wonder if she can feel my heart hammering, my breathing ragged, the way I don't want to move from her. We're pinned together, our eyes locked to see who will give up first.

"So you like to cheat?" she asks.

"Not cheat," I say. "Unless it involves winning." Because right now, the only person I want to win over is her.

She pushes up, and I roll to the side so she can stand.

"Let's play again," she says, rising.

I don't know what just happened between us, but where our bodies met, the force of friction is still sparking, like a live wire.

From the side of the ice rink, a throat clears before Brax says, "Looks like you're pretty well matched."

I'm not the only one who noticed what happened on the hockey rink.

The only question is: *What am I going to do about it?*

FIFTEEN

Mia

Ever since our hockey accident, Jace's texting has veered into dangerous territory. Like *more than* casual acquaintance territory.

Now he's sending me a daily morning text before I wake up, which is so sweet and strangely addictive.

This morning's text included a sleepy-face emoji with the words: *How did you sleep?*

Ever since a pipe burst over my room, I've been sleeping on the sofa, a sagging, thirty-year-old couch that should've been taken to the dump years ago.

Mia: Except for this crick in my neck, not bad!

I can't tell Jace that I wake up in so much pain I wear a heating pad on my neck for the first hour of my day. Since Mom can't afford to repair the ceiling, I probably won't have an actual bed until I return to South Carolina.

Jace: I have three extra guest rooms. Allan uses one when he's in town. But you're welcome to one until your bedroom is fixed.

Mia: Blackie and Tabby would be so offended that you are not offering one to them.
Jace: The cats have a luxurious cat house outside that is probably nicer than your sofa.
Mia: I'm good! Mostly.
Jace: I'm serious about the offer.

I let out the haggard sigh of a woman who desperately wants a firm mattress. But there's no way I can say yes to his offer. Not after what happened at the Pine Paradise. Even though we wouldn't be in the same room, and Allan lives there sometimes, things feel different between us. In a matter of weeks, I've gone from arguing with him incessantly to thinking about him nonstop.

My phone rings. It's Ella, probably with another question about the festival.

"Clear your afternoon schedule," she demands. "We're kidnapping you and taking you away to the spa, even if it means we drag you kicking and screaming."

I have approximately a billion things on my to-do list. I do not need a spa day; I need a break from Jace. Because he's getting under my skin in the worst way.

"So, I'm a hostage?" I ask. "What kind of friends are you?"

"The kind who make you have fun," Ella says. "Isn't that the agreement you made?"

Why does Jace's happiness dare keep coming up? It's like everyone thinks I've turned into a dull workaholic who needs to be forced into some holiday cheer.

Ella goes on, "Listen to the description of this place. *A posh mid-century spa on a mountaintop, boasting sweeping views from the hot tub, guaranteed to take you away.*"

Which is exactly what I need right now. To get away from these feelings for Jace.

"Can you be ready by two?" Ella asks.

"I guess," I grumble, even though my to-do list can't wait.

I'm good at working hard. I'm even better at running away from things that scare me.

And that's almost impossible when Jace keeps invading my thoughts.

———

When we arrive at the dreamy Japanese spa tucked on the top of a hillside, it's like someone has transported me to another world. Calming pan flute music plays through hidden speakers in the plants, while a stone waterfall in the entry gently bubbles.

The lady at the desk greets us with a serene smile. "Welcome to the Lotus Flower Day Spa," she says in a hushed tone. "I'll take you to your waiting room where you can prepare for your detoxifying bath."

She waves us down a dark hall lined with closed doors, and I wonder what mysterious luxury treatment lies behind each door. It feels like a game show where everyone wins.

The doors are labeled with metal plates engraved with flowers and leaves, instead of numbers. She stops at a door with an orchid plate and shows us inside where fluffy white bathrobes await and an essential oil diffuser fills the air with calming lavender.

Our hostess leaves as Jaz touches the robe. "This place is amazing already. Aren't you glad Jace gave you the day off?"

"Jace doesn't know I'm here," I admit sheepishly as I strip down to my underwear. "I told him I had some other things to do and wouldn't be around. He also offered me a room at his place until mine is fixed."

"He did? You're going to take it, right?" Ella asks, slipping on her white robe.

"Don't you think that would be weird? I work for him."

Ella ties her robe and looks at me. "He lets Allan stay there when he's in town. What's the difference?"

The difference is that Allan doesn't have feelings for his boss.

Maybe Jace's offer is strictly professional, but could I keep my feelings in check?

Ella goes on, "You're miserable sleeping on the couch. No offense, but your mom's home is way too chaotic for work."

"Tell me about it," I say, blowing my bangs off my forehead and removing my glasses. It's one reason I couldn't wait to move out. Mom hoards everything—old newspaper clippings from the Mistletoe Festival, my brothers' hockey trophies and scrapbooks of her life with Dad. It's like she never wanted to let go of the past, even when it hurt her to remember it. But all those boxes jammed with memories are like a millstone around my neck.

"You need to say yes to Jace's offer," Jaz urges.

"I'm perfectly fine," I say, dismissing the issue.

"Is that why your neck is hurting?" Jaz grabs my phone. "I'll tell him you'll take it."

"No!" I leap forward and try to snatch the phone from her, but she sweeps it out of reach.

"I'm doing this for your own good," she says, texting him *yes* before I can stop her.

"If you're just working for him, then what's the problem?" Ella asks.

I look at my two friends. "There is no problem," I say, feeling the heat crawl up my neck.

"Unless that night at the Pine Paradise Motel has something to do with your red face?" Jaz says.

"Or that viral video of you slow dancing?" Ella adds.

I hate that every time I'm embarrassed, my face lights up like Rudolph the Red-Nosed Reindeer.

"I may have felt a little something," I insist.

Jaz raises an eyebrow. "A little?"

"Okay, so he's grown on me. But it's like I said before, he's a big star. The chance of us ending up together is zero." At least, that's what I keep telling myself.

"Are you saying that because you believe it?" Ella asks,

studying me. "Or because that makes it easier to run away from things that scare you?"

"I'm not running," I insist. "Just because he's not bad to look at doesn't mean I'm going to fall for him."

Jaz wraps her arm around my shoulder. "We'll support you no matter what. I mean, I wouldn't judge you if you wanted Jace to be your first kiss."

I shake my head. "Jace could kiss anyone. I don't think I'm even on his radar."

Just then, there's a knock at the door and our hostess peeks in. "There's been a change of plans. Instead of the detox bath, we're starting with your hot stone massages. Follow me, please."

She leads us to a large room with three massage tables and more pan flute music and lavender oil. She motions toward the tables. "Just remove your robes, get comfortable, and your massage therapists will be in shortly."

When she leaves, I realize I'm still wearing my necklace. I slip it off and hurry to the door. "I'm going to run this back to our changing room."

When I sneak into the empty hall, I'm suddenly confused which way we came from. I'm directionally challenged, and without my glasses, all the doors look the same, with various flower and leaf emblems on them.

I glance around the corner, hoping to find our hostess, but she's gone. When I finally stop by a door with a flower that looks somewhat familiar, I go with my gut instinct and step inside, closing the door behind me. The room is darker than I remembered, and everything is a blur, but I know exactly where I left my bag. I spin around and immediately slam into something warm and soft. Not something, but *someone.* I stumble backward, the scent of pine and musk overwhelmingly familiar.

"Mia?" a gravelly voice says, confirming my suspicions. "Is that you?"

"Jace?" I squint at the blurry, shirtless man with tousled hair falling over one eye, wearing only a pair of ripped jeans.

My face heats when my gaze lands on a chest so perfect it begs to be on the front of an album cover. For one horrifying moment, I stare at him in shock. Staring isn't even the right word. I'm like Pavlov's dogs at the sound of a bell.

"What are you doing here?" I ask, gripping the collar of my robe, pulling it shut. Of course, it's *him*. Because running into anyone else would be too easy.

"I'd like to ask you the same thing," he says, his eyes dropping to the short robe I'm wearing before flicking to my face. "Especially since you're in my changing room."

"I thought this was *my* changing room," I say. "I lost my way and ran into you."

"I noticed." When Jace smirks, his dimple deepens and that little fluttering feeling brushes against my chest. "But that still doesn't explain why you're here."

I feel like a kid who's been caught playing hooky from school. "My friends encouraged me to take a day off. But I promise I'll still get my work done. And I honestly didn't know you were going to be here."

For a moment, Jace studies me in amusement. "I'm not taking attendance, Mia."

"Then why are you here?"

Jace shoves his hands in his pockets and leans against the wall, like he's posing for a photo shoot. The man doesn't even need to try to look hot, he just does. "Ella was the one who asked me for spa recommendations, and I gave her the name of this place since I'm a regular here. Guess I forgot to lock the door." He lifts a shoulder, and his mouth curls on one side, while my heart spins like a pinwheel.

"Anyone could have walked in on you," I say.

"But they didn't. *You* did. Guess I got lucky."

I'm the lucky one. "If I move into your guest room, we'll have to be more careful so it doesn't happen again," I say with a blush, thinking about the idea of living that close to Jace.

"The invitation's still open," he says. "And it would make it easier for us to work together. Allan is only there a few days a week, and I'm practicing during the day, so you'd have the house to yourself."

I bite my lip. I can't believe I'd choose sleeping on a sagging couch that gives me a neck ache over staying in Jace's luxury home. I'd be crazy not to take him up on it.

"I guess we could make it work. Just lock your door, okay?" I half-tease.

"Got it," he says with a grin. "Are you free to move in tonight? My chef prepped an amazing meal, and I'd hate to see it go to waste."

Everything in me feels knotted up, tight. "If I have time to pack tonight. I still have work to do and an endless list of emails to respond to."

"I'll send someone over to help. The sooner you can move in, the better for your neck."

Does this man have a small army I don't know about? It's like he snaps his fingers and things get done instantly, like royalty.

I rub my neck and feel the dull ache from last night. Despite my better judgement, the answer tumbles out before I can stop it. "In that case, I'll be over tonight."

There's a familiar knock at the door, and the same hostess I met earlier glances into the room. "Oh, I'm sorry, Mr. Knight. I thought you were alone."

Whatever this lady thinks, she hides it well, keeping her expression fixed. "Will both of you be indulging in our detox bath today?"

Heat floods my face as I realize what she's suggesting.

"No!" we both say quickly.

"We're not together," I stammer.

Then I tighten my grip on my robe and hurry past her, unsure how I'm ever going to get Jace's image out of my head.

SIXTEEN

Jace

Inviting Mia to stay with me might have been a little rash. Especially when I'm determined not to get involved in any complicated relationships since the whole Ava blowup.

"Too late now," I mutter as her car pulls up.

I'm suddenly thrust back to feeling like an awkward, gangly seventh grader. I wipe my sweaty palms on my jeans and glance at my open grey flannel layered over a T-shirt.

Mia lugs a laundry basket of clothes from her trunk as the cats skitter around her feet.

"Let me take that for you," I say, taking the load from her.

"You don't have to," she stammers. "You already sent one of your crew over to help."

I ignore her protest, then realize why she was so reluctant to hand it off. Silky pajama sets line the top, with something lacy peeking out from underneath. I pretend not to notice, but from the way her face is flaming, it's obvious she's as uncomfortable as when she walked into my dressing room.

"I'll show you to your room," I say, as we head inside to the biggest guest room on the second floor. "The room Allan normally stays in is at the opposite end, so you'll have plenty of privacy."

I put her laundry basket on the king-sized bed with the silk duvet I picked up in India. "The view in here is stunning. My band members always fight over it when they stay here."

I walk over to the blinds and hit the button for them to open automatically. As they disappear, the valley opens up outside the window, and her mouth drops open.

"This is gorgeous." She swings around and drags her fingers across a large desk facing the windows so she can look outside as she works. "I'm not really used to all this space. This is too much."

"You deserve something better than a couch, Mia."

"Shouldn't you save this room for someone in your band?"

"I have another room available. If you don't take this one, you'll get one equally as nice."

I lead her to an enormous bathroom with a whirlpool tub, a walk-in marble shower with two showerheads, and a double vanity that could accommodate a large family. "You have your own bathroom, so you don't have to worry about what happened earlier today. Why don't you unpack while I finish dinner? Feel free to put your clothes in the closet over there." I nod toward a gigantic closet.

Her eyes widen. "This is as big as my bedroom." She spins around, like she's a lost child in a department store. "I don't even have a single nice dress to hang in this closet," she says, fingering a wooden hanger. "I've spent the last year mostly wearing jeans and T-shirts, like a broke college student."

"How was the spa?" I didn't run into her the rest of the time I was there, which is probably for the best.

"Fabulous," she gushes, falling on the bed. "My neck feels so much better. The massage therapist said my back was like a brick wall, probably from the couch."

"This mattress will be perfect for your back. You can adjust the firmness by hitting a button," I explain, pointing out the remote control. "And there's a hidden fridge in the end table, too."

"I have a remote-controlled bed *and* a drink fridge?" She

shakes her head in wonder. "What else is hiding here? Are there any trapdoors or secret passages I should know about?"

I laugh. "No, but that's a great idea."

"Jace?" she asks, and I stop in the door. "Thanks for this. Having a decent bed and some quiet means more than you know. This is the first time I can check off something that makes me truly happy."

"I hope it's not the last either," I say, feeling a swell inside my chest. "I have a feeling this is just the start."

I leave her to unpack while I finish dinner. As I skim over the notes the chef left for me, she sneaks onto a barstool at the island. "Are we eating in front of the TV?"

I spin toward her. "No, we're sitting at the dining room table." I nod toward an immaculate table that's gleaming from the lights of the chandelier overhead.

She holds up the paper plates I left on the island. "It seems a shame to use paper plates on that table. Do you own any actual plates?"

I nod toward a row of cupboards behind me. "I think they're in there."

"You think?" she asks.

"I never use them except for parties. And only because my chef pulls them out."

She opens the first cupboard and gasps. "What is this?" She pulls out a sparkling goblet with gold trim that catches the light.

I glance over my shoulder as I check the pasta in the oven. "A glass."

"Do you ever use these?" She turns the goblet around in her hands.

"Not really. I usually drink from a can."

She shakes her head in disbelief. "I can't believe you eat on paper when you have china that probably costs more than all the furniture I own. This one still has the sales sticker on." She points to the white sticker.

"I only pull out the fine china when my agent bugs me to throw a fancy party."

"Which has been . . .?"

"Twice . . . total," I admit, pulling the baked pasta from the oven.

"That's a shame," she says.

"Ironic, coming from the woman who didn't even pack a dress."

"You have so many beautiful things here, and no one uses them."

"Allan uses them when he's in town. My band stays over occasionally. But I'm careful about who I let inside my home."

I can't tell her I believed one day I'd have a full, bustling home with lots of company. Fine china might have been impractical, but I thought my future wife deserved the best.

"Not even your family?" she asks, pulling out two plates.

"I don't invite them over." I avoid looking at her as I concentrate on cutting the steaming pasta. "We're not like other families. My parents started pushing me to perform when I was a kid. But then it got to be too much. They only cared about what I accomplished and how it made them look. For my eleventh birthday, all I wanted was to order pizza and have a pool party. Instead, my parents told me I had to perform for a county fair eight hours away. They'd signed a contract that I couldn't get out of. So instead of celebrating, I had to work. And that's how I spent the rest of my time at home until I left at eighteen."

She leans against the counter, the crease in her brow deepening. "No kid should have to miss their birthday."

"The hard part is that they pretend things between us are good, and they're just too busy to visit." It's a problem I've tried to push to the back of my mind.

"Do you have any siblings?" she asks, grabbing silverware.

"I occasionally hear from my brother. But he's often backpacking in some remote section of the country. Living off the grid. That's his way of dealing with our parents."

It's not like I wanted things this way. Somehow, my parents' obsession with my career took over our lives. Having a normal childhood was never an option for me.

Mia sets the silverware neatly next to our plates. "Mom loved having you over, and you're welcome back anytime. Granted, we're loud and chaotic and crammed together like sardines."

"I don't know how your brothers felt about having me there."

"After you left, they gave their approval."

"Really?"

"They told me they'd teach you to play hockey."

"Even after our epic accident?"

"Our whole family is very . . . *physical*." Our eyes catch, and something ripples between us. The memory of our bodies crashing into each other. My hand cradling her back as I hovered over her.

"That's better than never seeing each other." I set the pasta in the middle of the table. "Do your brothers talk about your dad?"

"They never bring him up. It's like he never existed." She stops behind a chair, gripping the back. "My family is spontaneous and fun, but they also pretend that nothing is wrong—that my dad didn't walk out a few days after Christmas and leave forever. For years, my mom acted like it didn't happen, and everyone could go on with their lives. She pretended things were fine, because it was easier than facing the truth. The only time I saw her cry was when I found her sobbing silently in the bathroom, wiping mascara-striped tears from her cheeks."

I shake my head. "I'm sorry, Mia."

She shrugs, then sits down. "That's why I don't like to come home for Christmas. Too many memories that I don't know how to deal with." She tucks a strand of hair behind her ear and then waves her hand. "Enough about me. This looks delicious."

She digs into her spicy mostaccioli pasta. "Was it weird leaving home at eighteen and heading to Nashville on your own?"

"It was so freeing at first. Nobody to tell me what to do. So I started playing my songs any place that would take me. I eventually met my agent, and he helped me to get a record contract and told me I needed a makeover."

She laughs. "You mean you weren't always a hot country star?"

"You think I'm hot?" I ask, and she glances away quickly.

"That's what all the magazines say."

"So you're stalking me online now? I thought you didn't do that," I say, giving her an amused grin.

"I've looked up a few things since I started working for you," she admits.

"But that still doesn't answer whether *you* think I'm hot."

She shrugs. "You're okay."

"Just okay? That's not what you said before. You said *hot*."

She throws up her hands in defeat. "You're hot, all right? A woman would have to be blind not to notice." Then she leans toward me. "What I want to know is why your agent thought you needed a makeover."

"I was too clean cut," I say. "He wanted me to look like a rock star. You know, the bad boy image. So I changed my wardrobe and dated a bunch of celebrities so people could see me at important parties."

She frowns. "Is that why you're in the news a lot?"

"In this industry, all press is good press. But after last year, I don't think so."

She tilts her head. "Did his advice work?"

"At first. But when I met Ava, things changed. I didn't want the bad boy image anymore. I didn't care about parties. Maybe that's why the press kept following us. I was trying to stay out of their way. The more I resisted, the more they hunted me down."

Her eyes flick to me, like she's thinking this over, but treading carefully. "Is that why you broke up?"

"Not exactly," I say, rubbing the back of my neck, not wanting to explain what happened. "But it made it worse. The press blew up the whole thing."

"That's terrible, Jace," she says, holding my gaze. "Just for the record, I don't think your career is over. I bet there are people willing to give you another try. If you still want to make over your image, you should."

"What are you, my PR person now?" I laugh.

"Not me. But my brothers know a professional hockey player who got himself into a mess with a girl, and he turned things around with a PR makeover."

"How?" I ask, curious.

"He showed up at some charity events with a friend, a gal nobody knew."

"And it worked?"

Mia nods. "She was the one who turned him into everybody's favorite hockey player."

"I'm not sure this Christmas concert is going to help."

"All I know is hiding in your house is definitely not doing you any favors."

When I glance at Mia, I get an idea: What if she helped me with my PR solution? What if we went out a few times and made people think there was something going on? There's a reason our slow dance video went viral. "If our charade worked on Ava in Evergreen, then why wouldn't it work here?"

Her head snaps up. "Wait. I wasn't volunteering for *that*."

"I meant for fun. That's what we agreed to, right? To have more fun?"

She shifts uncomfortably in her seat. "Yes, but . . ." She rises from the table, carrying her empty plate to the kitchen. "Maplewood is different. I know people here. And what happened in Evergreen, stays in Evergreen."

"Mia," I say, following her. "That's because they forced us into an awkward situation. In Maplewood, we can attend a few festival events together as friends. No strings attached."

Mia freezes, her plate still in hand, eyes narrowed. *"For your PR makeover?"*

"Not just that. You said I need to get out more."

She narrows her eyes. "And to repair your reputation?"

"It couldn't hurt."

She turns to wash off her plate. I reach over to take the plate from her, but she won't let go. "I have a housekeeper who will clean that."

"I can do it," she insists, scrubbing the plate vigorously.

"You know, you should really go out with *someone*," I tell her. "It might as well be me. Or am I that terrible of a date?"

She lifts a shoulder and drops it. "It's just weird that you'd want to be seen with me."

"Why would that be weird? You can set the rules if that makes you feel more comfortable."

"Like?" she asks, eyes still narrowed.

I run my hand through my hair, my brain scrambling to come up with an arrangement that would make her happy. "Like, we only have to act like a couple when we're in public."

"And what does that involve?"

I look away, then back at her. "I didn't know I'd have to come up with the rules right now."

She crosses her arms. "I'm not considering it until I know."

"For example, if someone wants our picture, we play along."

She bites her lip, thinking this over. "So, some physical contact may be required?"

"Maybe," I say, shifting. "We have to act like we enjoy being together."

She lifts an eyebrow. "That might be difficult."

"Difficult?" I chuckle.

She frowns. "It wouldn't be difficult for you?"

Not really. "It should be fun."

I can feel the spark of heat between us, how she's resisting this idea, even though it's the answer for both of us.

"I'll think about it," she says, turning back to the sink.

"Think about it?" I say, incredulous.

"I take it most women don't turn you down?" she asks with a smirk.

"Yeah," I say. "They don't."

"Just because you have an effect on most women, don't think that your persuasion works on me."

"Oh, so you think I'm persuasive now?" I grin playfully. "Kind of like you think I'm hot?"

She won't even look at me, just scrubs away at the plate. "I'll do it. But just so you know, you're having zero effect on me, Jace Knight."

Her lips fight a smile, and I feel the thrill of victory. I'm finally getting through.

SEVENTEEN

Mia

It's our last meeting before the festival setup begins, and it's obvious the committee is unhappy about the changes I've made.

Mom glances over at me nervously before going on. "This year we're trying a mistletoe booth instead of a contest. That way, people can post their pictures on social media, and we get free publicity." She looks around at the committee.

"Why didn't we bring back the original mistletoe contest?" Bob asks.

I shift uncomfortably in my seat. We need everyone on board, and judging by their frowns, it's not going well.

"I liked it the way it was," Judy says.

Several heads nod. Mom looks around for support. The committee has been less than enthusiastic about the changes that Jaz, Ella, and I have proposed for this year's festival. Mom glances at me for help.

"Social media is easier for people," I say. "And it has a global reach. A win-win for publicity and for the town."

Judy crosses her arms. Bob mutters under his breath. Mom looks like she's about to throw in the towel. Every single change to the festival has received this kind of opposition. Making over a town festival is a lot harder than I thought.

I plow ahead. "This festival isn't profitable, which is why we're trying the fundraising auction with a front-row date for Jace's concert. We've had two committee members volunteer so far."

"But there's still one spot left," Bob points out.

Mom shifts uncomfortably. "Um, yes, someone is still considering it." Her eyes sweep over to me. "Mia."

I turn and give Mom a look. Even though I said I'd think about it, I'm still opposed to the idea that I'm going to be auctioned off like some kind of livestock animal.

Mom ignores the daggers shooting from my eyes. "Mia suggested we do a fundraising auction, so it only seems appropriate . . ."

"I didn't suggest it," I correct, bristling at the term. "Jace did."

"She is going to fill our final volunteer slot," Mom finishes.

I turn to her. "Mother, could we talk about this . . . alone?"

"If you need to." Then she pastes on a smile. "Let's take a five-minute break."

As everyone shuffles from the room, I direct Mom to a corner away from the door.

"What in the world?" I ask, the frustration in my chest about to boil over. "You know I didn't want to do this." I can't say the real reason: Because it's humiliating. And if there's anyone I want to date, it's Jace. Not a stranger.

"The other two volunteers from the committee are ecstatic about it."

"That's because they didn't have tickets before."

"In case you didn't notice, we need this festival to go well," Mom says. "Otherwise, all our hard work will be for nothing. If we don't make this a smashing success financially, we won't have another Mistletoe Festival."

"Isn't there anyone else?"

"There's only one ticket left. And you've worked so hard on this festival. You deserve this ticket."

"What about Brax or Vale?"

Mom's gaze shifts to the floor before she looks back up at me. "I can't."

"What do you mean?"

She pauses. "I made an agreement with Jace. He made me promise you would use it. He wants you in the front row for the concert."

I look at her and frown.

I know how nervous he is about this performance, and if we're going to be seen together around town, people will expect me to be in the audience. It won't matter if I'm there with the winner of the auction—no one will consider that a threat to Jace. But I still don't want to do it.

Mom puts a hand on my arm. "Don't be mad at him. He's doing this for the festival . . . and he values your friendship. He's trying to give you an experience you could never afford otherwise."

I shake my head. I already know what would make me happy. And I can't have him.

———

Ella stretches on a ladder, placing a shiny silver Christmas bulb on a tree. The old drugstore building hasn't been used in years, but we're dressing up every single shop window with a holiday display so that all the storefronts look full of life. It's part of my friends' collective genius. Fill the town with so much Christmas cheer you don't see the empty buildings.

I've hardly seen Jace this week, which is probably for the best. Since he's been practicing nonstop for the concert, I haven't had to avoid him, which makes it easier to pretend I don't have feelings for him.

The door opens and Brax carries in a box that's filled to the top with decorations and sets it next to Jaz.

"Are you still mad at me for beating you last weekend?" she asks, looking at him under lowered eyelashes.

I nearly drop the Christmas bulb I'm hanging. "What happened last weekend?" I glance between them.

"Oh, nothing." Jaz bites down on her lip, hiding a grin.

"Wait, what's going on here?" I demand.

I've seen this shy smirk of Jaz's before. I just didn't think I'd see it now—with my brother, of all people.

"A late-night game of pool at Charlie's," Jaz admits.

"She totally cheated," Brax interrupts, not taking his eyes off her. "We need a rematch."

If I didn't know better, this banter would almost sound like . . . *flirting*. I can't believe I've been so consumed by the festival that I didn't see this coming.

I frown. The way they're both smiling at each other is sickening. "Brax, don't you have something better to do?"

He glares at me before turning back to Jaz. "Tonight at seven?"

"She is not available tonight," I interject. "She's filling in for me so I can help Jace."

"Again?" Brax frowns. "You spend a lot of time with him."

"Because I'm working for him," I argue and dig through the Christmas decorations. Brax saw my unfiltered reaction when Jace fell on top of me on the ice. He knows something is going on.

"You heard how he cheated on his ex, right? It was all over the internet," he says with a warning.

Something pinches inside me. "You can't believe everything you see online," I mutter, not looking at him. Even though I'm a grown adult, my brothers still want to protect me.

I look up at him, my jaw set. "Aren't you supposed to be helping Nolan?"

"I feel like you don't want me here," he says.

"Then your instincts are correct." I take him by the shoulders and lead him to the door. "Now, go."

On his way out, Brax waves to Jaz through the store window, and her face lights up.

I smack her on her arm. "Stop staring. It makes me want to throw up." Even though my twin brothers are only two years younger than me, I can't tolerate them flirting with my friends.

"I'm having fun. You should try it."

"Well, find someone else to have fun with."

"Who? His twin?"

"No," I warn. "My brothers are *off-limits*."

"Your brothers won't stay single forever."

"As long as they're living with my mom, they will."

"Did you know they're planning on moving out soon and almost have the money saved?"

"They do?" I always thought that as long as they were hockey players, my brothers would live at home, struggling for money. Like me.

"Why are you so opposed to them dating?" Ella asks.

I pick up another Christmas bulb and hang it on the tree. "As long as it's not my friends, I'm totally okay with it."

"Do you hold the same rule for your own dating life?" Jaz asks.

"You mean dating friends?" I glance away. "Depends on who it is."

"Do you know a guy named Cal?" Jaz asks.

My head snaps up. "Wait . . . Cal Perkins?"

She nods.

"He's not a friend," I say, shaking my head. "More like my childhood nemesis. Cal once poured his school milk on me to get my attention. That was the beginning of his many failed attempts to flirt with me. He even tried to trick me into kissing him under the mistletoe once."

"I'm guessing you successfully evaded him?" Ella asks.

"The twins nailed him with snowballs so I could run away.

One good thing about brothers . . . they're always going to have your back."

"Well, rumor has it he's going to bid on you," Jaz says.

I stare at her. "He's the last person I'd like to win that auction."

"Is there anyone else you'd like to win?"

"No," I say, immediately thinking of Jace. But Jace can't bid on his own ticket. He's not even attending the auction because of a meeting with the record company.

Jaz looks at me, like she's reading my thoughts. "What about Jace?"

"What about him?" I say, ignoring their pointed looks.

"He offered you a room at his house," Jaz says. "And I've seen the way he looks at you. He's pretty closed off with everyone but you."

"That's because I'm helping him with his concert. He has to be nice to me. And he gives Allan a room when he's in town. It's not like we're alone all the time."

"But he wants to be seen together around town." Ella finishes hanging a bulb and looks at me. "That doesn't sound like a guy who's just being nice. It sounds like a guy who actually wants to spend time with you."

I shake my head. "I'm probably his Christmas charity case."

Ella sits on the ladder. "If you were his charity case, he would hand you a check, not let you live with him. I mean, he even makes you coffee in the morning. That's *not* a random act of kindness."

"He knows I like coffee," I insist. "And he drinks it, too." At least, I assume he does. But now that I think about it, I haven't seen him with a cup of coffee.

"He has millions of fans," Jaz says, leaning against the ladder. "But he wants to be seen around town with *you*, not some model."

"It's a PR stunt to improve his reputation. If he cared, why would he arrange for me to be part of the auction? He wants me to go out with someone else."

Ella frowns. "Did you ever think that he wants you at his concert?"

I turn away from both of them and focus on the tree. "He thinks I work too much. It's his attempt to force me into having more fun."

Lately, the only fun I'm having is searching for pictures of Jace around his house. So far, I've found pictures of Jace surfing, posing with an injured eagle at an animal rescue, and sitting on the porch next to Blackie and Tabby. Who could resist a man who takes in stray cats?

"Or maybe there's something more between you," Ella suggests. "Have you felt any vibes from him?"

"No, because there isn't anything between us." Not that I would know what vibes to look for. Now that I've fallen down a rabbit hole of learning everything I can about Jace, that doesn't mean he feels the same way about me. "So now you're both on Team Jace?"

Ella takes my hand. "We're still on Team Mia. We just want you to be happy, that's all. You're really good at running . . . especially when a guy even looks your way."

"I'm not running," I insist. "And Jace isn't just any guy." Even if my friends are right and Jace is interested, I don't want to get my hopes up that this could lead to something. It would be a fling for him, and that's it.

Would I be okay with being a fling? Just a few weeks ago, I would have said no, but now I'm not so sure.

My phone buzzes with a text, and Jaz grabs my phone before I can. "Speak of the devil," she says with a grin. "Guess who's texting you to meet him at the barn?"

"It doesn't mean he likes me," I say, grabbing my phone from her. Whether I'm saying it for her benefit or mine, I'm not sure. "Can you finish up here? I'll swing by later to check on things."

When I hurry out the door, I can already feel the excitement building in my chest. *Jace wants to see me.* I've always prided myself on staying in control of my emotions and being the strong one, but Jace has this way of making everything in me crumble like a fool.

When I arrive at the barn, his car sits outside. He doesn't hear me come in because his eyes are closed, his face tipped toward the piano. Watching him play under the lights, it's no wonder he's a star. He begins to sing:

I was running from echoes of the past,
But you caught up with me at last.
I fought against it, but love's too strong,
I'm surrendering to you, where I belong.

In that moment, all my resistance evaporates, and I'm left with only a soft feeling in my chest for this sweet, tender-hearted man.

This is why people love him. How could I not fall for him, too?

I move, and Jace immediately looks up. "Mia, I didn't hear you come in." His face softens as he rises from the piano.

I've already forgotten my promise that I wasn't going to melt when I saw him. Right now, I want to watch his concert so I can absorb every part of Jace from the front row.

"That was incredible," I gush. "Is it for the concert?"

"Yes, I need to work out a few details, but this is the second new song I've written for it. I'm hoping this is the end to my writer's block." He walks down the aisle toward me, wearing a grin that makes my heart trip and stumble. "I think I've found my muse again."

The way his eyes roam over me with approval gives me a thrill.

I lift an eyebrow. "But it's not a breakup ballad or party song. It's another love song."

He rubs his hand across his shadowed cheek. "I know. Do you approve?"

"It doesn't matter what I think."

"It does to me. You're the only person who tells me the truth. Do you know how rare that is in this business?"

I shift because I haven't told him the truth about my feelings. "That's because I don't treat you like some special snowflake," I say, trying to lighten the mood.

He laughs. "I'll try not to take it personally. Would you listen to the whole song? I need to run it in front of someone and get my nerves out."

It's hard for me to imagine that someone as famous as Jace would ever get nervous. I sink down next to him at the piano, our legs brushing where they meet, the sparks running up my legs.

"I need you here, Mia. To help me get rid of the fear." His eyes meet mine, and it's like a weight I can barely hold. The pressure builds under my chest, that slow, deep longing every time he's close to me.

As he begins the song, I try to pack up my emotions, but it's impossible. As soon as he sings about falling in love, I'm the one who's completely gutted. I turn into a hot mess, and it lasts until he hits the final chord.

How does Jace have this effect on me? He makes me feel hollow and full, overwhelmed and completely satisfied, all at the same time.

When he finally lifts his hands from the keys, he glances over at me with a shy smile. "What do you think?"

"Honestly?" I swallow down the lump in my throat. *Right now, I'd like to kiss you so hard.*

"Yes, I want your brutally honest opinion."

"You really don't," I say, shaking my head, afraid he's going to see through this thin mask.

"I can handle it, Mia."

"It's . . . beautiful, Jace."

His mouth curls into a smile. "Really?"

"I felt ripped up inside. You're going to make all the women ugly cry. Everyone wants a love like you described."

He rubs the back of his neck. "That's pretty high praise, coming from you. Now . . . tell me what you're really thinking."

If only he knew I'd like to jump in his lap right now.

"I can't find one thing wrong with it," I say instead. *Or with you.* And that's the problem. How am I going to sit through his concert and pretend like he's not wringing out my heart?

He glances over uneasily. "Mia . . ." he says, then pauses. "What I asked you the other night, about being seen around town with me—I wasn't trying to put you in an awkward position. You don't have to do it."

I look down at my knotted hands and decide I don't care if Jace is only pretending. I don't even care if this is a temporary fling. This is the first thing that's felt right and made me happy. "Jace," I say, interrupting. "Don't apologize. I'm all in."

EIGHTEEN

Jace

I knock twice and listen, but there's still no response. I've hardly seen Mia over the last week. She's been busy preparing for the festival and helping me with final details while I've been practicing with the band nonstop. Allan has been staying here on and off, flying back and forth between his home and our rehearsals to make sure everything is going well.

Mia and I haven't had time to hang out or get dinner together, and I've missed those small moments of connection. I still haven't forgotten our agreement to go out in public, and the festival is the perfect opportunity.

I leave a cup of coffee on the hall table outside her bedroom, along with a Reese's Cup, and step away as her door creaks open. She rubs one sleepy eye and looks at me with confusion. "Is it morning already?"

"You worked really late last night decorating the downtown. Allan already boarded his plane this morning."

"What time is it now?" She grabs her phone and squints as she attempts to read it without her glasses. She's adorable in her red flannel pajamas, her hair still tangled from sleep.

"Does that say ten a.m.?" she asks. "Why didn't you wake me?"

"You didn't get in until four. You've been working nonstop this week."

She leans against the doorframe, like she's carrying the weight of the world on her shoulders. "We had to get everything done. Then Ella flew home early this morning." Her eyes flick to the coffee and candy on the table. "Is that . . .?"

I hold out the coffee and chocolate. "For my special snowflake."

She smiles and looks like she could kiss me. "God bless you, dear man."

"If it makes you feel better, I attempted a snowflake design in the coffee, but it turned out like a blob."

She peeks into the cup and holds back a laugh before dunking the Reese's Cup into the coffee. "Thank you. But where is your coffee?"

"I can't today. Bad for the voice." She thinks this over as I shove my hands in my pockets. "This is your big day, right? The official kickoff to the week-long Mistletoe Festival."

"Yeah, *that*." She takes a bite of chocolate as her brow tenses. "Only if I can get the committee on board before tonight. I offended them by not using the Ugly Santa this year. A few are even considering not showing up to the community tree lighting this evening." She runs her hand through her hair. "I can't lose the committee's support. That will get everything off to a bad start. We've worked so hard."

I study her for a second. "I have an idea that might help, but I have a few things I need to take care of first. How about if I meet you down there later?"

She narrows her eyes. "Don't you have a concert to prepare for? A million things to do?"

"I'm ready to go. Just a few details to wrap up. And don't tell the committee I'm coming."

She frowns. "What secret do you have up your sleeve?"

"Don't you know you're not supposed to ask questions this time of year?" I grin. "I have to practice with my band first and then do two live interviews, followed by a meeting with my manager."

"Just a few details, huh?" she asks. "You should really get an assistant to help you."

"I already have one, and she's great." I smile and play along. "She lined up the interviews today and emailed my crew about practice details. She even ordered my favorite snacks for rehearsal. Apparently, she really is my minion of happiness."

Mia smiles, cradling her coffee mug. "Can you at least give me a hint about what you're planning today?"

"Nope," I call over my shoulder as I head downstairs. "Just trust me."

"Jace, that's what you said before we slid off the road."

I stop and turn around, giving her a crooked smile. "And look how that turned out."

———

The rest of my day is a blur. Between a three-hour rehearsal and back-to-back interviews, the last thing I feel like doing is solving a dispute over the town's Ugly Santa. But I know this is an easy win. Not just for Maplewood, but for Mia.

When I arrive downtown, I slow down to check out Main Street's decorations. I've been so busy practicing for the concert, I haven't seen Maplewood's transformation. All the shops are draped in lights while silver tinsel trees and shiny Christmas bulbs sparkle in the windows. Light poles are wrapped in evergreen with bright red bows. Gone are the empty storefronts, replaced by endless Christmas lights, like something out of a movie.

By keeping all the best parts of the past and adding some new touches, Ella, Jaz, and Mia have brought out the classic features of Maplewood.

A crowd gathers next to a gigantic live evergreen in the town square that's decked out in multicolored lights—and Mia's standing near the towering tree. Based on the unhappy expressions, the dispute over the Ugly Santa still hasn't been resolved.

I park on a side street and grab my guitar from the back seat, hurrying toward the square. I can't guarantee this will change things, but it's worth a try.

As I approach Mia from behind, Judy holds the faded plastic Ugly Santa next to her, like a prop.

Mia points to the tree. "This is the focal point of the entire festival, not the decorations. We don't have room for Santa if we're going to hold events on the square."

"Then move Santa," Bob suggests.

"Where?"

I step up to the square and open my guitar case.

One lady points and whispers, "Is that Jace Knight?"

That's all it takes for all eyes to shift to me.

"Jace?" Mia spins around and looks over my guitar with a questioning glare. "What are you doing?"

I play a few chords. "Impromptu concert on the square," I say, loud enough for everyone to hear. A few snowflakes tumble down, setting the perfect mood. I move closer to the tree as several people snap pictures.

Mia leans toward me, trying to hide what she's saying. "I'm kind of in the middle of something right now." Based on the look she's giving me, she thinks I'm nuts.

I lean toward her, faintly catching her sweet scent. "Just trust me." Then I wink.

I turn to the committee. "Mia wanted to give you a special gift before the tree lighting tonight as a way of saying thank you."

Mia frowns. "I did?"

I give her a look. "Yes, a very special gift. A Christmas singalong with Jace. Anyone have a request?"

The committee members look at each other for a second before I suggest one. "Do you know 'Santa Claus is Coming to Town'?"

Judy says, "Except that we don't have our Santa!"

"Good point." I grab the Santa hat I stuffed into my guitar case and slide it on. "How's this for you?" I point to my hat.

A few people chuckle.

"I don't look like the plastic Santa," I say, nodding toward Ugly Santa.

"You look better!" someone from the back yells, and everyone laughs.

"Thank you," I reply, smiling. "I hope I sing better than him, too."

As I roll into the song, everyone joins in singing. Mia lifts an eyebrow, unsure of where I'm going with this.

After that carol, another person suggests "Jingle Bells," then "Silent Night," and "Let it Snow."

By the time we're done, the committee is laughing and singing like they've totally forgotten about the Ugly Santa dispute. Then they ask me to sign autographs and take selfies.

Mia approaches while I'm putting away my guitar, her arms crossed. "That was impressive. Did you know it would distract them?"

"I hoped it would. It's the only time that being famous actually works in my favor."

"If I'd known it was that easy to sway the committee, I would have brought you around a long time ago."

Jaz carries over the Ugly Santa under her arm. "Jace, thank you for saving us from Ugly Santa. Can we hide this before they return?"

"Let me take care of him," Mia says, looking at her friend. "You still need to pack."

"Actually, I decided to stay a few more days," Jaz says.

"To help with the festival?" Mia asks.

"That . . . and your brother asked me to," she says with a shy smile.

Mia frowns. "You're staying for him? What about me?"

"He wanted to take me to the festival. And we'll see each other after Christmas, right?"

Mia nods but doesn't respond, the reality of the holidays without her friends finally sinking in.

"I'll carry Santa," I volunteer, taking the plastic figurine from Jaz.

Jaz gives us a quick wave before leaving. As we walk along Main Street, the snow falls lightly, like a softly shaken snow globe swirling around us.

For a long stretch, we're silent, taking in the lights and the calm before the storm of tourists. "You're going to miss your friends for Christmas, aren't you?"

She stops on the street as the snow catches in her lashes. "It's weird to be the one left behind. Especially at Christmas."

"Hey, it's gonna be okay." I brush some snowflakes from her cheek with my thumb. "Jaz is still your friend, and you're not alone. I'm here."

Her eyelids flutter when I touch her, almost like she can feel the electricity between us.

"I'm probably overthinking things because of lack of sleep," she says. "I need to get through this Christmas festival first." She pulls out the key to unlock the back door of the empty storefront where we're housing the decorations.

The storage room is almost empty now, except for a few light strands.

I've never been here when it's so quiet. Mia shuts the door behind us, and I'm suddenly aware that it's just us in this dark room.

I put down the Ugly Santa. "What'll we do with this guy?" I nod toward the hideous figurine. "If we leave him here, Judy might find him and put him on the square."

"Are you saying I should throw out Ugly Santa?" she says with a concerned frown.

"Better yet, destroy him so he can't be reused."

Her lips quirk at the edges as she looks from me to Santa, considering if this is crazy or my best idea yet.

"But how?" she asks, looking around for something to smash him.

"Use Santa as your personal punching bag," I say, standing him up so she can take her best shot.

She gives me a conflicted look. "It feels wrong to destroy Santa."

"Or fun."

She hesitates, then drops her coat on the floor. "As long as you don't tell my mom."

Then she lifts her fist and flattens Ugly Santa with a punch. The plastic figurine falls to the floor, his face dented neatly from her knuckles.

I pick him up. "If you want to make sure they never use him again, you need to do better than that. The sooner we put him to rest, the sooner we can buy a new Santa. One that will not scare small children."

She laughs, then surveys the plastic Santa again. It only takes a second for her to decide to kick him a few more times, before picking him up and throwing the dented Santa in the trash can.

She turns around with a satisfied grin and a spark in her eyes that I've only seen a few other times. "Man, this feels great!" she says with a triumphant smile. "It makes me so happy to destroy something. Is that weird?"

"No, it means you need to do this more often."

She lifts an eyebrow. "Destroy more Santas?"

"I meant doing things that make you happy . . . and are out of your comfort zone."

"That's the problem. I always end up talking myself out of things."

"What do you mean?"

For a second, a look passes across her face. "Like the reason I've never been kissed. I overthink it. And then I get nervous. It's so paralyzing."

I hesitate, wondering if she's thinking the same thing. The

solution is right here in front of her. I could solve this problem so easily for her.

"What if you didn't run away?" I suggest. "What if you let it happen when it's meant to?" I step next to her, my heart beating wildly.

She pauses, her eyes dropping to my lips. "Remember when you asked me to watch you rehearse so you could get your nerves out?" I can see her chest rising and falling.

I brush my finger across her jaw. "Are you asking me to help you get your nerves out?"

She hesitates, then nods slowly. "Only if you want to."

Do I want to? "I don't even need to think about my answer."

NINETEEN

Mia

I *can't believe Jace just agreed to give me my first kiss.* "Even if we're . . ." I glance around. "In a storage room?"

"You were expecting somewhere else?" Jace asks.

"I thought it would be a little more romantic than this."

He snaps his fingers. "Hang on a second." He hurries over to the electrical outlet and flicks off the Christmas lights. With a quick movement, all the lights go dark so we can't tell we're in a storage room anymore.

I'm not sure if this is better or worse. If Jace had tried to kiss me yesterday, I would've explained why this is an incredibly bad idea.

It's *still* an incredibly bad idea. But I'm sleep deprived and just punched a plastic Santa, so I feel like I could do anything.

As his hand slides from my cheek to chin, he tips my face up to his. "You're thinking about backing out of this, aren't you?"

I feel so called out right now. "How do people kiss someone they hardly know?"

"You mean without thinking of the consequences? Happens all the time." In the dark, I can barely make out Jace's smirk.

"Willingly? Without being under the influence?"

Jace laughs, which makes my stomach feel funny in a good way. "Yes, really. Some people even find it fun."

"I'm sure I'll find it fun with the right person."

"Just relax." He's still touching my chin, sending chills down my body.

"Did you know that when you tell someone to *just relax,* that makes them do anything *but* relax?" I say.

"Okay, then focus on something else."

The only thing I'm focused on is the closeness of his skin, the way his fingers stroke my jawline, making everything in me whimper.

"For me, I think about the other person," Jace says. "Like right now, I can't see the green in your eyes, so I'm imagining it."

"You remembered my eye color?" I don't know why it surprises me that Jace would know this. Until now, I didn't think he paid any attention to me.

"Of course I knew. I also know what you look like when you sleep. It's the only time you look peaceful."

I tilt my head. "When did that happen? Are you the Edward Cullen type?"

"Only the one time at the Pine Paradise."

"You mean . . ." I let the words hang between us, because I'm too afraid to ask.

"Yeah, I know what happened that night . . ." He gives me a sheepish look. "It wasn't intentional, but I also didn't hate it."

I laugh with relief. "Good. Because I didn't hate it either."

I can see the inky black of his eyes, the dark pools I want to fall into. He steps forward, wraps one hand around my waist, and slowly closes the gap between us.

"Anytime you're not enjoying this, we can stop . . ."

"No, that's okay," I say quickly. "I need to get this over with."

"Over with? You sound like you're getting your teeth cleaned."

"Believe me, this is so much better than the dentist," I say, seriously.

"Is it weird that we're talking about the dentist before your first kiss?"

"No weirder than the fact I just punched Santa." If we're going to do this, it might as well be now. Since Jace has probably kissed hundreds of women, he won't even remember it. Which means if I mess up by bumping his nose or missing his mouth and hitting his chin instead . . . *I can't even go there.* There are too many things that could go wrong right now.

Jace tilts my chin up. "You're doing it again."

"Okay, I'll stop. No more overthinking. I figure if I can kiss you, I can kiss anyone. Except Cal. I will definitely *not* kiss Cal, even if he wins that auction."

"Cal?" he asks.

"A creep from high school who tried to kiss me under the mistletoe a long time ago. When I refused, he told me he didn't like girls who wear glasses, anyway."

"What a jerk," he says. "For what it's worth, I think your glasses are hot."

"You do?" I say, touching them. "In the movies, the nerdy girl in glasses is never the hot one, unless she gets a makeover. But I'm not doing that."

"Good. Don't stop wearing them," Jace says. "They're your superpower."

"I've never thought of them as an asset."

His hand sweeps down my neck lightly, sending chills down my arm. "You have so many superpowers you don't even know about."

"Like?" I say, barely able to form the word.

"Do you want to talk about superpowers or . . ."

"Yes," I interrupt, because I already know what the other option is, and that's the one I want.

His hand sweeps around my back, lightly grazing my spine, before landing on my lower back. The scent of pine and musk envelops me as the warmth of his body hovers against mine, sending the room spiraling. He looks down at me and brushes his fingers lightly across my cheek, like he's memorizing me.

When I wrap my hands around his neck, his palm moves to the curve of my waist, pulling me against him. As my fingers slip across his shoulders, I tip my chin up. Just as I lean forward, a faint click sounds behind me, and a sharp intake of breath.

"Who's here?" someone asks as a light blinds me.

I spin around. "Mom?" I jump away from Jace.

I can't make up a good excuse about why we were plastered against each other, and based on her astonished look, she knows exactly what we were doing.

"I was . . . um, looking for something . . ." She glances around helplessly.

"It's not what it looks like," I blurt, even though that's not technically true. It's exactly what it looks like. My face is so hot right now, I could probably microwave a frozen dinner.

"I misplaced my wallet," she says, pointing to her missing wallet left on a table. She smiles awkwardly.

I take a step forward. "Mom, I can explain . . ." Even though I'd rather not. Mom doesn't know that I've never been kissed. And that's not a conversation I want to have right now.

"You don't need to," she insists, waving her hand. "You're a thirty-one-year-old woman. I respect your privacy. And there are some things I'd rather not know." Then she leaves out the door as quickly as she came in.

I rub my forehead. "Now what'll we do?"

"I don't think there's anything we can do."

"She's going to assume we're dating. The whole committee will find out."

Jace shrugs. "Why does that matter?"

"Aren't you worried this news will spread to everyone in town?"

He glances at me before I realize this is a dumb question. He's not worried about it. That was the whole point of us pretending to date. I'm supposed to fix his PR problems.

"Why don't you just explain to your mom?"

I stare at him for a second. "What do I tell her? That I've never been kissed, and Jace Knight offered to be my first?"

"It's true, isn't it?" he asks with a smirk.

"That might work for you, but as long as I'm in Maplewood, I won't hear the end of it." The frustration builds in my chest. Jace doesn't understand why this is problematic.

"I don't see why this is such a big deal."

"Jace . . . my mom doesn't know."

Jace pauses as it sinks in. "That you've never been kissed?"

I shake my head, then turn away, feeling stupid for letting things get this far. "My mom has certain ideas about love, and one of them is that you do not let someone kiss you unless they're seriously interested. Now she's going to get her hopes up, and I don't want to ruin things by telling her I was just fooling around with you. And if my brothers find out, then it's game over for you . . ." I push my finger into Jace's chest to make my point.

Jace grabs my hand, trying to reassure me. "What if we don't explain? If we're going to be seen together anyway, we just let people believe what they want."

"Which is?" I ask, frowning.

"That there *is* something going on between us."

"My family would see right through it . . ." I hesitate.

"Unless it's believable," he finishes with those penetrating eyes that make my heart stumble.

"But how?" I'm a terrible liar. Even though with Jace, I don't have to lie. The way he makes my body light up like a Christmas tree, it's clear how I feel about him.

He studies me. "The real question is how far do you want to take this charade?"

I pause. "Until Christmas." I'm walking a dangerous tightrope between what my heart wants and what's best for my future.

I'm a single woman who's never been kissed. Maybe a risk is exactly what I need.

The agreement I made to myself was to do things that made me happy. And Jace makes me crazy happy.

I finally meet his eyes. "Whatever it takes to make people believe we're a couple."

"You sure?" he asks, still holding my hand.

"Positive," I say, wondering whether I can see this through without running off like a scared cat.

His dimple deepens as he smiles. "Then let's finish what we started."

TWENTY

Mia

He grabs my hand and pulls me outside, where the snow is falling harder.

"Where are we going?" I ask, confused by our sudden change of plans.

"The town tree lighting," he says. "Did you forget?"

I pretty much forget everything when Jace is around. The committee scheduled the tree lighting as a special event for the community, a way of saying thank you before tourists descend on our town.

Once we open the festival tomorrow, it's going to take an entire village to pull off this event.

"The perfect chance to be seen together," he says, squeezing my hand.

"Oh, right," I murmur, pulling away. *I'm his PR improvement project.* Whatever almost happened in that storage room wasn't real, even though every cell in my body was screaming, *Kiss me like you mean it.*

I glance over at Jace, suddenly shy. "We went over a few rules before . . ." I let the words dangle in the air.

"The rules?" His eyes search my face, like he's already forgotten our previous conversation.

"How believable do you want this first event?" I ask. "I think we need to make sure it's obvious I'm not just one of your crew."

His mouth hitches up on one side. "That won't be hard," he murmurs, taking a step toward me.

My whole body tenses when he moves next to me. It feels weird to be standing this close to Jace under the bright lights where anyone could see us. I need to get comfortable with him in my personal space.

"Are you okay with me touching you?" Jace asks carefully, brushing a strand of my hair behind my ear. "Holding your hand, putting my arm around you . . . that sort of thing?"

"Yeah," I say breezily, even though I want to bite my fist. He's being so respectful of my feelings instead of surprising me, like I did to him in front of Ava.

"Is this comfortable?" He takes my hands in his, and a shiver runs through my body. This is going to be harder than I expected.

"It's great," I say while my heart does backflips in my chest. I've been starved for this kind of touch. "As long as it's not crossing the line."

"And what line is that?" he asks, still holding my hand.

"Kissing in front of my mother."

Jace bursts out with a laugh. "Even I'm uncomfortable with that."

"What if there's a reporter who approaches us?"

"There's nothing you can do to make things worse," he says. "Or make me uncomfortable."

"I could embarrass you by saying something totally stupid. When I get nervous, I talk too much, and that's when it all goes downhill."

"You won't," he assures me as we stroll past lights in the shop windows. I'm so glad he puts so much trust in me when he's only known me for a short time. "If you do, I'll just give you a gentle squeeze to let you know you should stop talking. Like our own secret signal."

"What's the secret signal I should give you?" I ask.

"You choose."

"I'll just look at you like I'm going to kill you."

"So subtle," Jace teases. "At least I won't miss it."

As we wander past the storefronts filled with decorations, it feels like we're in a Christmas movie. Even the snow is cooperating for my imaginary movie set by falling down so lightly, it looks like we're trapped in a snow globe.

It almost seems *too* perfect. And that makes me worry. Because nothing is ever perfect in my life.

As we walk through town, people turn to give us a second glance. Jace squeezes my hand and smiles, like he wants me here. When we finally reach the enormous Christmas tree, we stand toward the back, waiting for the mayor to start the tree lighting countdown.

A few people turn to look at us, and Jace grabs my hand again, sending a hit of dopamine through me.

I thought I'd feel nervous appearing at an event with Jace. Instead, I feel like I'm right where I'm supposed to be.

"Ten . . ." the mayor begins. "Nine . . . eight . . ."

As the townsfolk continue counting, I catch Jace looking over at me with an amused half-grin.

"What?" I ask, suddenly self-conscious. That dimple slays me every time.

"I like being here with you," he says. "You make me feel human again."

"Thanks . . . I think?" I frown.

"It's a compliment," he says. "There are sacrifices I've had to make for my career."

"Two . . . one!" the crowd chants.

As we reach the final number, the Christmas tree springs to life as the crowd erupts with cheers.

That's when it hits me—why Jace is smiling. Because he never gets to hang out in town like a normal person. He can't even date like a regular guy.

As we look at the breathtaking lights, the glow reflects from

Jace's face, and I want to bottle this moment, to tuck it away in the scrapbook of my mind forever.

As I lean my head on his shoulder, a reporter steps in our way, blocking the view.

"Can I ask a few questions?" she asks.

Jace shoots me an apologetic look. No matter how hard he tries, being normal is remarkably short-lived. That's the price you pay for fame.

"Who's this for?" he asks, and I can see his mask slip back on, the one that makes him standoffish and grumpy, like when I first met him.

I'm the only one who gets to see the other side of him, the soft side he keeps hidden.

"*Maplewood News*," she says. "I wanted to ask about your upcoming concert."

"As long as it only takes a few minutes," he says. "And no personal questions."

I love it when Jace switches into his stage persona. There's such a clear distinction between who he is around me and how he acts in public. The fact he trusts me enough to show his real side makes me fall even harder.

"How about hot chocolate?" I ask, trying to give Jace some space for his interview.

He nods and promises, "I'll keep it short."

I leave Jace with the reporter and head over to the gourmet coffee truck to order a white hot chocolate for each of us. The barista tops off our drinks with whipped cream and a sprinkle of cinnamon so that it looks like a heavenly cloud of white.

When I return, he's finishing up with the interview.

"I'll meet you over there," he tells her before turning to me.

"What was that about?"

"She wants a picture of us."

I take a sip of my drink. "Together?"

"You're the genius behind this festival. But you might not want to wear whipped cream for the shot." He brushes his finger across my nose and licks the whipped cream off his finger.

My cheeks heat. "Definitely not," I say, trying to hide how much I enjoyed that. Everywhere Jace touches me, it's like my body turns into a heat map.

"I'll pass on the picture," I say.

"You're not getting out of this," Jace says firmly. "You've worked harder than anyone on this festival." Jace takes my hand and pulls me along, leading me toward the park hill where there are games, more decorations, and food.

"Jace, I don't want to be in the spotlight," I explain. I'm the one who's always been in the background, orchestrating things behind the scenes. Never the girl out front.

"I know," he says, and his face softens. "It's what I like about you. You don't demand the spotlight. I think we make a good team."

I'm part of Jace's team? Something about his comment sends a thrill through me. I want to be part of Jace's team, even if I'm just his assistant.

Jace holds my hand as we thread through the crowd, and I almost have to jog to keep up with his massive stride.

When we make it to the top of the hill, the wind hits my face, and I stop feeling my fingertips. "I'm going to look like an icicle for this picture."

"I'll make sure you don't. I'll hold both hands if I have to," Jace says, shooting me a look that makes my heart knock against my rib cage.

Until now, I hadn't been paying attention to where we were heading, but as soon as I see the mistletoe booth, I stop.

I frown. "Here?"

Jace turns to me. "She said she wanted to feature the new mistletoe booth. I thought you wouldn't mind, since this was your genius."

"I know, but . . ." *It also means we'll be under the mistletoe.* Does he realize what this means? This is why I hate mistletoe. As much as I want to finish what we started, I don't want to do it here. *In front of everyone.* It only brings back memories of Cal the Creep.

I pull my hand from his and shove it into my coat pocket.

Jace notices my hesitation. "It was the reporter's suggestion. But there's no requirement to . . . *you know.*"

"Actually, there is. It's an unspoken requirement of the festival. If you get caught with someone under the mistletoe, then you *have* to kiss them. That's why I hate mistletoe. It's forced PDA."

Jace looks at me. "Seriously?" Then he shakes his head. "But they can't enforce it."

"No, but people usually keep the tradition. And not kissing isn't an option."

I want to kiss Jace under the mistletoe. But the thought of being forced to just doesn't feel right. Especially given my history.

"Well, we don't have to if it makes you uncomfortable. We make the rules here. I'll tell the reporter to meet us somewhere else." He pulls out his phone to send her a message.

"Thanks," I murmur. "Oh, and, Jace . . ."

He looks up from his phone. "It's not that I don't want to . . ." I shift, trying to figure out how to explain myself.

"Mia, it's okay to say no. I won't take it personally." Then he smiles.

The fact that he's so aware of my feelings makes me like him even more. Maybe this is just a PR stunt, but he won't force me into something I don't want to do.

After what feels like a hopeless search for the perfect picture spot with no crowds, the reporter mentions she has access to the lobby of the old theater. When we arrive, she unlocks the door, and we dash inside the gigantic lobby where there's a Christmas tree decorated with excessive amounts of tinsel. It's the perfect spot for a quick shoot where no one will bother us.

As we stand next to each other, the reporter frowns. "Could you move together?"

I take a step closer to Jace, and our shoulders brush, making me aware of how close we are. I shiver, and Jace takes my hand.

"Your fingers are still freezing." He rubs them between his palms. "Does that help?"

I nod, trying to ignore the little sparks he ignites every time he touches me. It's so unfair how easily he can make me light up.

We take a few pictures before the reporter gets a text on her phone. "I need to run. There's an accident on the corner of Forest Street and Pine Hill. No one's hurt, but I might need to interview a few people. Could you shut the door behind you when you leave? It will lock automatically. Thanks so much!" Then she hurries out, leaving us alone.

As soon as she's gone, Jace spins around, checking out the old lobby with its giant chandelier and impressive woodwork. "They don't make them like this anymore. We should check this place out while we have the chance."

"Is this legal?" I ask, jokingly. "We're not supposed to be in here when it's closed."

"Of course it's legal. She told us to shut the door. She didn't say we couldn't explore." He dashes to the door of the theater and swings it open. A dark, cavernous space opens up.

"Is this where the fundraiser auction is going to be held?" he asks, standing in the doorway.

I peer inside at the empty stage. "Yes," I say, my stomach feeling sick at the reminder. "Unlike you, I hate to be in front of people."

"It always helps me to spend time in a theater before an event," Jace says. "Empty theaters are my favorite. They calm me down."

Right now, I can't imagine feeling calm. Standing this close to Jace puts all my senses on edge.

Jace looks around at the rows of chairs. "I bet we could get to the roof pretty easily. And the view will be worth it. I just need to find the staircase."

I gape at him. "We shouldn't be sneaking around here."

"It'll be fun . . . and you said you wanted to have more fun."

He turns on his phone's flashlight and heads down the aisle, climbing onto the darkened stage before helping me up. We sneak backstage, where he shines his flashlight across the back wall.

"What are we looking for?" I ask.

"A staircase." He pulls back a curtain revealing a hidden door and opens it.

A metal staircase rises into the darkness and Jace starts up, taking two steps at a time. I follow, trying not to trip in the dark. When we reach the top, he opens another door, and the wind catches it, whipping it open, leaving me breathless with the shock of cold.

"Bingo," he says, his eyes gleaming as he looks onto the roof.

As we step outside, I blink a few times before realizing the entire sky is lit up by the town's Christmas lights. Jace rushes to the railing at the edge of the roof, eager to take in the view.

From just behind him, I stop and peer across the landscape, my breath catching. I feel like I can see the whole world up here.

"Isn't this incredible?" he asks.

The entire downtown is luminous, like a miniature Christmas village. Church spires rise in the darkness, towering above tiny nativities. Pine trees dot the landscape between rows of houses aglow with Christmas decor. It feels like the universe is gleaming with light.

"This is amazing," I whisper.

"I knew it would be," Jace says, leaning across the railing. "And we're the only ones who get the best view in town."

"You can't even tell which buildings are vacant. It's like a new place."

"You did this," Jace says, turning his face to me.

I shake my head. "It was a group effort."

"But the committee couldn't have done it without you. This is something special." He's staring at me with a silly grin, like he's proud of me. It's almost unsettling how much he believes in me.

The wind picks up and snarls my hair, and I wrap my arms around my waist to keep warm.

"Are you cold?" he asks.

"I'll get used to it," I say.

"I don't believe you," he says, snaking his arms around me, snuggling me from behind, his chin tucked into my shoulder. "How's this . . . any better?"

"So much better," I say.

Even though we're only supposed to be pretending, I'm not breaking any rules by wanting to move closer to him. I have a practical reason for needing him to block the wind, because otherwise, I'll turn into a frozen statue.

Jace tucks his face into the curve of my neck, trying to keep us both warm, which is a total distraction.

"So, this mistletoe rule . . . do you always hold to it?" Jace asks.

"Yeah, it's a Maplewood tradition."

"That's interesting," he says quietly, like he's thinking something over. "Did you notice the mistletoe hanging over us when we were standing in the entrance to the theater?"

My head snaps toward him. "What? How could I have missed it? I'm usually trying to avoid it."

"I know. I think that's the point. Someone thought it would be a brilliant spot for unsuspecting couples."

"Then why didn't you say anything?"

Jace lifts a shoulder. "Because I didn't want to force you into anything," he says gently. "I want you to choose the right time. For your first."

Now that he's giving me the option, I want to break all the rules. I want this moment now, not later. The way Jace is making me feel with his arms wrapped around my waist, how could I *not* say yes to him? And if it's just this one time, am I really breaking *any* rules? Because you can't break rules for a relationship that doesn't exist.

"In that case," I begin, shifting my body around so I'm facing him. "What if I choose now?"

His smile drops. "Are you sure?" he asks, suddenly looking nervous.

If he could feel the way my heart is exploding inside my chest, he'd know for sure. "You promised we'd finish what we started."

"I did," he says, not letting go of me. "And I always keep my promises."

"I need someone to guide me through this. For when it really happens," I say, pretending like I've got so many guys lined up at home. Jace doesn't have to know there's not a single guy I'm interested in but him. "You're a stage performer, right?"

Jace laughs, then rubs the back of his neck. "I've never had to instruct anyone on . . . *this*. I don't even know where to start."

"Start at the beginning," I say. "What would you do first?"

"Like right now?" he says, his eyes darkening.

I nod.

He hesitates, then levels his gaze on me. "First, I'd make sure you were close to me, so we don't awkwardly lean forward from too far away. From a practical standpoint, it's so much easier if you're close."

"Like this?" I take a step forward so our bodies brush.

"Then I'd make sure I was touching you." He wraps one hand around me, while the other one sweeps the hair away from my face. "I want to see you. In my opinion, there's nothing more beautiful than a woman's face."

I can feel my cheeks flame as he tucks my hair behind my ear. His hand tightens around my back, while his fingers caress my cheek.

I can barely concentrate, and I haven't even kissed him yet. "What do I do?" I ask, feeling like limp spaghetti under his touch.

"Whatever feels comfortable."

I slowly wrap my arms around his neck, and suddenly my heart is beating frantically, like I've been pushed down a black diamond slope.

"Then what?" I say, looking up at him.

He swallows, his eyes turning into dark pools. "This is the part where there are no rules. You kind of figure it out as you go."

I frown. "Figure it out . . . how?"

"Close your eyes and go for it."

"That sounds like jumping off a cliff."

"It is. Kissing is like jumping with no parachute. You just hope the other person catches you."

He reaches up and cups my face. His eyes hold mine before they close, and he leans forward and hesitates. For a second, I forget to close my eyes, I'm so transfixed by him. I want to remember this moment, this feeling of being so happy in his arms. I'm ready to jump, even if there's no guarantee he'll catch me.

As his lips meet mine, they're tender and soft and not demanding at all.

Without even realizing it, I close my eyes, focusing on the pressure of every place he's touching me. One hand moves across my face, sliding down my neck, while the featherlight stroke of his thumb sweeps across my cheek.

I run my fingers through his curls around the edge of his neck, and it's like my hands are controlled by something outside my body.

One hand finds the warmth of his collar, stroking it lightly, while my other hand explores his jaw and the sharp cut of his cheekbone.

Everything about this man is perfect, and I'm suddenly eager for more of him. I press into the kiss, every part of me wanting to know what Jace likes, what makes him deliriously happy.

If this is what it feels like to fall for someone, then I want more. More of Jace. More of kissing him on rooftops at Christmas.

I push my body toward him without notice, causing him to step backwards and catch himself on the railing.

Suddenly, Jace's hand slides up to my other cheek, and he pulls away, holding me back before I realize it's over.

Jace's face flinches slightly, like it's taking some effort to stop himself.

"We probably should go," he says, his voice thick.

"Oh, I didn't mean to . . ." *Kiss you so hard I almost knocked you over.* Because I absolutely meant to.

I shove my fingers in my pockets, humiliated that I let myself get out of hand like this. I'm usually so responsible and controlled. Not the type who falls apart.

But Jace has that effect on me.

His crease deepens as he looks out over the town.

Did he think I was terrible? Is he mad at me?

"Jace?" I look away, unable to face him. With just one kiss, I crumbled like a tower of blocks. I need to make sure things are still good between us, or I'll never be able to look him in the face again. "I think, for a first kiss, that was pretty good."

Jace lets out a low laugh and leans against the railing, our arms brushing as we take in the lights one last time. He glances over at me, his eyes glittering, his mouth hitching into that dimpled smile. "I think that was pretty good, too."

Even though I've tried to hide my feelings, every time Jace looks at me like that, everything comes undone.

TWENTY-ONE

Mia

I can feel the energy as soon as I step out of my car, and it's not because of last night's kiss. After yesterday's tree lighting, the town is buzzing with anxious anticipation for this morning's grand opening of the Maplewood Mistletoe Festival.

I stroll by the outdoor Christmas market, where vendors unpack sugar-laden treats and fill tables with handmade gifts. Evergreen decorations and twinkle lights adorn every building, and there's more mistletoe than I've ever seen in my life. If we weren't the kissing capital of Christmas before, we are now.

"Mia!" Jaz calls from the storage room where Jace and I almost had our first kiss. I'm still replaying that rooftop kiss from last night, Jace's smell lingering in my memory, the way his hair felt threading through my fingers.

"You look bright and cheerful this morning," I say, looking my friend over. Jaz is sporting her pink fur again.

"And you look . . . sleep deprived," she says, her brow furrowing.

"I am sleep deprived." I tug at the hat Jace bought me in Evergreen, which doesn't hide the obvious bags under my eyes. "I was going over all the festival details until three in the morning." She doesn't have to know how late I was out with Jace. Since he's flying to Nashville with Allan to meet with record executives and won't be back until tomorrow, it means I'll have the house to myself. A twinge of loneliness twists inside me.

I sip the cappuccino Jace made me with his expensive espresso machine. It's like he's enjoying spoiling me, and I don't mind the attention, even if it is temporary.

"Well, everyone is looking for you," Jaz says. "Mayor Jenkins is worried about the parking situation for tonight. A committee member told me at least three tables didn't show up."

I rub my forehead. "How about I talk to the mayor and you track down tables? Beg, borrow, or steal, if you have to."

"Got it," she says, turning away before swinging back to me. "Oh, and your mom is looking for you."

I nearly choke on my coffee. "Did she say why?"

Jaz shakes her head. "Something to do with Jace, I think."

The one thing I don't want to talk about.

When I walk outside to look for Mom, I'm swarmed by people. One volunteer needs emergency tape. A shop owner complains his Christmas lights stopped working. Someone wants another table for her pies, even though I've explained there are no tables left.

My to-do list piles up like mail to Santa, leaving my head aching after a few hours of solving everyone's problems.

Just as I'm rushing through the warehouse searching for another strand of lights, someone grabs my arm. It's the mayor, looking frazzled. "Mia, did you hear the news? We're changing the schedule for this week. The fundraising auction is now right after the children's choir performance tonight."

"What?" I gasp. "I didn't approve that change."

"Several national TV networks want to publicize this festival and all the changes we've made. They're coming today for some live footage, and they're going to cover tonight's events."

My stomach clenches. I've tried to put the auction out of my mind, trying to forget I ever agreed to it, but now my anxiety is soaring.

"I don't really think we need media coverage about the auction."

"This is huge," the mayor says. "We could bring in more money for next year's festival."

"But couldn't they just focus on Jace's concert instead?"

"They will," he says, "but the concert is sold out. Cal even sold tickets for tailgating outside the barn since the seating is so limited."

"Cal Perkins? What does he have to do with this?"

The mayor chuckles. "He owns the barn, Mia. This event is a cash cow for him."

I had no idea Cal the Creep, the annoying nemesis from my past, was the one who turned the barn into a performance space, but it all makes sense now. It was the Perkins Farm before. His grandparents.

"He struck a deal with Jace about it recently," the mayor adds.

"He did?" I say, feeling a sting that I didn't know this before. Why would Jace make a deal with Cal and not tell me? Probably because it was a business transaction and had nothing to do with me. If Jace can sell tickets for fans to sit outside the barn while they tailgate, why wouldn't he? It's a win-win for him and Cal.

But if he's doing business with Cal, that also means he might have known that Cal wanted to bid at the auction. Maybe that's why Jace was pushing for it. It's one of those unspoken things in the business world: *I'll scratch your back, if you'll scratch mine.*

If he's hiding this, what else is he hiding?

"The tailgating tickets are already gone too," the mayor says. "But we can promote winning a concert ticket through the auction tonight. The TV networks are eating up the town's new look."

He seems immensely pleased by this, even though I'm frustrated by the last-minute schedule change.

"Don't you think we could keep the auction scheduled for tomorrow?" I suggest. "We've had this plan in place for weeks . . ."

"I already told them to change it. Your mom agreed. The town needs the publicity."

"My mom?" I spin around trying to locate her, but there are too many people. When I turn back, the mayor is gone.

Why does it feel like everyone is happy about this auction, except me? And why is it now that I've kissed Jace, I don't even want to think about going to his concert with anyone else?

———

When five p.m. hits, my mother tracks me down and stops when she sees my disheveled appearance.

"What are you still doing here?" she asks, her brow creasing beneath her glasses. "You're supposed to head home and prepare for the auction tonight." If she's thinking about what happened last night, she doesn't show it.

"In case you've forgotten, we opened the Mistletoe Festival today. I've had a million things on my plate."

Her face relaxes into a smile. "Today has been a smashing success! But now you should let the committee take over your job."

"My job *is* the festival," I say. "You hired me as the event planner."

"And you've completed that task. Now your job is to look presentable." She places her hand on my back and scoots me toward the door.

"Actually, my job is to be Jace's assistant," I remind her.

"You're a little more than his assistant, right?" She lifts an eyebrow.

I can see the hope in her eyes—and the unspoken question of whether I'm making a terrible mistake by having a holiday fling . . . or whatever I've gotten myself into.

"Yeah," I say with a smile.

She smiles and takes in a deep breath. "Well, for tonight,

you're the star of the show. Get yourself cleaned up for the auction. You're going to be on TV."

My worst nightmare.

When I get to Jace's home, Blackie and Tabby meet me at the door, sweeping around my legs with their soft tails. I stroke their backs, glad someone is here to greet me since Jace is gone. I crack open the door, and both cats push through. They skitter up the steps toward my room, and I don't even try to stop them.

They'll keep me company while Jace is gone with Allan. As soon as he gets home, I'll put them back outside.

Even though I'd like a nap, I force myself into the shower and let the hot water wash away all the stress from the festival's opening day.

When the doorbell rings, I check Jace's security camera and discover Jaz waiting outside, holding a large plastic bag.

"What are you doing here?" I ask, looking over the mystery bag. "I thought you were hanging out with Brax at the festival."

"I thought I'd surprise you . . . with a new outfit and a makeover for tonight."

I glance at the bag but don't take it. "Does this involve pink fur?"

"No, but don't keep me waiting. Open it!" She steps into the foyer and holds out the mystery bag.

I peek inside. It's a stunning red dress that's fitted at the top with a knee-length skirt that's perfect for spinning in circles.

"It's gorgeous . . . but I don't do red dresses." I attempt to hand it back to her, but she stops me.

"Why?"

"I don't know. I just don't like people noticing me. I'm the girl who's behind the scenes, making things happen. Not the center of attention."

Jaz holds the dress up to see if it will fit. "Try it on so I can send a picture to Ella. You know the last thing she told me before flying back? *Don't let Mia show up in jeans.*"

"Now you're my fashion coach?"

She nods. "That concert ticket is going to go for big bucks, and you need to dress like you're worth a million of them."

"As long as you don't tell me to take off my glasses."

"I wouldn't dare," Jaz says.

"I don't want to do this," I moan.

"I know," Jaz says. "Which is why I'm going to do it for you."

She loops her arm through mine, and we head to the gigantic bathroom in my guest room.

When she walks in, her mouth drops. "Why didn't you tell me you had the royal family's bathroom?"

I shrug. "I don't spend much time in here. It's kind of a waste."

"Not tonight. This is the bathroom of my dreams," Jaz says, as she yanks my hair into a clip.

An hour later, Jaz finally steps back and looks me over. After having my hair pulled, my eyebrows plucked, and so much makeup applied I can't believe I'm not a clown, I slide my glasses back on and stare at myself in the mirror.

"What do you think?" Jaz asks, clearly pleased with her work.

My knee-length red cocktail dress fits me perfectly, a miracle since Jaz guessed my size. My hair falls in waves around my shoulders, and my makeup highlights my best features and isn't clownish at all.

"Give me a minute to get used to it," I say, twirling in the mirror. "Because I feel like a stoplight."

"It's Christmas, Mia," Jaz says. "Aren't you excited about tonight?"

"If there was any way to get out of this, I would."

Jaz studies me for a second. "Does this have anything to do with Jace?"

I pause, feeling the weight of my secret. "I may have done something stupid."

She frowns. "How stupid?"

"I admitted to Jace that I'd never been kissed and . . . asked him to be my first."

"Wait. You had your first kiss with *Jace*?"

I slowly nod.

Jaz lets out a relieved sigh. "Finally."

"Finally?" I frown. "You expected this to happen?"

"Like two weeks ago. You really held out on him . . ."

"I did not hold out. I'm not even sure how Jace feels about it."

"Are you happy?" Jaz asks, looking at me in the mirror.

"I am," I murmur, even though there's this niggling feeling in my stomach warning me to be careful. I know I should tell Jace how I feel when the concert is done. But the thought of admitting my feelings makes me sick. Someone as famous as Jace could never fall for me.

And if he doesn't feel the same, then what? Is it over between us? It's so much easier to pretend we're dating—to live in this dream world—than to face potential rejection.

This feels like the first holiday I could be happy again. But that realization is also incredibly fragile. One mistake and it all could come crashing down.

———

By the time I reach the auction downtown, my stomach is in knots. All traffic is stopped, cars barely inching along through a heavily congested three-block stretch.

"I've never seen this many people in Maplewood before," I say in awe. People are everywhere, inside every shop and across the main square.

Hundreds of people, perhaps even thousands, have arrived for the grand opening of the brand-new Maplewood Mistletoe Festival, and the surge of visitors for tonight is overwhelming our tiny town. I stare in wonder at the crowded sidewalks and the smiling faces of the visitors.

"Look at the mistletoe booth." Jaz points to the pergola on the hill decorated with white lights and evergreen boughs and a sprig of mistletoe tied with a red bow. The line of couples waiting to take a picture is at least thirty-deep.

"It worked," I marvel. This exceeds even my own expectations. As much as I've been dreading this fundraiser, I have to do it for the people of Maplewood.

"Do you see a place to park?" Jaz says. "Because right now, we're not making it to the auction unless you walk."

From here, the line of cars is not moving, and the theater is several blocks away.

"Pull over," I instruct. Jaz wedges into a no-parking zone and I throw open my car door and jump out. I hurry down the sidewalk, dodging pedestrians as I rush toward the old theater.

I glance at the clock on the bank building—I'll make it with a few minutes to spare.

"There you are!" Mom says as I push my way backstage, still panting from the sprint. "I was beginning to think you bailed on us."

"Believe me, I wanted to," I mutter.

Mom puts her hands on my arms. "I'm glad you came. You look incredible." She cracks open a stage curtain so I can see the audience through a slit. "We have a packed house."

"I can't look. I might throw up." I try to focus on the memory of sneaking in here with Jace and the kiss that followed, but right now, the butterflies in my stomach won't let me.

"The auction is up next, right after the children's choir finishes," she whispers.

I glance at the audience and see the white auction signs scattered across rows. "Is it too late to back out?"

She frowns. "Yes, the other two committee members will go first, and then you'll be the last one."

"Last?" I swallow down the acid taste in my mouth from my nerves. Applause erupts as the children's choir finishes and the emcee waves out the first person for the auction. Backstage, I can hear the bidding begin, but I try to block it out by checking my messages. A text from Jace pops up on my screen.

Jace: Ready for tonight?

I might as well pretend that I'm excited about this fundraiser. Otherwise, he might suspect that my feelings are more than just friendship.

Mia: Yep. Fingers crossed that whoever wins is not named Cal and is a good kisser.

Knowing my luck, it will be someone who's as old as my grandpa, but I can't help but tease Jace a little. After all, I don't want him to think he's the only one who'll ever kiss me. After a pause, Jace finally responds.

Jace: I thought kissing you was my job.

A surge of energy courses through my body. *Is this more flirting?* Or does everything feel like flirting after you've kissed someone?

Mia: If someone else doesn't get to me first.

I shut off my phone, feeling a twinge of triumph. I'm not planning on kissing anyone. But I don't want Jace to think I'm so easily won over just because I let him be my first.

Loud applause pulls me back to the moment as my mom pushes me toward the edge of the curtain. "Your turn."

"Next up, we have Mia MacPherson," the emcee announces as I step onstage, blinded by the lights.

Remarkably, I make it to the emcee's side without tripping. I give him a shaky smile, hoping to get this over with as quickly as possible.

The emcee looks at his notes. "This front-row ticket has a minimum bid of at least one thousand dollars."

There's a murmur from the audience as I glance over at his

notes to see if he made a mistake. That's higher than the other starting bids.

Who would be crazy enough to bid that amount for a ticket?

"Who would like to start the bidding?" the emcee asks as he looks over the audience.

For a few agonizing seconds, no one responds. I fold my hands together to keep them from shaking. I don't know how long I can stand here and endure this. If no one bids on this ticket, I'll be horrified . . .

A movement catches my eyes. Someone on the aisle lifts their auction number. I squint to see a shadowed face toward the back of the theater. *Cal.*

My stomach drops. The thought of spending an evening with Cal is as appealing as finding a dead rat in my pantry.

The emcee smiles. "We have our first bidder. Would anyone like to bid fifteen hundred?"

I turn my head toward the emcee. *Are you crazy?*

Another hand goes up on the opposite side. "I'll do fifteen hundred."

It's Nolan Whitmore, the elderly handyman who's been instrumental to this festival. I let out my breath. I'm sure Nolan's doing this as a favor to me, and I could kiss his cheek.

"How about two thousand?" the emcee asks, his eyes scanning the room.

Cal's hand goes up again, and I have to restrain myself from reacting.

"Twenty-five hundred?" the emcee says, suddenly eager to jack up the bids as high as possible.

"I'll bid that," the mayor says, lifting his hand with a smile. I already know the mayor has a ticket, which means he's forcing the bid higher in order to raise more money.

The emcee points at the mayor. "Who's going to bid three thousand?"

Cal's hand rises again.

"How about thirty-five hundred?" the emcee asks.

The mayor accepts.

Cal frowns before he says, "I'll bid five thousand."

Whispers erupt across the room. Everyone knows that five thousand dollars for a concert ticket is nuts. Even a Jace Knight concert ticket isn't worth that much.

The emcee pauses, searching the murmuring crowd. "Anyone want to go higher than five thousand dollars?"

Everyone looks around as heavy silence fills the room.

It's impossible that anyone would bid higher than five thousand dollars.

"One last chance . . ." The emcee pauses. "Going, going . . ."

"Seven thousand." A hand goes up in the very back, opposite from Cal.

I can barely make out a man in a suit, standing in the shadows against the back wall.

"Eight," Cal shoots back without turning to see who is bidding against him.

"Ten thousand," the other man replies.

An audible gasp comes from the audience.

No one in their right mind would bid this high.

Cal shakes his head, the anger flashing across his face.

"Do you want to bid higher than ten thousand dollars?" the emcee asks Cal.

Cal's jaw clenches, the crease on his brow deepens. "No," he finally grumbles.

"Then the winning bid is ten thousand dollars," the emcee announces as applause erupts and everyone tries to figure out who just bid five figures for a concert ticket.

As I'm shuffled offstage by the emcee, Jaz bursts through the backstage door. "I got here during the bidding war. I couldn't see who won."

I shake my head. "He was in the back, and I couldn't see him either."

Mom hurries over carrying a small paper in her hands and

beaming with a smile the size of Texas. "Ten thousand dollars! Can you believe it?"

"Did you catch who the guy was?"

Mom shakes her head. "No, but he came over after he won and told me to give this to you."

She holds out a folded note.

I open the paper and find one sentence:

I couldn't let Cal win.

-Jace

TWENTY-TWO

Jace

Mission accomplished. It's the only message I received from my manager after the auction.

Never mind that it cost me a fortune to fly Allan back to show up at the auction in my place. There's no way I was going to let Cal win.

I open the door as quietly as I can when I arrive home, trying not to wake Mia. Two cats scurry past me. "What are you doing inside?" I mutter as they slip outside.

As soon as I flip on the light, she rises from the couch, dressed in a stunning red dress that looks nothing like her usual faded jeans and oversized sweatshirt. As my eyes sweep over her, my body forgets how tired I am. Seeing her again is like downing an energy drink.

She freezes as she turns to me, and we don't say anything for a moment.

"I let the cats in," she confesses. "I thought you weren't coming home until tomorrow, and Allan was already in bed when I got back after the auction. The cats made me feel less alone."

"I'm glad they kept you company. At least they're good for something." Right now, I don't even care about the cats being inside. She's the only one who captures my attention.

"Why are you home early?" she asks.

"I couldn't wait to see you, so I took a late flight."

She holds up the folded paper I left for her. "Is this note true?"

I nod. "I only gave Allan one instruction for the auction. *To win.*" Even though I want to close the gap between us, I stay in one place, unwilling to cross that line, afraid of what might happen if I do.

"But why would you pay so much for a ticket to your own concert?"

"The town needs it," I say, though that's not entirely true. I don't want her to date anyone else.

"You could have made a donation without putting me through that," she grumbles.

"Originally, I wasn't planning on bidding."

"Then why did you?"

I let out a ragged sigh. "After hearing how much you despised Cal, I couldn't stand seeing you miserable."

She lifts an eyebrow. "So you paid ten thousand dollars so I wouldn't be miserable?"

"Mia, I'd pay anything to see you happy."

She hesitates, her eyes rippling with something I can't read.

I shove my hands in my pockets. "I'm the one who donated the ticket and got you into this mess. I never intended to hurt you."

She walks toward me, her gaze leveled on me. "That was a *very* expensive apology."

"Believe me, I know," I say, rubbing the back of my neck. *But you're worth every penny.*

She stops in front of me. The light green flecks in her eyes have turned to a dark moss.

"And you infuriated Cal, which was priceless," she adds with a satisfied smile. "He really wanted that ticket."

"I wasn't going to let him have the ticket . . . or you."

For a moment, her eyes narrow.

I shake my head. "Now that we've been seen together, we need to keep up the charade."

For a brief moment, she almost looks disappointed.

I can't tell her I want to keep her all for myself. Sharing her with Cal, or anyone else, is not an option.

She crosses her arms. "It almost sounds like you're *jealous*."

I laugh it off. "Maybe I am. I was afraid he'd try to make a move, and I might have to stop the concert and ask him to leave."

"Well, thank you for saving me from a date with Cal and giving me the best seat in the house. Speaking of the concert, how were your meetings today?"

"Long and terribly boring," I say. When I was listening to the record executives, I could only think about how much fun we had the other night. The view. The kiss. *Her.*

She makes a small move toward me, and I want to pull her closer, but I stay in control. *For her.*

Next time I kiss her—if there is a *next time*—I want the real thing.

The sound of a motor grinding up the drive catches my attention, and Mia's eyes stray toward the door.

"Are you expecting someone else?" she asks.

"Not at this hour," I say, checking my watch. It's after eleven.

"Stay right here," I tell her. "I'll make this quick." I stride over to the door, eager to get rid of whoever is on the other side.

As soon as I open it, my stomach drops. "Ava," I mutter.

"Hi, Jace," she says, standing on the edge of the porch, looking like a lost puppy who's found her way back.

Her smile makes me feel like I've been socked in the gut.

"What are you doing here?" I look past her in the dark. "Is Benedict with you?"

"No," she says, tucking a loose strand of hair behind her ear and hesitating. "We broke things off recently, and . . . I thought I'd make a trip to see you." She steps forward, like she hopes to come in, but I don't move from the door.

She shrugs in this helpless way, like it's entirely normal to show up at your ex-boyfriend's house after a year apart. "With your Christmas concert this week, I thought you might need some support."

I cross my arms. Is she feeling nostalgic because it's Christmas, and the holidays are the worst time to be lonely?

I feel Mia's presence, watching our exchange. All I want is to rewind time. To kiss her again. *Why did I open the door?*

A throat clears behind me.

Ava's gaze flicks to her. "Oh, hello. I didn't see you." Her mouth twists slightly.

Mia awkwardly folds her hands together and looks at me, a furrow deepening in her brow. She's waiting for me to do something. Say *something*.

The moment drags on a beat too long before Mia says, "I probably should head up to my room."

Ava looks between us. "Oh, I didn't mean to interrupt. I can go . . ."

"It's okay, I'm tired anyway." Mia turns away.

"Mia . . ." I say, trying to stop her, but she darts up the stairs.

Ava crosses her arms and lifts an eyebrow. "She's living here?"

"Temporarily. She's working for me until the concert is over." At least that was my plan until things spiraled out of control. I hadn't been planning on letting things get this far.

"Is your band here too?"

I shake my head. "Just Allan, when he's in town."

"The band is staying somewhere else because of her?"

I don't answer, and she nods, drawing her own conclusions. "She must really be special."

I don't know how to answer her without giving too much away. When she saw us in Evergreen, we were pretending to date, but now, my feelings are anything but an act. And since I haven't told Mia how I feel, it's especially tricky. I don't want Mia to feel like I'm using her to get back at my ex. But if I tell her now, she won't believe me. Either way, I'm screwed.

I rub the back of my neck. "Maybe we could talk about why you're here instead."

She gives another helpless shrug. "Things have always been complicated between us."

Not for me, they weren't. A few months ago, I would have done anything to have her back in my life, but not now.

My eyes skirt over her dark jeans, the leather jacket that's not nearly warm enough for a New England winter. A strange feeling rises in my chest, like a wall slowly rising. I've come a long way since then.

I rub my jaw. "Listen, Ava, this isn't really the best time."

"Tomorrow, then?" she asks.

"I don't know. My schedule is really busy with the concert later this week."

"At least tell me you saw the article," she says, fishing through her purse. "Even if you don't trust me, I still have your best interest in mind." She pulls out a section from *The New York Times* and hands it over.

I frown. "What article?"

She points at a headline buried in the entertainment news. "Can Jace Knight Make a Comeback?"

I shove the paper into her hands. "I'm not reading a stranger's opinion on whether this concert is my comeback. I'm just ready to make music again."

"It's not just that, Jace. Somebody leaked info on you."

I frown, trying to figure out why she'd come all this way to give me bad news.

I scan the article, my eyes catching on one part: "Someone close to the artist who wished to remain anonymous says his new songs don't have his usual magic touch. 'It's a mediocre love ballad,' the anonymous source states. 'It's like Jace Knight is selling out.'"

My heart sinks. *Who would even know this?* I wanted to save my new music as a surprise for my fans. Now, someone ruined the surprise.

The article ends by saying, "This Christmas concert is the final straw to Jace Knight's flailing career and will likely end up as a Christmas flop."

I crumple the paper, trying to block out what I just read. My new song is already getting panned before I've even had the chance to play it publicly.

"I'm so sorry, Jace," she says with a sympathetic look. "It's unfair they included this person's opinion before the fans have spoken. Do you know who would leak this?"

"I've only played that song for a few people—my band, Allan, and a few of the record executives. They wouldn't say anything . . . not when their incomes rely on it."

"What about her?" Ava murmurs, nodding toward the stairs.

"Mia? She would never . . ."

"Are you sure? Jace, how well do you know her?" She folds her arms and studies me. "Do you know she wouldn't do something to hurt you?"

"That's ironic, coming from you," I shoot back. "So maybe I'm not the best person to ask."

Ava's face flinches. "That wasn't what I was asking."

"She wouldn't do it," I repeat. Mia and I haven't always been on good terms, but I can't imagine her stooping this low.

Ava's gaze moves to the staircase, where Mia has changed into a grey sweatshirt and jeans. Her backpack is slung over one shoulder, and she's carrying her suitcase.

"Where are you going?" I ask.

"Heading to my mom's," she says, brushing by me. She opens the door and heads to her car before I realize what's happening.

I follow her to the car. "Why are you leaving?"

Her eyes flick from me to Ava. "I get the feeling I'm in the way."

"Mia, we need to talk about this." I don't know what she heard inside, but I don't want her to go now.

"Don't leave tonight," I insist. "Not until we've talked."

She circles the car and stops. "I think you need to talk to her first. After that, we'll see if there's anything left."

"Mia, there's nothing to talk about."

"Then why did she come back tonight? Her timing is impeccable."

I can't tell her about the article yet. Not until I know who leaked the information.

"She's here to support me . . . as my friend." But even I can hear how disingenuous that sounds. *Who am I kidding?* Ava hasn't been around this entire year.

Mia lets out a humorless laugh. "*Friend*?"

I don't know what I can say to keep her here, to convince her that whatever Ava and I had is long gone.

"Mia, it's not like it looks. Just stay."

She shakes her head. "I can't."

"Mia," I repeat one last time as she slides into the driver's seat.

As I watch her taillights fade away, a terrible emptiness drills into the center of my chest.

How is it possible that my life went from the *best kiss ever* to losing the one thing I really wanted?

I glance over my shoulder. Ava waits in the door, her body silhouetted by the glow behind her.

I thought this concert was going to be my comeback moment.

But I was wrong.

Mia

"You're quiet today," Mom says, as she puts away groceries, hardly aware of my emotional state. "You must be tired from all the festival planning."

"Yep," I mumble. I hide my emotions well. I also eat my emotions, which is clear from the empty Ding-Dong wrapper next to me.

Mom studies me for a second and then puts another can of soup into the pantry. "Everyone is raving over the festival. Today's numbers are projected to be even bigger than opening day."

I stare at the TV. Apparently, I can organize a giant festival, but I can't get my own life together.

Mom gives me a concerned glance. "Aren't you meeting Jace for his last dress rehearsal?"

"I'm swinging by to organize some things," I say vaguely. "Then I'll head downtown for the festival." Not that I'm needed by the committee. Everything is running so smoothly, my job is done.

Until the concert is over, I'm doing everything to stay out of Jace's way. It was clear from the look on Ava's face why she returned. Now he needs to decide if he wants her back.

None of this should surprise me—Ava's always been the right

one for him. A star who's beautiful, successful, and the perfect sidekick for his comeback moment. The reporters are going to eat up this news.

Mom frowns, holding a box of spaghetti. "Is something wrong? I thought you and Jace looked so happy the other night."

"Unfortunately, you're mistaken," I say quickly.

"Oh," Mom says quietly. "Well, that might be a problem."

I swivel toward her. "Why?"

"Another newspaper reporter wants to talk to you."

I stare at Mom, suddenly concerned. "What did you tell them?"

"I didn't tell them anything . . . *specific*," she says carefully, but the way her eyes dart away makes me suspect something.

"You didn't say anything about Jace and me, right?" I shake my head slowly. "Please tell me you replied with *no comment*."

"I didn't say you are dating," she says defensively.

"But did you imply we are?"

Mom bites her lip. She doesn't have to. Her face tells me everything I need to know.

"No, no, no, noooooo," I groan, dropping my head into my hands. I knew our PR stunt was a risky idea, but I didn't think my family would make it worse.

"What?" Mom exclaims. "Aren't you together?"

I lift one shoulder and drop it. "I'm not exactly sure what we are."

I know what I want. But it isn't even realistic to dream about being Jace's girlfriend.

"If you don't know, then why were you . . . ." She can't even say it.

I roll my eyes, frustrated that this is growing more complicated. "Do you have to ask so many questions?" I shove my computer into my backpack. "I was stupid, okay? I thought there could be something more. But I was wrong."

"Then why didn't you tell me before?" she asks, propping a hand on her hip.

"I don't know. I was embarrassed? Humiliated? Feeling like a total loser because I had to return home?"

"You are *not* a loser," she says firmly. "Look what you did for this town. You brought it back to life."

"But that's just it. I didn't change Christmas *for us*."

"What do you mean?" Mom asks frowning.

"Never mind," I mumble, heading toward the door.

"At least meet with the reporter today. Say something nice about the festival . . . for Maplewood."

I stop mid-stride and stare at my mom. "Don't you understand that I've already done everything for Maplewood? I gave up my Christmas for this. I was trying to make this year different for our family. For *me*. But I realize I can't."

I bolt toward the door, suddenly feeling constricted by all the memories here. I can't keep reliving the past.

"One last thing," I say, turning to face her. "Please stop trying to orchestrate my life. No matter how much you think I need someone, I don't. I won't make the same mistake you did . . ." *Even though I probably already have.*

Like mother, like daughter.

Mom's mouth drops, like she wants to say something, but can't fix things between us.

There's too much that's already gone wrong.

———

I spend the rest of the week avoiding Jace. Since he's busy with his band, it isn't difficult to stay out of his way. A few times during practice, I catch him staring at me, his eyes flicking away when I look his way.

Inside, I'm dying to talk to him, but there are too many people around. Add to it the fact he's working about sixteen hours a day to prepare for this concert, and there isn't time for us to talk, even if we wanted to.

Several times this week, Ava has stopped by to watch him

practice, her face lighting up while everything in me crumbles, like I'm splitting apart, piece by piece.

When I arrive early to set up for his dress rehearsal, I don't see him anywhere, much to my relief. His band and tech crew are checking final details, so I wander backstage, making sure Jace has everything in place for the concert.

Water bottles. *Done.* Costume changes. *Done.* Erasing my feelings for him? *Impossible.*

I don't want to forget that moment on the roof. Not ever.

I lay out his clothes, resisting the urge to think too much about the fact that this is the last time I'll be his assistant. I drape the shirt across his chair, close my eyes and try to dash out of the room.

As soon as I wheel around, I ram into something hard and buckle backwards.

"Mia?" he says as I catch myself on his chair, knocking his clothes to the floor.

"Sorry," I mumble, picking them up in a hurry. "I was just leaving." I can only hope he didn't see me standing there like an idiot holding his shirt.

"Leaving?" he asks, his face pained. I can't read the look in his eyes, and I know why.

It's her.

Ava's surprise visit turned back the clock for him. Every emotion he'd tried to destroy was resurrected by seeing her again. Why wouldn't he choose her? She's a star, like him.

Not like me. For one night, I pretended to be his girl, but I'm the only one living in this fairy-tale world.

"I'll get out of your way so you can get ready." I hurry to the door.

"Mia . . ." he says.

I spin toward him, trying to make sure my face is a blank slate, and cross my arms.

"The night Ava stopped by . . ." he begins, and then hesitates. "I'm sorry if things were weird."

I shake my head, pretending it was no big deal, even though she highjacked our fairy tale—the one that ends with a real kiss.

Apparently, I'm in the wrong fairy tale.

Jace looks at me from under his hat. "There's a lot of pressure on me to make this concert matter—for my career. And my sales."

"You don't have to explain," I say. "I know your career comes first."

"It doesn't. It's not as important as it used to be. But I have to figure out who I can trust, and who will stick around."

I slowly nod, pretending to understand, even as something in me flickers and then dies out. Is he trying to tell me he doesn't want me around? Seeing him one last time is making everything inside me feel stretched to breaking, like a rubber band about to snap.

"It's none of my business." I shake my head.

"It is," he begins. "You're my . . ."

"Assistant," I complete for him with a nod. *Nothing more.*

He clamps his mouth shut. Jace can't let everyone get close to him. Because there never was supposed to be anything between us. I'm the one who broke the unspoken contract. I never should have let my feelings get this far.

"The pressure's on to make this concert everything I need for my career. Ava showing up wasn't what I planned." He rubs the back of his neck, like he always does when he's stressed. It's strange that I know this detail about him—how I know every little nuance about him. Right now, I want to tell him how I feel, but I also want the best for him. If he chooses Ava, then that's what will make him happiest. I won't get in the way.

At least I wasn't stupid enough to confess my feelings to him. I can still walk out of here with my chin held high.

I stop near the door and look at him. "Jace, I hope tonight is everything you dreamed it would be. Not just for your career, but for you. And I hope you find the happiness you're looking for."

Jace looks like he wants to say something, but just then his manager appears in the door. "There's a reporter out here."

"I didn't know about any reporter," Jace says. "I'm not taking interviews before my last rehearsal."

"She's not looking for you," Allan replies. "She wants to talk with Mia."

"Mia?" he repeats.

"My mother arranged this," I stammer, glancing at Allan.

Jace gives me a questioning glare. I want to reassure him I did nothing wrong, but so many things are wrong right now, I can't handle one more strained conversation.

Jace shakes his head, like he doesn't care. "I've got a concert to get ready for." Then he dismisses me with a look.

I storm out the door and nearly run over the reporter in the lobby.

"Miss MacPherson?" She's not the same reporter who took our picture in the theater. It's a middle-aged woman I don't recognize.

"Are you from the *Maplewood News*?" I ask.

She shakes her head. "*The Boston Globe*."

Why would *The Boston Globe* want to interview me? An uneasy feeling swirls inside me. The woman gives me a practiced smile, like we're old friends. "I have connections to your local newspaper. We heard that you and Jace Knight have been seen together?"

I blink. She's digging for news on his personal life and she found the picture from our local paper.

I straighten my spine. "Of course we've been seen together. I'm his assistant."

She keeps her frozen smile leveled on me. "Some people are speculating you're in a romantic relationship. Is it true?"

I shake my head. "No," I say without wavering. At least now I don't have to lie.

"Can you explain what your connection is, then?"

I fold my arms. "It's *none of your business*."

I turn to go, but she keeps talking. "What do you think about the comment in *The New York Times* about this concert being a Christmas flop?"

I wheel around to face her, angry she'd call Jace a flop. "They don't know what they're talking about."

"An undisclosed source indicated his new songs were entirely different. He's not known for love ballads."

"He hasn't played any of his new songs for a crowd yet."

"But a few people have heard the early versions. Are you one of them?"

For a moment, I consider denying it, because I want her to leave. But something stops me. A surge of energy rises inside me, a desire to make one last sacrifice for Jace.

I've got to change the angle of this story, for his sake. He's clawed his way out of career setbacks and depression and, finally, gotten brave enough to write new music. He won't ever see my comment.

I swallow hard. "I've heard his new music."

"And what did you think?" she says. "Are these new songs going to ruin Jace's career?"

"Whoever made that comment is dead wrong." I step toward her to make sure she records every word. Even if we're not meant for each other, I won't let someone else destroy him again. "These are the best songs he's ever written. Probably his biggest hits yet. His fans are finally going to see the *real* Jace Knight. And they're going to love him even more."

I should know. Because that's what happened to me.

TWENTY-FOUR

Jace

They say when it rains, it pours. But tonight's forecast isn't rain. It's snow. Twelve inches of it.

But that won't stop my concert.

I hold up the phone to make sure everything is in place for tonight. "Can you get here early? Your ticket will be at the will call desk," I say, confirming one last detail.

Allan enters my dressing room, red-cheeked and snow-covered. "Who's that?" he mouths as I hang up.

"A surprise for tonight."

He nods, but doesn't press me for details. "Despite the snow, folks are lined up outside the barn," he says with a smile. After months of declining sales, he's more than eager to share good news.

"How are people going to get home if the roads are bad?" I ask, thinking of the time Mia and I slid off the road. If it hadn't been for that freak snowstorm, we wouldn't have ended up in our motel room. I can't say I'm sorry. That night changed everything for me.

Allan shrugs. "Beats me. Says a lot that they're willing to risk their lives for you."

"I don't want anyone risking their life for me."

"You can't stop them," he says, grabbing a water bottle from the mini-fridge. "Your super fans would show up in snow, sleet, or hail. The rest will stream it. This might be the biggest event on YouTube."

"I don't care if it's the biggest," I say, taking a sip of water. "I want it to be good."

A knock at the door cuts me off. I glance over my manager's shoulder as Mia walks in, still dressed in her jeans and sweatshirt. Did she forget there's a concert in an hour? Why hasn't she changed yet?

She looks at me uneasily. "I finished everything for the concert tonight."

"Thanks." I pause, unsure what else to say. Things have been so awkward ever since Ava arrived in Maplewood.

"Good luck tonight," she says before leaving.

"Wait." I step toward the door to stop her.

She pauses, her eyes flicking from my manager to me.

"Can I talk to you out in the hall?"

She nods and follows me to a vacant corner where no one will bother us. "You're coming tonight, right?"

For a moment, she hesitates. She shakes her head, her strawberry waves falling down her shoulders. "I can't."

"What about your tickets?"

Her eyes drop to the ground. "Give them to someone else. Now that Jaz flew back, I don't really have anyone to hang out with."

I need her at the concert, but I can't explain why or I'll ruin the surprise. "Mia, I arranged for someone to take the extra ticket."

A look of hurt flashes across her eyes. "You mean Ava?"

That's why she doesn't want to come. She thinks I gave Ava the extra ticket.

"Not Ava."

"Then who?" She crosses her arms. "I'm not looking for a date."

I grip her shoulders gently so she'll look me in the eyes. "Mia, I wouldn't let anyone else be your date. I'm the one who won the auction."

She narrows her eyes. "Why does this matter so much to you?"

"Just trust me, okay?" I tell her. "And be back here in an hour."

She juts out her chin. "If I can't?"

"Mia, please." I lower my voice. "I need you here, especially when I play these new songs."

She narrows her eyes. "Another publicity stunt?"

I level my gaze. "It never was about the publicity."

For a second, her face wavers before she hurries out the door.

———

"You nervous?" my manager asks backstage.

"Is it that obvious?" I say, cracking my knuckles.

There's so much riding on this concert. Not only is my team counting on this to bolster our sales, my future in the industry might depend on it.

"Is it the concert?" Allan asks. "Or the girl?" Just beyond the curtain, the noise of the crowd grows. Everything is ready. We're just waiting for the cue from the stage manager.

"Both."

"Is she here yet?" he asks.

"I don't know. But if she doesn't show, I don't know how I'll get through tonight."

"She'll come," he says. "Did you read this?" He hands me a newspaper.

I push the paper back to him. "I don't want to read more predictions about the concert."

"It's not about the concert." He gives me a firm look before shoving the paper in my hands. "She'll come tonight." He slaps my back before leaving to join the audience.

"It's go-time," the stage manager announces. The band lines up as a surge of nervous energy pulsates through me. I throw the newspaper to the side. Tonight, only one thing matters.

As I step out on stage, the crowd erupts into cheers. Even though I'm used to stadium shows, the small venues are still my favorite. The barn is glowing in white Christmas lights, and my eyes immediately dart to the front row.

Her seat is empty.

Suddenly, there's movement from the back of the barn. That's when I see a red dress—the same one Mia wore the night of the auction. She glances at me, but I can't read her expression because the stage lights are blinding. For a moment, I forget what I'm supposed to do because I can't stop staring.

She doesn't see the two people behind her until they slide into their seats at the last minute. Without Mia's knowledge, I arranged for both Jaz and Ella to attend the concert, flying them in at the last minute.

Tonight, I wanted to make Mia happy.

When she turns and sees her best friends, her mouth drops and her face shifts from shock to elation.

She looks up at me and mouths the words, *Was this you?*

I give her a quick wink as Jaz elbows her in the side. Maybe tonight can be the start of changing her Christmas memories. You can't rip out pages from your past, but you can make better memories, ones that will eventually outshine the parts that nearly break you.

As the band rips into the first few songs, the music and energy in the crowd is electric. People rise to their feet, clapping to the beat, forgetting about the rest of the world outside the barn. When we change to the familiar carols, the energy is still present, especially when we sing "Silent Night." Something deep inside my chest vibrates, giving me a warm glow that stretches across my body.

I stop for a moment and let the crowd take over, listening to the gentle harmonies as they echo across the space. *Sleep in heavenly peace, sleep in heavenly peace.*

I don't care what the critics say. I don't want to stop making music ever.

When the silence settles across the room, sweat pricks the back of my neck. I sit behind the piano, stretch my fingers across the keys, and take a deep breath.

Never have I been this nervous to perform a new song. As my heart bangs against my chest, I search for her in the front row.

"I've got a new song to play tonight," I tell the audience. "And I'd like to ask someone to join me onstage." I look out at the expectant faces in the dark. "Tonight, I'd like Mia MacPherson to come up here."

I don't care if I had to pay a million dollars for this date. I'd do it all again.

Mia stares at me while Jaz and Ella push her toward the stage.

She slowly joins me onstage, and then shoots me a nervous smile as she sits next to me.

At first, I'm too nervous to look at her, so I close my eyes, letting the piano echo across the space.

Beneath the mistletoe, by the glow of Christmas lights,
With you in my arms, it's a magical night.
Snowflakes softly falling as our fingers entwine,
I can't wait 'til we're alone, because this year, you'll be mine . . .

I feel her eyes on me, giving me a surge of confidence, until the band hits the instrumental part.

I lift my hands, and lean close to her. "Will you dance with me?"

She glances at the audience. "In front of all these people?"

"Yes, Mia, in front of everyone," I say, loud enough for only her to hear. "It's not pretend this time. It's for real. I've been waiting for this moment ever since we danced before."

I walk her to center stage as the band continues to play. The hesitation swirls in her eyes, and I give her a reassuring smile, gathering her in my arms and pulling her body close, like we were made to dance this way, swaying gently under the Christmas lights. As I rest my head against her hair, we slowly find our rhythm and let the audience melt away. It's just her and me and a lifetime stretched out before us.

Closing my eyes, I imagine what it would be like to have this every day. To wake up every morning with her in my arms, to kiss her every night.

As much as I love music, she's worth losing everything for.

When the band plays the last note, there's a stretch of silence—the whole audience caught up in our moment.

When I turn to Mia, her eyes are shining. Whatever is happening between us—she feels it too. She's the reason I found my muse again. No matter what happens after tonight, this song will always be hers.

As the crowd rises to their feet and applause fills the room, the only thing that matters is her.

I brush my lips across her cheek before letting her sneak back to her seat.

With a final wave, I slip offstage as Allan runs over with a huge smile. "Jace, you're not going to believe it."

"What?"

"The entire field outside is full of tailgaters, and so many fans watched online that YouTube temporarily glitched."

"That's crazy."

"The news outlets are reporting already that your concert was a massive success. Your new songs blew up the internet, especially that last one with Mia." He holds up his phone to show me the comments pouring in.

"That's great," I say, feeling an urgency to tell Mia. "I need to talk to Mia before she leaves."

"You're finally ready to tell her?" he says, his lips curling into a smile.

"You knew?"

"Every time you looked at her," he says with a chuckle. "You're not good at hiding your feelings." Then he rushes out the stage door to look for Mia.

I don't even know what I'm going to say to her, but I need to do this while I'm still riding this high after the concert. I shoot her a quick text.

Jace: Can we talk? Allan is looking for you. Meet me backstage.

A hand lands on my shoulder.

"That was fast," I say, spinning around.

I frown. Ava stands before me dressed in leather pants and an off-the-shoulder sweater.

"You were expecting someone else?" she asks, raising an eyebrow.

My smile fades. "I thought you were leaving early."

She shrugs. "I changed my mind. One of your band members had a ticket. After the way things ended the other night, I wanted one last shot to change yours."

I thought I'd made things clear with her. But apparently, she didn't get the hint when I told her to go home.

I open my mouth, but she holds up a hand to stop me. "Can I finish talking first?"

I nod.

"After seeing your show, I realized you were right." She pauses. "When I saw you singing to her, you looked . . . different. Through our entire relationship, you never looked at me that way."

I glance away. "Was it that obvious?"

"Only to me," she says. "That's the look I always wanted from you."

I drag a hand through my hair. "I'm sorry, Ava."

"For what?" She shakes her head incredulously. "You didn't cheat on me. And you took the blame when we broke up. But look what it cost you." She can barely meet my eyes; she's so torn up by guilt. There's so much we haven't talked about, but it doesn't matter now.

I open my arms to her, and she steps into them. This is the one thing she's desperately wanted, and I've refused to give . . . until now.

A curtain shifts nearby and I pull away from her. "If things hadn't been in such terrible shape the past few months, I wouldn't have come back here or agreed to a concert. Even though it's been the worst year of my life, I ended up at the exact place I needed to be."

Ava lets out her breath, relieved. "Thanks for that. I needed to know that you won't be mad."

"You know I'm not good at staying angry," I say. An understanding settles between us. We've both moved on.

"So, what's next?" she asks.

"I need to talk to Mia," I say, glancing around. Allan should have found her by now.

"Then go get her," Ava says with a grin. "And don't let her go."

"I don't plan to," I say, heading toward my dressing room, hoping she's there.

I glance at my phone on the way. No messages. It seems odd that she hasn't responded yet.

Suddenly, Allan rounds the corner in the hall.

"Did you find her?" I ask.

He frowns. "I sent her back here a long time ago."

I check my dressing room as Allan follows. She's not there, either.

"A couple of her friends are still around," Allan says. "I'll ask them."

I wish I could find Mia myself. I hate that I can't go out in public and hunt her down.

A dam is going to burst in my chest if I don't tell her now.

A few minutes later, a knock sounds at my dressing room door. Jaz and Ella wait outside.

"Where's Mia?" I ask.

Jaz frowns. "We thought she was with you."

"She's not here. I texted her and she hasn't responded. She didn't say anything after the concert?" This isn't like her. A growing sense of urgency builds in my chest.

The women glance at each other uneasily before Ella responds. "Listen, Jace, we really appreciate the surprise for Mia. But she told us something privately, and I feel like I'd be breaking her trust if I told you."

I stare at them, feeling alarm over the way they're looking at me. "But I was going to tell her tonight how I really feel . . . about us."

Ella glances at Jaz, before her eyes flick back to me.

"What is it?" I ask.

"I'm only doing this because I think you deserve to know . . ." Jaz says slowly. "Before Allan sent her back here to find you, she told us she wasn't staying. She's heading home."

"To her mom's house?"

"No," Jaz says. "Not that home."

I stare at them, shaking my head. "She's headed to the airport?"

Jaz sighs. "A red-eye to South Carolina. She said she couldn't stay for Christmas. That it was too hard to be here with you . . . because of Ava."

"But I don't want to be with Ava. I thought I made it clear tonight," I say, suddenly driven by an urgency to catch her before she leaves. "Why would she go without saying goodbye?"

Jaz shrugs. "I don't know. When Allan told her to meet you backstage, she left us, and we haven't seen her since."

I replay how I could have missed her. The only time I wasn't looking for her was when Ava was here . . .

That's when it hits me: *Ava*.

My stomach twists like I'm going to be sick. "Do you think she saw me with Ava?"

Ella's eyes widen. "Ava was here with you?"

"Yeah, just for a few minutes to say goodbye. Do you think that would scare her off?" I remember how the curtain moved when I was hugging Ava. I assumed it was just my crew.

Jaz looks at me like I'm an idiot. "Your ex shows up for your biggest event of the year . . . how would that *not* scare her?" She tilts her head to see if I'm understanding. "Every girl would feel threatened by her. Mia's so selfless, she'd never want to interfere with your happiness."

How did I not see this before? She saw Ava and ran like a skittish cat. "How soon does her plane leave?"

"Don't ask questions," Jaz says, hustling me toward the door. "Just find her."

I stop in the door, looking at them both. "Do I have a chance?"

"If you hurry," Ella says.

Jaz's phone buzzes, and she glances down at the message. "Looks like Mother Nature is on your side." She holds up the phone to show a message from Mia.

Mia: I just slid off the road. Can you pick me up and take me to the airport?

"I'll be right there." I grab my keys, beelining for the back entrance. "Will you tell her I'm on my way?"

"That will just make her run," Jaz says. "I'll tell her we're coming."

I frown. "Why would you do that?"

"Because she'll wait for us," Jaz says, her lips curling into a smile "And then she'll get the surprise of a lifetime."

TWENTY-FIVE

Mia

For the second time this winter, I'm stuck in the snow. It feels just like *Groundhog Day.* How lucky can one person get? Apparently, *very* lucky.

I check the time again. At this rate, I'm barely going to make my plane, and that's only if my flight hasn't already been delayed.

But I'm not going back to Jace's house. I don't want to face the memories—how it felt to see him bringing me coffee or think about how he agreed to kiss me for the first time and made every part of me come alive. When he slipped his hand across my cheek, then my neck, the slow graze of his lips over me like it meant something, makes me nearly buckle inside.

Because you don't fall for someone like Jace and forget it in a day, or a week, or even a lifetime.

My heart might never recover from this. And yet I'm the stupid one who fell hard and fast.

He dared me to be happy, and I dared to fall for him.

Why is it the things that make us happy are the same things that can crush us? I've seen what love has done to my mother, the way she cried in the shower after she thought I was in bed, the heaving sobs escaping her lungs until she couldn't breathe, her face a splotchy mess of red-rimmed eyes and mascara streaks.

When I asked why Dad left, Mom's response was barely audible: *Because he wasn't happy.* Whatever happiness deal my parents made, my dad reneged on it.

When we risk loving someone, maybe the expectation shouldn't be happiness all the time. Because isn't real love daring to say yes and sticking around even when life gets messy? Maybe that's when you find something better than happiness—in the commitment that comes when you say yes to the other person, no matter how messy life is.

For years, I've rolled this around in my head like a marble I can't corner. *Maybe happiness is just as much a dream as love.*

Lights flash in my rearview mirror as a car slows behind me, then grinds to a halt on the shoulder. The driver leaves their lights on, blinding my view.

A silhouette flashes behind me before someone taps on my window. When I glance up, my throat catches. I'd know that bearded jaw and tousled hair anywhere.

"Jace?" I roll down my window. "What are you doing here?"

"Your friends told me what happened."

I can't read his face, whether he's annoyed about coming to my rescue or amused that I'm stuck like before.

"Where's Jaz?" I ask.

"She sent me."

"You didn't have to save me," I say, rubbing my numb fingers together. "I could've called my brothers."

"And missed an opportunity to rescue you from the snow again? Not a chance." His eyes drop to my hands.

I forgot my gloves again.

"Climb into my car. You're freezing."

"I'm not freezing," I argue.

"Is that why you can't stop shaking?"

I hesitate, wanting to fight against his kindness. There's too much history between us. If I get into his car, I don't know where this will lead. It won't take him long to see it in my face. *I only want him.*

"Don't you have other things to do?" I ask, still stubbornly refusing to move. "Other people to see?"

He opens my car door and waits for me to step out. "Nobody more important than you."

When I don't move, he lets out a frustrated sigh. "Seriously, Mia, for once, let me help you."

"I don't need help," I argue.

"Then I'll carry you to my vehicle kicking and screaming if I have to. But I'm not leaving you to freeze to death."

I don't know if he's serious, but I know Jace is just as stubborn as I am.

I climb out and face him. "I'm sorry if I'm keeping you from spending time with other people. I'm not trying to annoy you."

He levels his gaze. "The only thing that's annoying me is the fact that you *assume* I want to spend time with anyone else tonight."

I dig my hands into my coat pockets and narrow my gaze. "Even her?"

He sets his jaw. "She's not you." Then he pauses. "Even she noticed how I looked at you tonight."

I hesitate, unsure if he's telling me everything. "So that hug between you and Ava meant nothing?" I can't hide the edge in my tone. That moment sliced my heart in two.

He stares at me for a long second, the car lights reflecting off his face. Then he shakes his head and exhales, the air rising like a cloud on this frigid night. "Is that why you didn't stay?"

"I walked in when you were hugging," I say. "I assumed you were getting back together."

"Well, you assumed wrong," he shoots back.

"That's not how it looked." I stride past him, trying to get away.

He grabs my arm to keep me from walking into the darkness. He knows me too well, and he won't let me leave without an explanation.

"Were you even going to tell me you were leaving?" A pained expression flashes across his face.

"I told you I was going home after the holidays. That was always the agreement."

"What about the happiness agreement?" he asks. "What about *us*?"

"There is *no* us," I say, more firmly.

The snow is swirling around us, like we're caught in the middle of a shaken snow globe, just me and him—and this thing between us that I can't erase no matter how hard I try.

He dared me to be happy, and I dared to fall for him. Look where that got me.

"Sully's Beach is where I belong," I say. "It's where I'm happiest."

He shakes his head, his gaze holding mine. "There's only one place where you belong. And that's with me."

His words pull everything tight inside me, knotting my emotions so I can hardly breathe. I close my eyes. "Jace, I can't. I always said this is how it ends."

"But this is *not* the end." He wipes snow from my cheekbone lightly with his thumb. "Not until you give me another chance."

"I gave you a chance. And then Ava showed up. What we had was only pretend."

His jaw clenches. "Not for me it wasn't."

"What did you say?" I ask, not believing him.

He pauses, then turns to face me, the headlights catching his dark eyes, the sharp cut of his cheekbone, the angle of his jaw. Everything in my body is pulling me toward him.

"There's no chance I'd go back to her. Not when there's a chance with you."

My breath hitches, the emotion rising in my chest. I pack it down hard, fooled by false promises before. "After what you did to her?"

It's a low blow to throw him off. If I keep the reason we can't be together focused on him, then we don't have to deal with my trust issues.

He looks at me warily. "I thought you didn't read things about me online?"

"I don't usually. But I had to know why you broke up. The article said you cheated . . . and I can't take a chance on someone who won't be honest with me."

Jace looks down the road, a faraway look in his eyes. "You want to know the truth? When Ava and I broke up, it was because she cheated on me."

I pause as this news sinks deep into my chest. "But I thought it was you . . ."

"So did everyone else," he says, looking back at me, his jaw set. "I promised myself I wouldn't leak it to the news. When I suspected something was going on, I trailed her for a few days and caught her with Benedict at his apartment. Someone at the building saw me there. I had to know if it was true. I didn't believe she was cheating, and I had to see for myself."

"So that's why you froze when you saw Benedict at Evergreen."

He nods. "It brought back that memory."

"But why did the articles report it was you?"

He drags a hand through his hair and sighs. "Someone came forward who had seen me at the apartment that day. They assumed I was there with another woman. Ava and I had argued in the hallway, and when the media caught wind of it, she was terrified of how this would affect her career. Even though I was angry, I refused to talk to the press and blame her. And they took my silence as a confession. I never told them I was guilty; they assumed it."

I stare at Jace in shock. "You took the blame for her? After what she'd done to you?"

He kicks the snow on the ground. "At the time, her dad was going through cancer treatment. Ava was financially supporting him so he could afford an experimental treatment that wasn't covered by insurance. I knew that however bad the rumors made me look, I'd be able to recover, eventually. My family doesn't rely on me for support. But Ava's family does. She didn't need any more stress in her life."

My mouth hangs open. "Still, Jace. *Why?* Weren't you furious at her?"

He rubs the back of his neck like he's wrestled with the same awful question. "It's strange what you'll do for someone even when you're livid. I've been angry about it for a year, wondering why I sacrificed so much for her when I wasn't the one in the wrong. It felt like a really stupid decision."

I shake my head, realizing that Jace has been hiding this for a year. No wonder he came across so grumpy when we first met. He had every reason not to trust me after what he'd been through. "I don't understand how I had anything to do with this."

He touches my chin. "Mia, you showed me why I had to make music again, why I needed to have fun and not spend all my time alone. All of that saved me. I still have a long road ahead. But I finally feel like things are right when I'm with you."

The happiness agreement. *Of course.*

I shake my head, the emotions welling up in my chest, even though I won't allow them to spill out. I can't let Jace convince me this is possible.

"Stop," I whisper, blinking back tears, nearly breathless. I won't get caught up in an emotional whirlwind that will rip me apart.

Jace tips my chin up so that I can't hide from him. "You were the one who gave me the confidence to go on stage tonight. I almost pulled the plug on my new songs so many times, especially when I saw *The Times*. Then I figured out who was the anonymous source. The one person who was bitter about me beating him."

"Cal?"

He shrugs, unbothered by it now. "I put two and two

together. As the venue owner, he stopped in occasionally while I was practicing. Before the show tonight, I told him I was performing the songs he hated. He knew I'd figured it out but was too much of a coward to say it to my face."

He steps closer to me and I freeze, not because of the cold, but because his gaze is so intense. He takes my hand from my coat pocket and presses his palms around it, his warmth sinking into my skin. "Allan showed me your comment in *The Boston Globe*." He pauses. "And that's when I knew I needed to tell you how I really felt. I can't stop thinking about you. I can't stop loving you. When I'm lying in bed at night, all I can think of is how I want you next to me, your body warm against mine. When I wake up in the morning, I want your smile to be the first thing I see. Because my first thought, my every thought, is always you."

I close my eyes, trying to hold the swell of emotions back, even though it keeps slipping out. "What if I can't make you happy? You might be happy now, but can I *keep* you that way? That's the problem with love. It never stays the same." I look at him while the snow catches in the headlights around us, framing us in white.

"For two people willing to make it work, there's only one option—*staying*." He brings my fingers to his lips and presses them softly to his lips, the warmth spidering through me. "I already know who makes me happy. That's not even a question."

My gaze skates away from his, looking for something to stabilize this emotional slide-off. "I'm still not staying."

"Then I'm coming with you." He knits his fingers with mine.

"No." I swallow hard. "I'm going alone."

He holds my gaze, searching for something. "Mia, you don't have to run like your father did."

"I am *not* my father," I insist.

"Then why are you scared?"

"Love couldn't solve my parents' problems. How do I know it's going to make us happy?" I try to pull away, but he refuses to release my hand.

"Is that what this is about? You're afraid that I'll leave?"

"More than dancing on stage. More than kissing you for the first time." Deep down, it's always what I've been afraid of. When Dad walked out, he left a hole in my heart too big to fill. And one message burrowed that hole deeper: *Love isn't enough.*

"I won't be enough for you," I say. "I'm not famous. I'm nobody special."

"I don't want someone famous. I only want you." Jace pulls me back toward him, and this time, I'm worn down so much, so emotionally distraught, that I can't resist. "Love isn't about happiness. It's about two people who stay together even when everything tells them to run. But I won't let you go this time. If you leave, I will chase you down, until you believe this one thing —" He presses me closer so that I can barely breathe. "I will always be here for you."

His hands wrap around my back as his lips graze my cheek.

When he stops and pulls away slightly, his eyes drag over me like a match. "Will you come home with me?" He asks it so tenderly, my heart aches.

This time, I know I want to try.

————

When we show up at Mom's, the white lights on the porch make the piled-up snow around the drive look like a winter wonderland. I'm not sure I want to have this talk now, but I've already missed my plane. If this Christmas is going to be different, it starts with having a conversation I've been avoiding.

When we sneak inside, the house is unusually quiet with only the glow of colorful lights brightening the corner where the Christmas tree stands.

Finally, an upstairs door creaks open, and Mom comes to the top of the stairs in a red bathrobe.

"I thought you were leaving?" she asks with a frown. When I told her I wasn't staying for Christmas, she already knew why. Ever since our argument, things had been strained.

"Me too," I say. "But I have something that can't wait." I look around. "Where are the boys?"

"Brax is out with your friend Jaz." A smile curls across her lips. "He was pleased to see her again. I think they've hit it off."

I shake my head. "I've warned her against dating a hockey player."

"I'm not sure Jaz will listen," Jace whispers with a sly smirk.

"You can't keep two people from falling in love," Mom adds with a sigh.

I wonder if she's talking about someone other than Jaz and Brax.

She steps into the kitchen and grabs two plates. "You hungry? There are fresh cookies."

The fragrant scents of ginger and cinnamon fill the air.

"You've been baking?" I look around for the gingerbread cutouts. Mom only bakes when she's down; it's one of her coping mechanisms.

She holds up a large plastic container stacked with cookies. "With the festival ending and you leaving, it felt like all the excitement was ending. And honestly . . ." She pauses to adjust her bathrobe. "Christmas never feels complete without everyone here."

I say it slowly. "You made cookies because I left?"

"We didn't part on good terms," she says, putting cookies on plates and handing them to Jace and me. "I pushed too hard."

"You didn't push me away." I shake my head. "I left. There's a difference."

Jace stays silent behind us, letting us have a moment alone.

I tuck my hair behind my ear. "Staying for Christmas seemed too hard."

"I know. I wish I could make things right and fix the past. I always thought your dad would eventually want contact with you. When he died last year, I realized you never got what you needed."

"I wanted an explanation. That's all." I set the plate down. "I wanted to know if he ever found what he was searching for."

She looks away uneasily. "I told you he wasn't happy here. But that's not the complete story. He *was* happy here . . . in many ways." She sighs. "I was wrong to make you think otherwise, because you blamed yourself."

I hesitate, realizing Mom has been more clued in on my feelings than I thought. All along, I've been worried I was the reason. I told myself a lie that became my truth.

She shakes her head. "It wasn't you or anyone here," she admits. "It was him. We were mismatched in a lot of ways. But you and your brothers made him happier than he ever was alone. He missed you so much."

"Then why didn't he visit?"

Mom draws in a deep breath and plays with the edge of the counter. "I suppose that was my fault. He wrote a letter about a year after he left, asking to visit. And I wrote him back and told him no."

"Why?"

"Over the years, he asked to visit several times. And I never let him because I knew that a once-a-year visit couldn't make up for his absence. He never pressed the issue. I wanted you to have a father. Not an occasional visitor. And that was wrong of me. By the time I realized it, it was too late." She shakes her short hair and adjusts her glasses. "A yearly visit might not have been enough, but it would have been something. I didn't understand how my hurt was affecting you." Her shoulders sag as she looks away, unable to meet my eyes.

She believed she was doing the right thing, but we were all running from the pain, from each other, from the things we couldn't face.

"It's okay." I wrap my arms around her shoulders. "I've got you and my brothers. And I'm not leaving . . . if that's alright with you?"

She pulls back from me, searching my face. "You're . . ." She can't even bring herself to say the words.

"Yes, I'm staying for Christmas. I don't know how long after that, but I can promise you Christmas."

When I glance over at Jace, he's leaning against the kitchen counter, arms folded, watching us with a goofy smile.

And he can see it written all over me. *This is what happiness looks like.*

———

The next few days are a blur of errands, buying Christmas gifts and celebrating a successful festival. Ella already left for Sully's Beach, eager to spend Christmas with her husband, Grant, and their extended family. Jaz made a last-second decision to extend her stay in Maplewood, and I have a feeling Brax had something to do with her change of plans.

Mom and I spend Christmas Eve making a feast while Jace heads into town for last-minute shopping.

"I bet he's buying a gift for you," Jaz hints as she scoops cranberry sauce into a bowl. Brax is watching her at the kitchen island, offering to taste-test everything.

I crack open the oven door. "I told him we're each buying something small," I say, checking the apple pie. "It's too soon for extravagant gifts."

Jaz looks at me like I lost my mind. "You will not turn down any gift that man gives you. If he wants to buy you a brand-new Tesla, let him."

"I will not accept a car," I say stubbornly. "I might be dating a celebrity, but I want to have a relationship that's as close to normal as possible. He knows I can't compete with extravagant gifts. If Jace wants to win me over, he will have to use something more than money."

He's already concerned about how he'll protect me from the press and the constant demands of being in the public eye. But I'm not worried about it. I might have to share him with the world, but when he returns to Maplewood or visits me in Sully's Beach, he'll be all mine.

Brax sinks a spoon into the cranberry sauce as Jaz slaps his hand away. He gives her a lopsided smile. "Do you think after dinner tonight we could have a friendly hockey competition?"

"I'm in," Vale yells from the living room.

"We aren't playing hockey tonight," I say, grabbing two hot pad mitts with a picture of Will Ferrell dressed as an elf. "It's Christmas Eve. We're stuffing our faces and hanging out. And tomorrow morning we're opening gifts in our pajamas and then having a wrapping paper fight, just like old times." As I slide out the pie, Mom checks the turkey.

"The bird is ready," she announces.

Brax looks at Vale. "I'm not cutting it."

Vale shakes his head. "Don't look at me. I did it last year."

As the boys argue about who's carving the bird, Jace enters, dusted with snow and bundled in a scarf and winter cap. I'm still wearing my *Elf* hot pad mittens when I give him a hug.

"Nice mittens," he says, kissing my forehead as I wrap Will Ferrell's face around his neck. "How much time do we have before dinner?" The anticipation in his expression makes him look like a kid on Christmas. But the heat in his eyes tells me he wants to be alone.

Mom peeks around the corner. "Oh, good. Jace arrived, just in time for dinner."

When I glance back at Jace, disappointment etches his face.

"What's wrong?"

"I'm just excited to give you your gift," he says. "I'm not good at waiting."

"Later," I promise, dragging him to the table.

The dining room table is overflowing with steaming piles of mashed potatoes, stuffing, and a decadent apple pie.

After Brax and Vale argue about how to carve the bird, they divide up the slices and we stuff ourselves with food. The conversation flows as fast as Mom's famous Christmas cranberry punch.

Brax recounts the Christmas he and Vale found their gifts hidden in the basement, and unwrapped them all, only to discover they'd need to rewrap them in order to hide what they'd done. Their poor wrapping job didn't fool Mom, and she made them do morning chores before opening Christmas gifts as punishment.

As we all laugh at the memory, I feel joy split me wide open, like it's bubbling out of me. *Is this what I've been missing all these years?*

Even before I look up, I feel his warm gaze on me. Jace is staring at me from across the table, a lopsided grin on his face. He's enjoying having a family to spend Christmas with, but even happier to see me with my family, laughing again.

As we're cleaning up, he comes up behind me and wraps his arms around my waist. "Come outside," he whispers in my ear, the sharp scent of pine and musk overwhelming me. It's enough to make me immediately stop what I'm doing and follow him to the porch, like my body can't help but follow him. Vale and Brax are still in high spirits recounting their childhood high jinks, and no one says a word about our absence.

Under a single strand of lights dangling from the porch roof, Jace looks at me with a smirk and finds the curve of my waist with his hands.

"You look happy," I murmur.

"I am, especially seeing you so happy. I forgot how much I loved being with family on the holidays."

I've finally won him over to the dark side of hanging out with my crazy family, but that can't be the only reason he wanted to bring me out here. "What are you hiding?"

Jace rubs his hand over his jaw. "Am I that bad at keeping things from you?"

"Only since we started dating."

"When it comes to you, I can't keep secrets." He kisses the top of my head, then levels his gaze. "One of the record company executives called today and said the concert was a massive success. Your new song is skyrocketing up the charts."

"It's not my song," I remind him, even though he refuses to call it anything else—something that makes me secretly happy. "I knew your fans would like it."

"You were the only one," he says with a laugh. "But there's more. Since the song is doing well, he wants me to go back on the road after the New Year."

I try to hide my shock. "Wow. That soon?" We hadn't talked about the future in definite terms yet. Jace was planning on writing and recording more music in January at his home studio. Since I'm back to being unemployed, I didn't have a plan, other than staying here until I figured out my next gig.

"He said we should ride this wave as long as we can," he adds. "Now everyone wants my band in town, which is a total switch from a few months ago."

I smile, the elation bubbling up beside another emotion . . . *missing* him. This news is a blow. I don't want to be left behind in Maplewood, pining for Jace while trying to figure out what I should do next.

"Congratulations," I say, wrapping my arms around him, trying to hide the mixed emotions under my smile. I *really* am happy for him. He deserves this. But I wonder what will happen to our relationship when he's gone. Will he miss me as much as I'm going to miss him? After he leaves, will there still be an *us*?

He pulls away and takes my hands. "I won't give them an answer until I know one thing."

"What's that?"

"Will you be my assistant on the road? Because I'm not leaving you behind."

I hesitate, unsure if Jace is doing this because he really wants me as his assistant or feels bad about me not having a job. "Jace, you don't have to hire me. I know you were desperate for someone before and I was available."

He shakes his head. "Maybe at first . . . but you blew me away with how determined you were to get everything right. You're way overqualified for this job. Incredibly smart and talented. I don't want to leave Maplewood without you by my side. I'll even make sure you have your own space on the tour bus."

"Are you sure?" I ask. "What if you tire of me?"

He shakes his head like this is a dumb question. "I could never tire of you."

"You haven't been on the road with me yet."

"Then let's test my theory," he says, pulling me closer. He smiles, and my heart feels like it's glowing as bright as the white lights above us.

He reaches into his pocket and hands me a tiny rectangular box. "For you."

"We're exchanging gifts *now*? But I thought . . ."

"I'm not good at waiting," he interrupts, holding it out. "And since you'll be with your family tomorrow morning . . ."

I stop him before he can go on. "You're coming over, right?"

He shakes his head. "This is your time with family. I don't want to interfere."

I level my gaze at him. "You're *not* spending Christmas alone. My mom is already expecting you."

"She is?"

"She told me, 'Make sure Jace knows we're opening presents at eight sharp.' I meant what I said about my family welcoming you. Maybe we have our faults, but I'm adamant that no one should be alone on Christmas. As your assistant, I insist."

With a heated gaze, he cups the back of my neck and tilts my face to his. "You're more than an assistant to me. You're the woman I love."

I can't help but smile. "That's an even better reason to come over on Christmas."

His mouth curls on one side, making his dimple show. "In that case, I'll do it if you'll open your gift."

I sigh, giving in to his demands and open the lid. Inside is a gold circular necklace that shimmers in the light.

Jace looks at me expectantly. "When I woke up beside you at the Pine Paradise, I knew that's what I wanted—someone who would stay with me, no matter what. Being there with you changed everything. After that, I didn't want to ever leave you."

I hold the necklace closer and discover words engraved along the curved rim of the circle: *He dared her to be happy.*

And I complete it without thinking. *And she dared to fall for him.*

"Jace, you are the only one who could make me this happy." I hold up the gold necklace so that it shimmers in the light. "Will you do the honors?" I ask and he takes the necklace.

When he finishes adjusting the clasp, he kisses the side of my neck, sending warm shivers down my body.

"Do you think my family will notice if we sneak away for a few minutes? Your gift is downtown."

A burst of laughter echoes inside the house, and Jace shrugs. "No, I don't think they'll even notice."

We climb inside Jace's car and head to Maplewood, parking along Main Street under the glow of Christmas lights. Even though the festival is done, all the decorations are still up, and the street is a frosty, silent Christmas village tucked away in the snow. Not a single car passes us as I grab Jace's hand and take him to our destination.

Maybe it was a silly idea, but I promised him something and never followed through on it. I only hope the committee hasn't taken down my surprise.

When we reach the top of the hill, I spy the wooden pergola draped in evergreen and lights, overlooking the entire town.

I stop and turn to Jace, grabbing both of his hands, leading him to the mistletoe booth.

"Remember when that reporter wanted a picture, but I refused to kiss you here? At the time, I was too embarrassed, afraid you'd see how I felt right away. But I didn't forget the promise I made to you. And I was hoping I would get a second chance."

His mouth curls into an adorable grin. "I thought you hated mistletoe?"

"I might be persuaded to change my mind."

"Then I'm going to put mistletoe all over my house," Jace says with a mischievous look. "Until you've changed your mind."

I lift an eyebrow, wrapping my hands around his neck. "Merry Christmas to me," I whisper as he pulls me close and kisses me.

I already know it's true. I don't hate mistletoe any more.

Epilogue

One year later
Jace

As soon as I drop my luggage in the foyer, Mia sees the surprise I arranged for her. "You decorated for Christmas already?"

The entire living room is decorated in evergreen and lights, thanks to my housekeeping staff. Since I started touring almost a year ago, I've hardly been home. But now that it's December, I'm planning on taking a couple of months off to write more music and spend time with the woman I can't get enough of.

Mia points at the mistletoe hanging above her. "Is this based on our conversation from last year?"

I arch an eyebrow. "I don't forget things."

She walks over to me and lazily wraps her arms around my neck. "Just so you know, I've already changed my mind about mistletoe."

I lean in, whispering in her ear, "Just in case you weren't thoroughly convinced, it's in every doorway of this house."

Her lips curl into a smile. "You never do things halfway."

"What would be the point?" I kiss her forehead. "Just for the record, neither do you. You're the one who gave the entire town a makeover last year."

I know Mia is eager to see if the festival is the same as last year. Since she's been working for me, she officially retired from her position as event planner and gave all her planning documents to her mom, who took over Mia's job. Now that the town agreed to pay Cora, she's actually able to cover her bills without Mia's help. It turned out to be a win-win for everyone.

I smooth a strand of hair behind her ear. "As much as I want to kiss you under the mistletoe, I wonder if we could head to the barn?"

She crinkles her nose. "And run into Cal? No, thank you."

"You won't run into him today," I promise.

"How can you be sure?" she asks, frowning.

"Just trust me," I say, winking.

A few minutes later, we're driving the winding roads through the snow-covered hills and finally arrive at the barn, which looks spectacular against the deep blue winter sky.

Inside, the piano is still sitting on stage, the Christmas lights draped across the rafters, twinkling above us like stars. We sit on the piano bench together, and I play a few chords, remembering last year's concert and everything that's changed since then.

The piano echoes across the cavernous ceiling, and I can't wait to tell her any longer. "When we danced together last year on this stage, it was like something shifted inside me. I realized I hadn't been this happy in so long. You are everything I've ever wanted—someone who has shown me how to have fun again. How to love with your whole heart." I stop playing, and look over, pulling a small box from my pocket, wrapped with a red bow.

She glances from the box to me, then slowly unties the ribbon so it falls to the floor. For what feels like an insanely long moment, she opens the lid and pauses.

"Jace? Is this . . .?" She's too choked up to finish and too scared to ask me the question I know is on her mind.

I take her hands in mine. "I want you to be my wife, Mia.

You're the only one I want to spend my life with. There's nobody I'd rather make dinner for, or talk about my day with, or go on the road with than you." I kneel. "Please, Mia," I ask in a soft voice. "Will you marry me?"

This time, she doesn't make me wait. "Yes," she says, her eyes shining.

I slide the square diamond set in a gold band on her finger, and then cup her face in my hands and kiss her mouth. This time, there's no hesitation between us. I want to kiss her forever—right here and now.

She pulls away gently, searching my face. "How long have you been planning this?"

"That ring has been burning a hole in my pocket for months, but I wanted to wait until the other surprise fell into place."

She frowns. "Other surprise?"

"When I was touring this year, I had this idea. What if I could be home more, but still perform? The concert last year in this barn is still my favorite. So I made Cal an offer he couldn't refuse. Remarkably, he agreed to it."

She glances around the barn. "Wait. You bought this place?"

"If the Maplewood Mistletoe Festival continues to grow, I'll have a Christmas concert here every year. Eventually, I want to start a concert festival in the summer, and in between, we'll still tour. But I want to make a life in Maplewood—to make memories together—so we have a place to call home."

She lets this news sink in. "As long as we can fly to Sully's Beach occasionally. Maybe after Christmas?"

I kiss the inside of her palm. "Traveling after Christmas is too long to wait. I know how much your friends mean to you. Sully's Beach is your home, too."

Her eyes widen. "Are we going to Sully's Beach now?"

"No," I say, shaking my head. "I brought Sully's Beach to you."

As if on cue, the doors to the barn open, and Jaz and Ella yell, "SURPRISE!"

Mia looks over at me in elated shock. "You brought my friends here?"

I brush her chin. "Anything to make you smile."

They climb up on stage with us, and we're suddenly caught up in hugs and tears and so much laughter.

"Did she say yes?" Jaz asks.

Mia holds up her left hand. "But how's it possible you kept this secret from me?"

"Let me tell you, it was hard," Jaz says, propping her hand on one hip. "I warned your brothers not to say anything."

"My brothers knew?"

"I may have told Brax . . . who then told Vale," Jaz admits with a grimace.

Just in time, because Cora's voice echoes outside the door. "Mia?"

Mia's mom appears, followed by Brax and Vale. "The traffic in town from the festival kept us from getting here sooner," she says, her face flushed. "Please don't tell me you planned the wedding date."

"Nothing has been planned yet," Mia says. "But I'm not waiting long." She squeezes my hand.

Cora throws her arms around her daughter's neck as Brax and Vale congratulate me, slapping my shoulder so hard it almost hurts.

"Now you have to learn to play hockey," Vale says.

I look to Mia for help, and she shrugs. "You knew you were marrying into a hockey family."

"Where will you get married?" Ella asks. "Sully's Beach or Maplewood?"

"Definitely here," Mia says, looking around the barn, her face tipped toward the lights. "This place would be perfect. And sooner rather than later." It seems appropriate the venue where we had our first dance would be the place we say *I do*.

"How soon?" I ask.

"Well, my friends are already here . . ." she hints. "Do you think we could pull together a wedding by the New Year?"

"Are you serious?" Cora asks, her mouth falling open.

Mia nods. "It's crazy, but with everyone's help, I know we could pull it off. If we're going to get married, why not do it while Jace is home? We have the time, and now, we even have the place." Then she turns to me. "As long as you're okay with it?"

Never agreed more. My hand slides across her waist as I give her a kiss on the cheek. "I'll marry you anytime, any place you want."

She gives me a smile so wide, it makes my heart skip. "Before we decide anything else, let's head to the festival," Mia insists, grabbing her girlfriends' hands and pulling them to the door, while the rest of us follow.

Cora discusses wedding dates, while Jaz begs to know what color she's going to wear as a bridesmaid.

I already know where Mia's headed before I even ask. She wants to show them the best view of Maplewood: the rooftop where we had our first kiss, the place where you can see everything more clearly.

Mia stops in the door and lets everyone go ahead of us. "Thank you for this," she says, nodding toward her friends. "You gave me the second-best present ever."

"Second?"

"You're the first," she says, reaching to wrap her arms around me.

"I could hardly consider myself deserving of your love if I didn't at least try to make you happy. After all, I'm the one who dared you to find it."

"And I'm the one who fell for you," she adds.

"We both fell," I correct her. I knew then that falling in love isn't a onetime thing. It's a forever kind of thing—something you do for a lifetime. "And I don't want to stop. *Ever.*"

———

A few weeks later
Mia

"It's time for the annual twelve days of Christmas singalong," Brax announces, handing us each a red plastic wine goblet. Even though it's New Year's Eve and the night before our wedding, he's wearing his ugly Christmas sweater with Darth Vader in a Santa hat. Although Mom wasn't told it was ugly sweater night, we all showed up in our hideous outfits. It's like someone threw Christmas in a mixer and spewed out our sweaters.

"Oof, this is gonna be bad," I say to Jaz as Brax hands me a glass labeled with the first day of Christmas, which means I sing all twelve verses as a solo.

"Get Jace to help you," Jaz says, elbowing me.

All of my friends are here for the wedding tomorrow: Jaz, Ella and her husband, Grant, Jack and Maeve—who left their kids to have a weekend alone—and Brendan, who came solo.

Along with Vale and Mom, we have eleven people, almost enough to cover all twelve verses.

Mom couldn't resist the opportunity to throw a big party the night before as our rehearsal dinner. And because I'm so good at planning events during snowstorms, nobody is amazed that we're currently getting a foot of snow dumped on our town.

We don't know how the storm is going to affect tomorrow's wedding plans, but as long as the minister shows up and our friends and family are there, we don't care.

"It's not even Christmas," Vale complains as he's given the "second day of Christmas" goblet.

"It's New Year's Eve," Mom reminds him. "With the storm outside, it still feels like Christmas." When Mom found the goblets in the attic while searching for old photos of me, she asked if it would be okay if we restarted this tradition, in memory of Dad. Knowing my complicated history, she wanted to respect my feelings. But if there's one thing I've learned, it's that I don't have to let my past define my future. My happy memories can coexist with all the other mixed emotions.

Brax hands Jaz glass number four with a grin, while Jace takes five, so he can play up the "five golden rings" part.

"Your family does this every year?" Jaz asks me, watching as Brax hands out the goblets.

"We haven't done this in ages, actually. When Dad lived here, we had this tradition of singing through "The Twelve Days of Christmas" as a family. It was Dad's thing. But Mom says we need to embrace having a singer in the family now."

Jaz laughs under her breath. "Your family is embracing all kinds of changes with you becoming the wife of a celebrity. Pretty soon, you're going to be all over the magazines."

"I will not be that girl," I insist. "Jace is determined to keep as normal of a life as possible. Living here in Maplewood will help. Few people want to tromp through the woods to take pictures of us."

From across the table, he winks at me, and my heart feels like the bubbles in a glass of champagne. After all this time, I will never get over that dimple.

Brax sits next to Jaz with glass number twelve and I point at his choice. "I see you saved yourself the last glass."

He holds up the goblet in a toast. "Saving the best for last. And since you're first, you get to start."

I shoot Jace my most desperate look, and he gives me a smile of support. "You want me to sing along?"

"I've trained you well, young Jedi," I reply before we launch into the first verse.

We sing through all twelve verses with Jace taking the extra verse since he's the only decent singer. Vale throws popcorn across the table during my part, and by the time we finish, we all raise our glasses.

"AND A PARTRIDGE IN A PEAR TREE!" It's off-key and horrendously loud, but nobody cares. We're too busy laughing.

Brax stands and sets his goblet on the table. "I think after that lovely number, we need a pre-wedding hockey match. Who's up for one?"

"No!" all the girls shout in unison, because the last thing we want are limping groomsmen tomorrow.

I point at my twin brothers. "I will not have my wedding canceled because my future husband injured himself playing against you two."

"I promise to take it easy," Vale says. "We'll just shoot around. No fighting or rough playing."

With that promise, Grant, Jack, and Brendan scramble to the closet to find skates while the girls circle up in the kitchen, digging into the lemon meringue pie and mixing more cranberry mule drinks. We talk about how Ella's design business is flourishing, while Maeve shows off pictures of her kids, who are adorably cute.

Only later do I look around and realize that Jace has disappeared without me noticing. I peek outside to see if he's watching the guys play hockey, but he's not there either. With our wedding tomorrow, I'm sure he has last-minute preparations to take care of, but when I stop at the bottom of the stairs, a gold wrapper flashes in the light.

"Did someone drop this?" I say to no one in particular, as I bend down and pick up a mini Reese's Cup off the floor.

All the girls stop and look at me.

"What is it?" I ask, confused by the way they're staring, like I'm the only one who doesn't get the inside joke.

Mom approaches and takes my elbow, turning me toward the stairs. "I think all the Reese's Cups are yours."

"They're not mine . . ." My voice fades as I follow her gaze. Reese's Cups line the steps, an obvious candy trail leading upstairs.

I pick up the candy, tucking them into my pockets before realizing they stop at my bedroom door, the same room that once forced me into Jace's home because it was flooded.

The door is almost closed, and when I push it open, Jace is

sitting on my old twin bed, waiting for me with a sheepish look on his face.

The candy leads right to him.

"What is this about?" I ask with a smile, holding up a chocolate.

"I see you found the candy trail."

"If you wanted to get me alone, you could have just told me." I sink onto the bed next to him.

"Remember when you said I don't do things in a small way?" His dimple deepens, and there goes my heart again.

"I like that about you."

"I'm glad you have a thing for Reese's Cups," he adds with a smirk.

"And you," I add, and his gaze heats.

"Tomorrow can't come soon enough," he says. "The candy is a peace offering."

"For what?" I say, frowning.

"That I wasn't more understanding. You needed to spend time with your friends before we left on our honeymoon."

I shake my head. "That's why Mom threw this big party tonight."

"I know, but I was selfish. I wanted to travel to Italy as soon as possible after the reception." He nuzzles his face close to my ear and it sends little sparks down my body.

"You don't have to apologize for that," I say softly.

Jace looks into my eyes, tipping my chin toward him. "I didn't want to start married life this way."

"What way?"

"With you wanting something and me keeping you from it. I realized I can fix this. Taking you to Italy one day later is not a big deal in the scheme of forever. We have the rest of our lives to be together, but our friends are only here for a short time."

"What?" I nearly shout. "You changed your plans for me?"

He brushes my cheek with his knuckles, featherlight. "Of course I did. Because I love you. If this one thing can make you happy, then this is the best gift I can give you." He kisses the tip of my nose and smiles.

I want to melt into a puddle, this man is so good to me. "What can I do to thank you?"

His eyes flick to the door lightning fast. "I think you should check the door."

"What for?" My gaze follows his. Hanging to the top of the doorframe is one sprig of mistletoe.

I hold out my hands so he'll follow me. Then I walk backwards to the door, pulling him with me.

"I know it's not Christmas," he says with a wicked grin.

"It doesn't have to be," I say, kissing him on the cheek and then making my way to his mouth, trailing kisses the entire way. "As far as I'm concerned, you never need mistletoe to kiss me."

I lean my body into his, kissing him gently but firmly, letting him know there's more to come. His hands slide up to my neck before he backs me into the door.

"Mia?" Jaz calls from downstairs. "Jace? What are you doing up there?"

Jace pulls away reluctantly, brushing his hand across my cheek. "I can't wait for tomorrow."

"Me too," I whisper.

"Come rain, or snow, or the apocalypse, I'm getting married to you, no matter what." He kisses my forehead as a promise, and warmth soars through me.

I look up at the mistletoe before we leave.

"Can you get that for me?" I say, nodding toward the green sprig.

He reaches up and plucks it off the frame. "I thought you said we don't need mistletoe?"

"We don't." I spin the mistletoe between my thumb and fingers. "It's just a reminder."

"Of what?" he asks with a curious smile.

"Of how much I love mistletoe."

I kiss him once more, and this time I don't have to wonder

about the future. Because I know, in a way I can't explain, that I've already found what makes us both happy.

———

Get Jaz and Brax's hockey romance, *The Roommate Remodel: A Hockey Sweet Romcom.*
This book introduces the Carolina Crushers hockey team (and the spinoff hockey series!)

Brax MacPherson is the hotshot player hockey teams only dream of having . . . and everything I'm trying not to get burned by.

Find it on Amazon!

———

BONUS MISTLETOE SCENE
(Hint: There's kissing involved.)
If you want to see a deleted scene of Mia and Jace *actually* kissing under the mistletoe, get it here.

Get your bonus mistletoe scene!

The Roommate Remodel

Sneak Peek of the next book in the series

Brax MacPherson is the hotshot player hockey teams only dream of having . . . and everything I'm trying not to get burned by.

I've already been burned once. When Brax kissed me last year at his sister's wedding—who also happens to be my best friend—and then ghosted me afterward, I swore off dating players like him.

When I advertise for new roommates to earn extra money, I never expected the hockey team would take me up on the offer.

Or that Brax would get switched to this team and end up as my accidental roommate.

As the team's new marketing manager, I've got a front row seat to the Brax show every. single. day.

I'm trying not to trip over my own feelings—for the sake of this losing team, who's fighting to stay alive.

Meanwhile, I have to pretend my heart is as cold as ice, even though this hockey heartthrob is the biggest distraction I've ever laid eyes on.

No matter how Brax looks at me or how real things start to feel, I know this is a temporary arrangement. He's too talented to stay on this team. And the roommate situation is too hard on my heart, no matter how good I am at pretending there aren't sparks flying between us.

But when my feelings for Brax heat up, I wonder how this game between us is going to end.

With me winning over the man I can't stop thinking about? Or losing everything, including my heart?

***The Roommate Remodel* is a closed door hockey romantic comedy with no spice, but all the chemistry and emotion to give you a happily ever after.**

Get The Roommate Remodel on Amazon!

Thank You

Thank you for reading this book! I'm truly humbled you'd choose it, and if you're reading this far, you deserve a medal! I'm so excited to give you Brax and Jaz's story next because it's my first sports romance and you'll get to find out what REALLY happened between them.

Now on to thank everyone who's been instrumental in this book:

Thank you to my Heavenly Father for showing me the most perfect love and giving me the life and breath to tell another story.

Thanks to my biggest fan, my forever love, Sam. I love that you read my books before anyone else. I couldn't do this without your support or your understanding. Thanks for making it possible even when it's hard and I forget to make dinner because I'm deep into writing a scene. You're hands down the best husband, and I'm so grateful to be married to you.

Thanks to my kids who mean everything to me. You're my *why*. I love being your mom and I love this adventure called life we get to do together.

Thanks to my phenomenal beta readers, Heidi and Joy. I can't get over how spot-on you are with your suggestions, as well as talented and smart. You both are incredible!

So much gratitude goes to the people who made this book possible: My editor, Emily Poole, my lovely cover designer Melissa at Alt 19 Creative, and my proofreader, Judy Zweifel. You all do amazing work!

Also, a huge thanks to the bookstagrammers, my ARC team/review crew, and my amazing readers who make this work a true joy. You inspire us all to keep reading and for me to continue writing. For this author, it means a lot.

Last but not least: I'd be so grateful if we could stay friends. Sign up for my email of awesomeness at graceworthington.com to find out about my next romcom release and gush about your favorite characters, as well as amazing book bargains and new releases.

LOVE ON THIN ICE / LOVE IN MAPLE FALLS

This is a multi-author hockey series with standalone romances and interconnected characters.

The Friend Face Off

The Icing on the Cake

Check out Grace's entire backlist here.

Grace Worthington is a three-time award-winning author who lives and breathes sweet romcoms.

A former musical theatre gal and playwright, she brings that same energy, heart, and comedic timing to her stories, crafting witty banter and lovable characters you can't help but root for.

She holds a master's degree in psychology and human development and has also completed graduate studies in creative writing. Her inspiration comes from charming coastal towns and classic romcoms from the '80s and '90s.

When she's not writing, she enjoys spending time with her husband and two kids.

Follow Grace on Amazon to be notified of future releases or follow Grace on Instagram.

———

FREE ROMCOM NOVELLA

Get a free novella or bonus epilogues at graceworthing-ton.com

www.ingramcontent.com/pod-product-compliance
Lightning Source LLC
Chambersburg PA
CBHW070455300726
48975CB00007B/2182